College

or

Not?

by Chad Grills

Books by Chad Grills

Non-Fiction:
Veterans: Rebuild America
Future Proof
Business Ideas

Fiction:
College or Not?

Short Stories:
Take These Pills
While You Were Bleeding
Call It Murder
Quick Fix
First Patrol

These books are available for free as part of Amazon Kindle Unlimited.

Paperbacks and Audio versions of most books can be found at:
www.amazon.com/author/chadgrills

For the latest updates, essays, ideas, book giveaways, and more, visit: www.ChadGrills.com

PART I

1

THE REST OF YOUR LIFE

"The hero and heroine both wake up and find themselves in boring lives."
–Mr. Moore

"Jay, your breakfast is getting cold!"

"I'll be there in a minute, Mom!" Jay yelled out of his room.

His Mom's voice fired back from downstairs, "You're going to be late for school."

"Gary's picking me up and I'll be down in a minute!" Jay grabbed his books and checked his phone. No text back from Ella. It had been a full day. Had he said something wrong? He tried not to think about it since he would see her at school soon enough. There was one new message waiting for him from his older brother Gavin. He tapped it and read,

"Ready to come visit, little bro?! Good news: I can get you that internship where I work, but that's assuming that you actually get into P&C."

There was that word... *actually*. Nobody thought Jay was *actually* going get into the prestigious P&C College, which was Gavin's alma mater. Whenever his parents or their friends heard P&C, they instantly assumed Gavin was a genius. Jay's parents ate this up, and always reminded him of Gavin's accomplishments: his GPA, SAT scores, sports, or now, his job working on Wall Street. Jay envied it sometimes, but a part of him wanted something more. He couldn't articulate it exactly... but there had to be something he could do with his life that mattered. In a corny way, maybe he was looking for his passion.

Jay glanced at his phone and texted back.

"I'm ready! I was going to bring Gary?"

The typing bubble popped up as Gavin texted him back. "WTF! Why is Gary coming?"

Jay tapped back. "B/C he's my best friend, he might apply to P&C, and he has a car."

Jay rolled his eyes. Gavin was always ripping on Gary.

"Why don't you find hot girls for friends instead of computer nerds?"

"Gary's smart, and I'm friends with Ella, who is hot."

"Then bring her."

"Shut up, Gary's cool. BTW: did you see how much P&C raised tuition? I don't know if Mom and Dad have that kind of money."

"Don't worry about them. It's what parents do, pay for college. You NEED to worry about getting accepted."

"Yeah, but I really don't think they have the money. Mom is only working part-time."

"They paid for mine. They can pay for you. If you want to

eventually get a job where I work, you'd better get into P&C."

"Yeah I know. We'll see you soon."

"Sounds good. If Gary is still lame, he might have to sleep outside."

Jay sighed and put his phone down. He hated the idea of being reliant on his older brother, but he wasn't sure what else to do. P&C was prestigious, and Jay figured if he went there, he might finally start getting some respect from adults. Gavin got that, and he made a ton of money at his job. Jay knew he hated the work, but so did almost every other adult he knew.

He might as well visit P&C, Gavin, and his co-workers to see firsthand. After all, the campus was only an hour away from their house. If Gary was going, they'd be able to make it fun.

Jay shuffled the papers around on his desk until he found his books for the college prep class. He had to retake the SAT's if he was going to get into P&C. He found the book he needed, stuffed it into his old book bag, and walked to the bathroom.

He paused in front of the mirror. One day he'd like his reflection, he thought. He splashed some water on his face, and popped his contacts onto his blue eyes. His eyes were his best looking feature, even though he didn't have great vision. He threw some water in his straight brown hair and attempted to style it. After some plotted messiness, he disguised the fact that he just woke up.

He was a late bloomer, but not quite as late as his best friend, Gary. Jay was average height and weight, and when he stood next to Gary's skinny 5'3" 105 lb. frame, he looked bigger.

Gary was, to put it mildly, eclectic. He was in home school until the 9th grade. Then, one summer before high school, he was in a family meeting with his parents and declared he, "must go to public school to learn about the public." Gary made broad, sweeping declarations and promises, and then scrambled to figure out how to deliver. He didn't have the most normal social habits, but he was the most loyal friend Jay had ever had.

He'd been gone for the last three months, and starting senior year without him wasn't fun. Today would be his first day back from his three month long trip to California. Gary's parents were technology entrepreneurs, and Jay assumed that they had had to do work out there. As for what Gary was doing the whole time, it was a mystery. When Jay asked him before he left, Gary had leaned forward until his glasses slid down his nose and whispered, "*it's a secret pilgrimage.*"

When Jay pressed him for details, he gave none, except that soon he'd, "return from the promised land with tidings of great joy!" This type of silly build up was Gary Weinstein at his best.

At first it pissed Jay off, but then it peaked his curiosity. What was Gary doing out there for three months?

Jay's phone buzzed, and he grabbed it. Speak of the devil. The text from Gary read, "Rollin. @ your house in 25 mins."

Jay smiled and rolled his eyes. "About time, you went completely dark! No texts, no calls? What have you been doing?"

"Sorry, but I already told you, it was a secret pilgrimage to the promised land."

"Lol, riiiiiight."

"No lie, and I'm back with the truth. Have you tried Drivr

yet?"

"Not yet, why?"

Gary's typing bubble popped up, lingered, and then a link to download Drivr appeared. He texted, "Download it with my link and get the first $30 ride free."

Jay typed back. "Cool, Drivr will be good to have when we visit Gavin at P&C."

"Yup, rollin w/ SICK surprise."

"Lol, whatever. See you in 25."

"Word."

Jay pocketed his phone in time to hear his mom yell, "Get down here and eat your breakfast!"

His heart jumped and his eyes widened. Good lord could that woman scream. It had to be her coffee talking. He grabbed his book bag and rushed down the steps. "Coming down now!"

He bounded into the kitchen and the smell of pancakes hit his nose.

"I'm up, I'm here!"

"Good morning to you too. Pancakes and sausage are on the table," said Debbie.

"Yum! Morning Dad," said Jay.

"About time you're up," said Jay's dad. At 48, Alan was already in his morning routine of the last 20 years. Wake up at 6:00, brew coffee, drink it black, read the paper, worry about the world's problems, and then commute to work.

Debbie walked over and slid a plate full of pancakes and sausage in front of Jay.

"Yum! Thanks, Mom."

As Jay dug in, his dad put the paper he was reading down on the table. He looked at Jay for a moment and asked, "So are you ready to visit Gavin and tour P&C College?"

"Yea, but I'm just not 100% sure I'm sold on P&C yet. I'm still not even sure what major I want to pick."

Alan let out a half sigh. "Well... Following in your brother's footsteps would be a good place to start."

"I know, I know, he's the greatest. I'm just not sure yet."

"You still have a few months before you have to apply and choose," suggested Debbie, with a smile.

Alan nodded and added, "But remember, to get a job like Gavin's, you have to actually follow through and get accepted into P&C."

Jay cringed. There was that word *actually* again. Did anybody have faith in him?

"Of course I can get accepted into P&C, Dad. Like I said, I'm not sure about what major I want to pick. The only reason I'd go is because Gavin could get me a job afterwards?"

Alan's paper came down again, and this time it knocked his fork off his plate. The metal fork clanged on the tile kitchen floor.

Alan squinted his eyes, looking exasperated. "Jay, P&C College is one of the best in the country. You should be glad your brother blazed a trail there instead of turning your nose up at it."

His dad was frustrated every morning after reading the paper. But today he was unusually argumentative. Jay just decided to drop it. "I'm not, that's why I'm applying and going to visit."

Debbie chimed in. "That sounds like the perfect place to start. Isn't Gary supposed to be back from his trip soon?" she asked.

"Yeah! He's driving me to school. It's his first day back

from his trip to California."

Alan scoffed again. "He's been gone from school? What kind of parents let their kid start senior year a month late?"

"I guess Gary's parents."

"Okay, smart aleck. Aren't they a bunch of computer nerds? Last I heard they worked from home or something."

"Yeah, they started their own business. Did you know they both dropped out of college?"

Alan's face grew red, and before he could say anything, Debbie cleared her throat and jumped in, "Please don't argue you two."

Alan put his hand up in irritation. "The only thing I'll say, Jay, is that your mother and I are the first ones in our families to graduate from college. Your brother worked hard to get where he's at on Wall Street. So you need to go too, bottom line."

"Dad, I know!" Jay finished his breakfast. He still knew what his parents didn't. Gavin grades and SAT scores all came from Adderall, which Jay wasn't willing to take. The satisfaction of knowing that helped him stay quiet while he listened to his dad drone on. Midway through Alan's lecture, one sentence caught Jay's attention:

"If you want to keep giving us such a hard time, why don't YOU step up and pay for college?" asked Alan.

Now he had Jay's full attention. His dad could be aggressive in arguments, but this challenge was new. The way he said it sounded like a threat.

"Well, you said you'd pay for college. You paid for Gavin's." A feeling of terror crept up Jay's spine. He knew money had been tight for his parents...but he didn't know how tight.

"We paid for Gavin's because he had things figured out. He did what he was supposed to do at P&C, and now he makes a lot of money. If you don't want to follow in your brother's footsteps, then you need to lay out a better plan. It doesn't sound to me like you even have one."

"I didn't know I was supposed to come up with one. I just thought you'd be paying for it!"

Alan took a long sip of coffee and put his mug down on the table. "I didn't say we wouldn't. I said if you keep giving us a hard time, you might find yourself paying. You know, P&C has raised tuition quite a bit."

Jay swallowed a bite of his pancakes. "I saw they did, which is why I'm trying to be sure I know why I'm going. I mean, I don't want to *just* find a job afterward. I want to find a job that I like... something that matters, you know?"

Alan laughed and picked up the paper. "Ah... young idealism! First get into P&C. Then get a job and we'll see what you think about changing the world." Alan looked back to his newspaper.

Jay felt the anger rising inside him. Before he could respond, Debbie sighed. "Can we please have a meal without you two arguing all the time?"

Alan sighed and pushed his chair back. "Sorry dear...ahhh... the hardship of youth. Everything paid for, and every possibility open. Call me old fashioned, but college is the place where you figure everything out. I don't know why you're not more appreciative that Gavin lined up so many things for you? Aren't you grateful for any of it?"

"Yes, I'm grateful for it all, Dad," stammered Jay.

"Good. Then get excited about visiting your brother and P&C. And until you show me a better plan, I don't want to hear about anything else." Alan stared at Jay for a second before getting up from the table. He shook his head and turned to Debbie. "Thanks for breakfast. I need to go."

Debbie jumped up and got Alan's plate. "Bye honey, have a good day."

Alan grabbed his briefcase and walked out the front door. It slammed shut behind him.

2

A SHOCK

"We just want what's best for you."
–Debbie Pencha

The door slammed, and Jay and his Mom sat silently for a few seconds. Jay finished the last few bites of his breakfast, and looked up at his Mom.

"I didn't mean to make Dad upset. I was just trying to talk things out," said Jay.

"I know..." Debbie said. She sat slumped at the table. She looked tired.

"Thanks for breakfast Mom, it was great."

"You're welcome. Jay, you know your father is busy lately. There's a lot on his mind, and we...we just want what's best for you. Isn't your ride going to be here soon?"

"I know, Mom. Yeah, it'll be here soon." He unlocked his phone and saw a text from Gary. "T-minus 5 mins. Prepare YO' SELF"

Jay smiled and picked up his plate, and put it in the dishwasher. From the corner of his eye, he noticed his Mom was leaning over the table. She was wiping her face.

Tears. She was wiping away tears.

He walked over and put his hand on her shoulder. "Please don't be upset. I'm sorry I was arguing with Dad. But P&C is expensive, and I'm not sure I even want to go."

Debbie turned to Jay from the table. "It's not that, and I'm not upset with you," she said. "Your father..." She paused and shook her head. Debbie looked at Jay with watery eyes. "Jay, your father lost his job last week."

Jay's stomach sank to the floor, and blood rushed from his face. His parent's budget was already tight, and his mom was only working part-time. Worst-case scenarios cascaded through his mind. As each scenario emerged, he saw himself as the central expense.

"What do you mean? Dad got fired?"

"No, he didn't get fired. His whole department was... replaced. Supposedly some technology company is making something new... I don't know all the details."

"Well, don't cry, it can't be that bad."

Debbie pressed her hands over her face for a moment. "I can't believe I told you. I wasn't supposed to say anything until we figured it out. Look, just don't tell your father okay?"

"Fine... I won't say anything, but why didn't you want to tell me?"

"We didn't want to burden you. You need to focus on getting accepted to P&C."

"But if we don't have the money, and P&C is so expensive, why should I apply?"

Debbie sighed. "Don't be difficult now. This is already hard enough on your father and I. We'll figure something out. We always do."

Jay heard the last sentence, but didn't believe it. Without his dad working, he knew there was no way they could pay for P&C. How could he even ask them to try? He took a breath and fought the urge to panic. Since he was little, they had always had enough money, but he knew it was a touchy issue.

His mind raced. "What if I get a job, or figure out how to pay for college?"

"Jay, you've never worked at a job for more than two weeks."

Jay's thoughts spun to generate ideas... Gary! His best friend's parents were never worried about money. Maybe his family knew something they didn't.

"Yeah, I've quit those jobs because they sucked. I'll talk to Gary! His parents are loaded." Jay heard himself say the words and immediately regretted them.

"Stop, I don't want to talk about it again until we figure it out. Gary's parents are college dropouts. And even if they did manage to get lucky with money, why would you listen to them? I have my degree and can't even find a full-time job. You know what every job application asks for? At least a Masters Degree." Her eyes started to water up again.

Jay didn't know what else to say without making things worse. All that came out was, "Fine. I'm sorry."

"I can't handle talking about this anymore today. It's overwhelming. We'll figure it out. If you do want to help, you could start by not bringing up Gary or his family around your dad. Okay?"

"Okay."

Debbie stood up and walked out of the kitchen, and then upstairs.

Fear percolated with anger as Jay stood alone in the kitchen. He fought back tears of frustration. It wasn't his fault that his dad got fired. Maybe he should start being more like Gavin, and stop caring so much.

This wasn't fair. But maybe his parents were right. Maybe Gary's family just got lucky. It was easy for Gary, thought Jay. As long as they had been friends, money was never a worry.

Now, Jay was walking into his senior year with no way to pay for college.

His phone buzzed, and the music outside let him know that Gary was here. He grabbed his phone and backpack and walked outside.

3

SENIOR YEAR

"What if it only took three months to buy your freedom?"
−Gary Weinstein

Jay opened up the front door, still in shock. No wonder his Dad had been frustrated lately.

Rap music and bass instantly filled his ears. He forced a smile, then looked up and saw Gary's "SICK" surprise.

It was a new, hybrid sedan. The bright blue car sat idling in the street with its windows down, and flashers on. Behind the driver's seat sat the 5'3", 105 lb., glasses wearing, rap music blaring, Gary Weinstein. He had a few loves in life. Among them were: books, coding, and gangster rap. Now one of his loves was loud enough for the entire neighborhood to hear. Jay cringed as he watched one of his neighbors, Ms. Johansen, out walking her dog. She stared at Gary with a look of confusion. As she walked by, she trained her gaze to Jay. He smiled and waved. Ms. Johansen squinted and kept walking.

Jay jogged up to the driver side door and yelled, "TURN IT DOWN!"

Gary mouthed the word "oops", then turned the music way down.

"My bad! Dude! Checkout the new whip!" He darted his eyebrows up and down, "Senior year is all about rollin' in style!"

Gary looked a bit ridiculous, but his energy was contagious. He spread his hands across the interior of the sedan, complete with leather seats and a double roof sunroof.

Jay was envious as he looked over the car. He was used to driving his families oldest car, which wasn't exactly nice. Now that his Mom was back to working part-time, he didn't even have that.

He pulled on the door handle to get inside. "It's nice man, but the door's still locked!"

"Uh, yea... you downloaded Drivr right?"

"Yea, why?" asked Jay.

"Well the first ride is free, but only after you leave me a nice review." Gary pointed to his phone showcasing a Drivr logo perched in the front window.

"Are you serious?" asked Jay, as he threw his hands up in exasperation.

"Gas isn't free and neither is this new whip! C'mon, request me on Drivr. I need the reviews!"

"Ha-ha. Dude, it's been a rough morning. I'm not in the mood." Jay pulled on the door handle again.

"I won't be in a good mood until you give me a good review. Help me help you chauffeur your broke ass around!"

Jay rolled his eyes. "Gary, you realize you're not from the streets...right?"

Gary whispered, "Then tell me why I hustle like it son!"

Jay couldn't keep a straight face. He laughed, pulled out his phone, and requested him on Drivr. Gary smiled, and then tapped his phone to accept.

"Wooo-wooo!!! Hop in man." He unlocked the doors.

Jay sat down in the passenger seat. Gary was completely ridiculous, but to his credit, he was an entrepreneur. Ever since Jay had known him, he was always scheming up new ideas, selling something, or starting businesses that puttered out and went nowhere.

As they drove, Jay admired the brand new car. "This is sick, congratulations man... But what the hell! It's been three months. What's so secret about this pilgrimage? You can't even text?"

"Thanks, It was a complete social media and phone detox. That, plus I got a new job! I was too busy working, but I'll fill you in on it later!"

"Fine... Did your parents get the car for you? This is yours?"

"Oh my parents didn't buy it, I bought this baby. They did co-sign, but only so I could get a loan with APR under inflation. I'm making the payments."

"You're gonna make enough money driving around here?"

"Yeah, I've already had a few customers since I got back. I should be able to bring in a couple racks a month."

"A couple thousand dollars?!" Jay stammered.

"Yea, a couple G's son! And that's just small change compared to what I'm working on," said Gary.

"And what's that? Why wasn't I in the loop?" asked Jay.

"Well, I haven't texted because I've been too busy. I've been working the whole time. My parents had to go out west for business, and I went out there to step up my coding game."

"You're already good, what'd you go out there for?" asked Jay.

"To become great, son! I went to a Bootcamp... it's like a year of technical training compressed into a 10-week course."

"So how was it?"

"Amazing. But, there was no time to do anything else."

"So why'd you take the social media detox?"

"I needed to focus. Didn't want any distractions, because I made a big bet with my parents."

"Okay, so what was the bet for?"

"The bet was that if I lined up something better than college by the time I graduated, I wouldn't have to go."

Jay felt his frustration return. "Wait, what? We've always talked about going to college together!"

Gary's eyes widened as he tried to explain. "But–"

Jay cut him off, now practically yelling. "We were supposed to go visit P&C this month!" His morning had gone from bad to worse.

Gary's face looked terrified and broke into a rapid explanation. "I'm sorry man... it was last minute. My parents brought up the challenge to me... I still want to go visit P&C with you, but I don't think I want to go anymore."

"What the hell? We talked about going to college together and now you're not going? What kind of hypocrite move is that?"

"Hypocrite?" asked Gary, shaking his head. "Oh nooo, I changed my mind when I found a better path! That's not being a hypocrite, that's being smart."

"I can't believe you."

"We talked about it, but I've been researching better options for a year. Now I found a better path, and I was excited to tell you about it. I'm the one who took the risk and spent the money on it! Isn't that what best friends do? Learn and help each other?"

"Look... I don't even care. It's been a rough morning. I don't want to hear about your trip." Jay blinked his eyes and put his head in his hands. Did his best friend really not want to go to college with him anymore? This was going to be a long year.

Now Gary was pissed. He squinted at Jay through his glasses. "What'd you think? That we were friends based on mutually assured mediocrity? The whole reason I went out there is because it's a great opportunity. For me... and for you!"

"Yea right. It sounds like you got the hookup for you. I don't need one more thing to worry about. My parents are screwed, I might be too..."

Gary's face turned from defensive to genuine worry. "Wait... my bad man... what happened?"

"Ah...nothing that major... but it sucks. It's kind of embarrassing," said Jay.

"It's probably not as embarrassing as having Mandy Steven's parents contact the school, and request that the student known as Gary Weinstein stop messaging their daughter."

Jay laughed. "Maybe that's worse. It's just my parents man."

"Annnd? Drop the worries on Doctor G."

"Well, my dad lost his job."

"Oh... crap. That does suck man. Sorry to hear that."

"Yea, and it's not just that... It's like... I don't want my parents paying all that tuition for P&C. And I don't know if I even want to do what Gavin does."

Gary put up his finger to interject. "That's why I'm trying to tell you about the Bootcamp!"

Jay shot him a warning glance. "Not now man. Information overload. My dad just lost his job. Not everybody's family has money for stuff like that."

Gary looked offended. "I'm sorry your dad lost his job... But I'm sorry I'm not sorry my parents busted their asses to start a business!" said Gary.

Jay turned and looked out the window. "I can't handle anything else right now. Just drive us to school, OKAY?"

Gary put his hands up defensively. "Fine! But eventually you might want to listen."

Jay crossed his arm and fought the urge to say anything he'd regret.

4

MYSTERIOUS MESSAGE

*"I'm back from the promised land, and they let me in
without college!"*
–Gary Weinstein

A few minutes passed as Jay and Gary sat in silence.
Eventually, Jay started to feel bad about yelling at Gary. "I'm
sorry I yelled. I just don't know what to do."

Gary nodded. "Thanks, but don't stress about this. All I'm
saying is we have thousands of options and opportunities in
front of us. Have some faith, and we'll figure it out."

"Maybe I do, but it doesn't feel like it right now."

"Dude, I learned more in 10 weeks in Cali than I did in all
four years of high school! There's this whole new wave of
jobs coming. It's not that big of a deal that your dad lost his.
There are tons of new ones."

Gary's phone vibrated with a new message. He turned to
Jay. "I don't want to check that while I'm driving, can you get
it?"

"Sure... It says you have a notification about, *College or*

Not? What's that?" asked Jay.

"Oh! That's Mr. Moore's class."

"Oh yea... Isn't he that new teacher?"

"Yup. He was in the military for a while, and now he's teaching. My parents know him, and they say he's legit. I saw for an elective I could take Pemberton's College Prep class, or Mr. Moore's *College Or Not* class. Easy choice."

Jay laughed. "Good call. Pemberton hates you, so why do you need *College or Not*? I thought you have everything figured out now?"

"I don't, but while I'm still stuck in high school, I'm going to learn everything I can."

"So what's the class about?"

"The syllabus looks like it's a survival course for the new economy. The course goals are to decide if college even makes sense, and show us how to pick and decide what skills to learn."

"How is anybody supposed to get a decent job without college?"

"Get skills that employers need, prove it to them, and get hired."

"And that's going to work?"

"Uh... Yeah! Why wouldn't it?" Gary looked at Jay as if he was asking stupid questions. He took the last turn into the school parking lot and reclined his seat.

"Oh my God, did you just recline your seat?"

"Yea, gotta let these shorties know what's up," said Gary as he bobbed his head and turned up the music.

Jay laughed and shook his head.

Gary made sure to drive around the parking lot several

times. In his words, he needed to, "peep the scene" and ensure everyone knew he was there. He rolled slowly through the parking lot, nodding to random groups of students walking outside. Jay couldn't keep a straight face and put his face in his palms.

"Good Lord! What did homeschooling do to you?"

Gary leaned even further back in his seat and turned to Jay. "No shame in my game. Gotta roll slow before you roll fast. You feel me?"

Jay kept laughing... "I feel you all right. You're gonna have to roll with a restraining order if you keep creeping like this. Just park already!"

"Don't hate, man!" Gary sat up slightly, and pulled into an open parking spot.

They got out of the car and walked through the parking lot. Students hung out in groups, and the last of the busses passed through.

Jay was walking with his shoulders slumped, and Gary shook his book bag. "Cheer up! I'm telling you, don't worry about that stuff with your parents!"

"Easy for you to say."

Gary turned his head to the side in mock thought. "Yes... yes it IS easy for me to say, because I'm making money now, and I have skills people want to pay for!"

Hordes of students walked around them and the bus brakes squealed loudly to their right. Jay stopped in his tracks and looked at Gary. "Wait I thought your job was just driving for Drivr?"

"Oh no, that's my secondary source of income. The Bootcamp I worked through in Cali helped me land a mobile developer job at a startup."

Jay was stunned. "Wait what? So you got a real job after just three months? There aren't any good jobs around here, how'd you manage that?"

Gary laughed. "Drivr's a real job too... but nooow you want to listen."

"Yeah I want to listen!" said Jay. "I had no idea, fill me in! In just three months? Do you think I could do it?"

"Told you I went out there for both of us!"

"So who are you working for? What are you doing?" Jay was ready to ask more questions, but Gary put up a hand to stop him.

"It's a mobile developer job for Livu. They were a tech startup, and now they're a full-blown company. They're well funded, and I have a six-month trial work arrangement. I'm making $50 an hour now and I'll be making over double that once I go full time."

Jay's head spun. "Are you kidding me? You're not moving there to work are you?"

"Not yet, for now it's remote work. There's no commute, and I can do it from anywhere. Plus, it's in demand, so I have options. Maybe I'll move there later, I dunno."

The first bell rang. Begrudgingly, they both kept walking into school.

5

AN ANGRY MAN

"If they figured it out, then why can't I?"
–Jay Pencha

As they walked up the side entrance to their school, the door swung open.

The school janitor, Mr. Regis, propped open the door. He was whistling as he mopped the floor. As Gary and Jay approached, he looked up at them and smiled.

"Morning, boys," said Mr. Regis. "Gary, how are your parents doing?"

"They're great Mr. Regis, what about yourself?" asked Gary.

"If I was any better, it'd be a crime."

As they walked away, Jay turned to Gary. "How do your parents know him?"

"When they built their new house, he did all the plumbing."

"Ah... I gotcha. That's sad he has to work two jobs to pay the bills," said Jay.

Gary shook his head. "Uh... Not exactly. He owns the

business. It's like 10 trucks and 40 employees. He's worth a few million dollars."

"What... a few million dollars?! Yeah right."

"At least. I'm telling you, man, skills are the path to financial freedom."

As Jay and Gary walked to their lockers, the school halls bustled with activity. Students scrambled to class, or huddled in groups along the walls. Jay and Gary navigated through the crowded halls to their lockers, which were only a few spaces apart. As Jay opened his, a girl's voice cut through the noise in the hall.

"HEY! Why didn't you text back?"

Jay turned around in time to see Ella punch him playfully in the shoulder. Her brown hair was in a ponytail, and she was wearing her soccer jersey. Jay knew he should have played soccer this year. It would have been an awesome excuse to hang out with her.

"Hey, I was going to ask you the same thing!"

She smiled and stepped back, holding her phone up to Jay's face. "So... I texted you last, and you never texted back. A bit rude don't you think?"

"Wait, I thought *you* didn't text back. I swear! Here look!" Jay fumbled in his pocket, grabbed his phone, and tapped his messages. "There... see? I was waiting for your text!"

Ella looked up from her phone and smiled. "Oh well. I forgive you... THIS time." She turned and smiled at Gary. "Hey Gary, I saw your car, is that new?"

"Hey Ella. Yep! New whip, new game this year."

"Uh... Cool. Yeah, my friends and I saw you driving it in circles around the parking lot."

Gary's face turned bright red... "Yea, I was just checking things out!"

Ella turned back to Jay. "SO. I've been trying to catch up on all the SAT vocabulary for College Prep. It's crazy, right?"

"Yea it is, but why are you worried about it? You'll get accepted early to P&C!" said Jay.

"Maybe, but might as well keep studying now. It won't be long before I have to take the GRE for graduate school."

The thought of graduate school made Jay's mind shut down. Thinking about more school after this was tough, even if it was college. Thinking about graduate school after college made him anxious. He grabbed his books, shut his locker, and turned to Ella.

"I don't think you have much to worry about."

"Yeah, well better safe than sorry," she said. "Hey you're still going to apply to P&C right? Didn't your brother go there?"

"Yeaaa, he went there. I'm still applying."

"You'd better!"

As Ella kept talking about their College Prep class, Jay noticed that Gary was captivated by a group of football players walking down the hall. The goon squad was led by Conor Trajan. Conor was Ella's ex-boyfriend, who was a full head taller then Jay. He was from a rich family, and was headed to P&C on a sports scholarship. He was, to put it mildly, an all around jerk. As Jay and Ella talked, Conor's eyes locked with Jay's in a stare that said, "I'm going to kill you."

Ella noticed Jay's attention drifting, and she spun around. "Oh! Hi, Conor."

"Sup Ella," said Conor. He nodded his head and kept walking.

Ella turned back and kept talking. Gary stared nervously at the rest of Conor's goons as they walked away. Gary had a theory that Conor had Traumatic Brain Injury from the hits to the head he had taken in football. The looks he gave, his constant readiness to fight, and Ella's break up with him, all supported that theory.

"I've gotta go finish homework for class. See you in College Prep, Jay! Bye Gary." Ella turned and skipped down the hall.

Gary leaned over to Jay and whispered, "YOU STUD! You didn't tell me Ella was so into you man! I leave for three months and you've already got a girlfriend! Now I know why you're so hung up on College Prep and P&C!"

Jay looked at Gary with a smile. "Yeah, I think she likes me, and it'd be cool to go to P&C with her, but I can't stand College Prep. It has to be the most boring class ever."

"Then switch to *College Or Not*? You already have a good enough GPA and SAT score to get into college. Why wouldn't you explore the real world now?"

"Yea, I'm still not sure..."

"What do you think will make Ella like you more? Being one of 4,000 freshmen at P&C? Or being the only guy your age that's making BANK at a sick tech job? We can visit P&C anytime, and showing up as ballers who work in tech is better than being starving freshman."

"Yeah I guess that'd be better. Do you really think it's doable... like could I get a job like yours by end of the year?"

"Maybe, but you would have to start working like crazy."

As Jay and Gary walked through the halls, they almost

bumped into Mr. Pemberton, the massive school Guidance Counselor and College Prep teacher. He stood in front of them, glaring at Gary.

"Mr. Weinstein, you've missed the entire first month of your senior year!"

"Mr. Pemberton, I wouldn't say I *missed* it!" Gary winked, gave a thumbs up, and Mr. Pemberton's face looked disgusted. Gary was physically small, but it didn't stop him from standing up to Mr. Pemberton's 6'3" frame. Pemberton had been a great football player in high school. He played a bit in college, got hurt, and eventually made his way into teaching.

"Gary, you're late for your senior year, you have yet to take the SAT's, and your GPA leaves a lot to be desired. I have no idea how you'll get accepted into a decent college." Pemberton shook his head as if Gary had failed.

"I'm not going to college!" said Gary cheerfully.

"Then good luck making any money or finding a decent job. If you ever plan to start a family, it will be very hard on minimum wage."

Gary's face turned to mock worry. "Family planning? Slow down Mr. P... I need to figure out how to get laid first!" Several students around them turned to stare at the scene unfolding, and Pemberton's face turned red.

"V-V-Very funny smart aleck." Pemberton turned swiftly to Jay. "I don't have to remind you that Gavin graduated summa cum laude from P&C... and landed a great job afterwards."

"No reminder necessary," said Jay.

"So, I take it you'll be ready to apply soon to P&C?" asked Pemberton.

"I don't know... they raised tuition again, and the only

reason I'd go there would be to get a job where Gavin works."

Mr. Pemberton sighed in exasperation. "Well first things first, and that means applying to P&C and some safety schools. You can figure out the tuition and all that later. Your GPA and SAT scores are good, but not quite up to par with Gavin's. And it's a shame you've gone through four years of high school without playing football. I'm worried you won't be as... compelling of an applicant as Gavin."

Before Jay could speak up, Gary jumped in. "Speaking about Gavin, Jay and I are going to visit him and P&C!"

Mr. Pemberton looked at Jay then back to Gary. "That's nice. Be careful Jay, you'll become like the people you hang around." He turned and walked down the hall.

Gary and Jay turned in the opposite direction. As they walked, Jay couldn't help but think about all the demands from his parents and Pemberton. They were all right about one thing; Jay was a lot like Gavin. But he was like Gavin *used* to be, imaginative. He still believed that there was something he could do with his life that mattered. Gavin had been like that until high school. Then he started to jump through all the hoops their parents and Pemberton placed in front of him.

Jay used to look up to his older brother for a long time, but he'd stopped in recent years. He watched Gavin get "serious" about college in the early days of high school. Hanging out with his younger brother turned into a burden, and all of Gavin's time went into studying for tests, playing sports, and prepping for the SAT. As he did, all the adults around him patted him on the back. It was an exhausting load, and to keep up with it all, Gavin turned to Adderall on weekdays, and alcohol on the weekends.

Jay watched his older brother's creativity get hammered until it fit neatly inside a cubicle. He thought about all the pictures Gavin posted online. If all he did was work 80-hour weeks and get wasted every weekend, something was wrong. Jay's mind snapped back to the present, and he turned to Gary.

"How do I transfer into Mr. Moore's class?"

"MY MAN!" Gary yelled. Some freshman in the hall turned and gave them both a weird look. Gary smiled at them, raised both arms in the air and proclaimed triumphantly, "HE'S BACKKKK!"

Jay chuckled and pushed Gary. "Okay, okay, so what do I need to do?"

"Go get the form from the guidance office, get Mr. Moore to sign it, and you're good."

"I'll do it tomorrow."

"Lazy, lazy, lazy."

"Oh come on, it's not –"

"Do it now!"

"Fine, let's go get the form," muttered Jay. They still had a few minutes before class, and he and Gary headed off to the guidance office.

6

A Virtuous One

"Most people won't show up or do the work. Force yourself to do both. If you do, you'll bypass the competition."
–Mr. Moore

Jay walked into the guidance office, glad to see Pemberton wasn't there yet. He found the form in a box on the wall, and quickly walked out.

"Got it?"

"Yeah. If I end up homeless in the gutter, I'm blaming it on you!"

"And what if I help you find a sick job you actually like?"

"I won't complain about that," laughed Jay. He looked over at Gary, who was squinting down the hall. He grabbed Jay's arm and pointed. "That's Mr. Moore! Go get him to sign it and let's bust you out of College Prep."

The two jogged down the hall, and caught up to the medium height teacher walking swiftly down the halls.

Gary called out ahead, "Hey Mr. Moore!"

The man stopped in his tracks and swiveled around. "Gary!

How was the trip to California? Your parents said you finished your Bootcamp."

"It was great, I got a job with Livu right after!" said Gary.

"Well congratulations" said Mr. Moore as he shook his hand. He turned to Jay and extended a hand. "Hi, Thomas Moore."

"Jay Pencha, nice to meet you."

Mr. Moore motioned over his shoulder. "I was on my way to class, is there anything I can help you with?"

"Yeah" said Jay, holding up his form. "I was wondering if you could sign this transfer form for your class?"

"Sure thing," said Mr. Moore as he took out a pen, placed the form on the wall, signed it, and handed it back. "Here you go."

"Thanks," said Jay. "That was easy enough. So Gary said your class is about finding a great job?" asked Jay.

"Kind of. I'd describe it as learning to navigate the new economy. We search and find the best options out there, then reverse engineer a path for students to break into those fields. That might mean college, or there might be a hidden path you can take."

"Sounds good," said Jay.

"Great! Well drop off that form in guidance, and class starts in 10! See you both there," Mr. Moore turned and started walking back down the hall.

7

UNLIKE ANY OTHER CLASS

"If it's hard to ask them for help, then they might not be your friend."
–Gary Weinstein

Jay and Gary dropped the form off and walked to Mr. Moore's class. As they approached from the hall, the classroom was bustling with noise. Makes sense, thought Jay, class hasn't started yet. He wasn't sure what he was expecting, but when he and Gary walked through the door to Mr. Moore's class, it wasn't at all what he imagined.

His classroom was one with a lab, and it had raised tables that were all filled with students, laptops, and papers spread everywhere. Nobody was seated. Everybody was either up walking around, talking, or writing on whiteboards. It didn't seem to be random, as Jay noticed the students were in groups of two or three. They all seemed to be collaborating on something.

He and Gary walked to their desks, and put their books down. Mr. Moore was standing at the far end of the room, talking to one group that seemed to be in some sort of a debate. He shook his head vigorously, then drew something on paper in front of three students, pointed to it, and they had an "aha" moment. The students took the piece of paper, listened, nodded, and then resumed their work. Mr. Moore walked up to Jay and Gary in the front of the room.

"Welcome!" he said. "Hmmmm... It's the first day for both of you. Let's see what you missed." He handed them each a class syllabuses.

"Thanks." said Gary and Jay.

Jay looked at everyone spread out throughout the room and decided to venture a question. "Doesn't class start soon?"

Mr. Moore grinned from ear to ear. "It already has! We *do* more than we *talk*. Not much sitting or lecturing here."

Gary rubbed his hands together. "Now THIS is the class I've been missing!" He pointed to each of the groups. "What are each of those groups working on?"

Mr. Moore pointed to one of the first bullets on the syllabus he handed them. "Right now everybody is working on finding and identifying 20 companies that are doing good work in the world. Ideally, they're companies who have products or services that help humanity."

"Okay, that sounds easy enough," said Jay, as he glanced at the syllabus.

Mr. Moore looked around the class. "So far it seems every student in here wants to uncover a meaningful job, opportunity, or career after high school. We're all on roughly the same page of finding work that's challenging and rewarding."

Jay and Gary both nodded, and Mr. Moore pointed to a quote on the whiteboard. "As a class, we've agreed that these subjects are worth fighting against."

The massive whiteboard at the front of the room listed:

Extinction

Disease

Economic Scarcity

Evil (In all of it's forms)

Gary and Jay glanced at each other in agreement, and Gary pointed to Economic Scarcity. "So, I just got a job as a mobile developer at Livu, a learning startup. That would fall under fighting Economic Scarcity?"

"Yes, and you're way ahead of the game," said Mr. Moore.

"And I'm still trying to figure out if I should go to college... I'm not sure what I want to do," said Jay.

"Perfect!" said Mr. Moore, with a grin. "First find some companies doing great work, and from there we'll figure out what skills they need, then calculate the most affordable and best way for you to acquire them. Maybe it's through college, an alternative, or... maybe it's... cue the evil music... no college at all!" Mr. Moore turned to make sure there wasn't anybody listening in and Jay laughed.

Mr. Moore tilted his head. "But eventually, we'll be reaching out to those companies and their employees to discover what it's really like to work there. Ideally, every student will go visit them in person to see firsthand if they want that lifestyle. For now, get started researching. I'm here to help. And Gary, if you have work to do for work, you can bring it to class."

Gary's eyes lit up behind his glasses. "Really? You're serious?"

"Sure," said Mr. Moore. "As long as you don't mind teaching a bit. You know, letting everybody know how you got the job, what the Bootcamp was like... stuff like that."

"Yea! That's no problem!" said Gary with a smile.

Mr. Moore nodded. "Great, well get to work, and give me a shout if you need something." He walked over to another group who had a question.

Jay looked over at Gary, still cheesing from ear to ear. "Good call on transferring."

"Told you this would be good," laughed Gary. He grabbed a notebook, and they stood at a lab desk. Jay researched while Gary read a book he needed to for work. After a few minutes Jay paused and looked up at Gary. "This doesn't feel like work. This feels like a scavenger hunt."

"That's the point!" said Gary. "If you just assume work has to suck, you're liable to stay at places that suck instead of searching for companies with big missions."

"Yeah I guess that makes sense," said Jay. He paused for a second, and then decided to ask what felt like a stupid question.

"I don't even know what work is like at a startup or tech company. I mean, what does everybody do there?" asked Jay.

Gary thought for a second. "Well...hmmm..." he took off his glasses and rubbed his eyes. "I guess it boils down to four main types of jobs inside them, you have: business, engineering, design, and science type stuff."

"Uh... Okay, but are all the jobs remote like yours?" Jay asked with a confused look on his face.

Gary shook his head. "Not all of them, plenty of companies have their teams on location, some half and half, or some are a mixture based on the job you do."

"Ah... I see," said Jay. "So this might be dumb too, but I just assumed a technology company or startup was filled with... no offense... computer nerds?"

"Hah! If by computer nerds you mean ballers, then, yes."

"C'mon, really?"

"Well it depends on your definition of baller."

"Okay, Mr. Technical... well let's see... Gavin and his friends party almost every night and they all drive ridiculous cars. That looks pretty baller to me."

"Have you met any of them?" asked Gary.

"Not yet, but we will when we go to visit."

"Perfect. What do they do again? Is it investment banking or consulting?"

Jay stretched and then shrugged. "Uh... I think investment banking. All I know is that P&C grads usually end up doing one or the other."

"So... go see what his job's like, then compare it to a tech co. It's not rocket science!" laughed Gary.

"Yeah but I don't know anybody else in technology besides you!"

Gary glared at Jay. "You know my parents started a technology company, why don't you ask them?"

"Ask what?" said Jay.

"Ask to go see their offices, meet their team, see what actually goes on at a tech co. I mean, they're entrepreneurs, they started it at their kitchen table and grew it. You're not gonna find a better one to tour in this town. We could stop by tonight?"

"Okay, let's do it," said Jay.

"Done. I'll text them now and let 'em know we're coming through tonight."

Jay felt stupid for never thinking to ask this before. For a while he wasn't sure what Gary's parents actually did. He just knew they were successful, assumed it was luck, and vaguely knew it had something to do with technology. Maybe seeing what they did in person would be a good idea? There wasn't anything to lose.

8

THE WEINSTEIN'S BUSINESS

"We can't hire good designers and developers fast enough."
–John Weinstein, Oxen Co-Founder

After school, Jay and Gary headed off to his parent's work. Their sleepy suburb town had started to boom in the last few years. Cheap real estate was abundant, as the biggest nearby cities were all overcrowded. Now, businesses like Gary's parents' were starting to call the downtown area home.

Jay never would have predicted his hometown would grow like it was now. As they drove through downtown, the streets were crowded with people who were just getting off work. The buildings along the streets were now filled with restaurants, new bars, stores, and even a gym. They continued to drive towards the fringe of the downtown where most of the new construction was happening.

Gary slowed down and pointed to a sign they passed that

said, "City Center Coming Soon."

Both sides of the street in the new city center where bordered by the tallest buildings in town. The first level of each building contained retail stores, and the second two levels appeared to be offices. But above the offices, it looked like apartments and condos were being built.

Jay rolled his window down and looked all around. "This is sick."

"I know, right?" said Gary.

"Where were they working before?" asked Jay.

Gary shrugged. "Out of the house for the first few years... wherever really. The team was remote before, but now they have enough local team members and profits to get an office."

They pulled up to one of the high rises at the end of the city center. Beyond it's border of sidewalks sat a park, and then a woods. Jay saw walking paths snaking through the park and woods. A few people were out running or walking their dogs.

Jay marveled at the location. It was hard to imagine he could work at a place like that. After all, didn't you need a degree to work at a place like this? Maybe not... If Gary was already working at a startup after a few months of training, why couldn't he?

Gary parked the car in a space on the street, and they walked up to the tall glass building. By the door, Gary punched in a security code and the doors unlocked. They entered the massive lobby and the afternoon sun spilled over everything inside. Jay followed Gary up the first flight of steps. They walked up onto the second floor, and up to another set of glass doors containing the simple words, "OXEN."

Gary paused at the doors and entered another security code.

He pushed the doors open and they both walked inside.

Jay knew Gary's parents were smart, but he wasn't expecting this. Over the last few years he knew that they did something with computers from home, but he didn't realize it was a full-fledged business. He had an image in his head of a very small side income stream, or a simple home based business. This wasn't at all what he imagined. His gaze stretched across an open floor plan of standing desks, cathedral ceilings, hanging light fixtures, and an entire wall of floor to ceiling glass windows that looked out over the forest and walking trails he had seen earlier. Hardwood floors covered the entire place, and each standing desk and work area rose like an island for each team member. Brand new, large silver computer monitors dotted the desks.

Gary turned around, arms outstretched while darting his eyes up and down behind his glasses. "So... what do you think?"

A huge smile spread over Jay's face. "Okay, this is ridiculous... This is your parents business? I had no idea man! This is insane!"

Gary dropped his arms. "Impressive, right? They lease the space, but yea, they started it all. Oh! It's profitable too! They self-funded OXEN from nothing to where they're at today. A bunch of customers, mostly big businesses, and they've got about 20 employees total now."

Jay's head remained on a swivel as they walked through the office. Each workstation's standing desk could be raised or lowered, depending on if the user wanted to sit or stand. The solid walls to their right were all painted so that they could be used as whiteboards, with a variety of sketches, drawings, and signatures dotted across them. The "team members", as Gary called them, were all scattered around the office. Some looked like they were working hard, and others didn't.

"How long have they been working?" asked Jay.

"Most of them get in after 10 or 11 to avoid rush hour, so not that long," said Gary.

The OXEN team members were a diverse bunch. Some stood with headphones on, furiously tapping away at computers. Some were stretched out with laptops on oversized lounge chairs by the windows. Two of them were outside the glass windows on the balcony, pacing back and forth while making lots of gestures about something.

Another small group sat inside a walled conference room. As Jay peered in, they all seemed to be discussing something serious, but they seemed to be having a good time.

From Jay's first impression of the OXEN offices, the team members were the exact opposite of the pictures that Gavin sent from his, "cubicle farm", as he called it. In his pictures, the ceilings were low, the florescent lights were bright, and everybody wore a suit and tie. The managers and bosses at Gavin's job even had offices that lined the edges of the building, blocking the employee from seeing out the windows. The thought of the "cubicle farm" made Jay claustrophobic. After seeing a workspace like this first hand, it made him hungry to figure out how he could get a job here... or at least at a place like it.

As Jay and Gary walked through the building, a few employees occasionally looked up, smiled, and waved at Gary. They approached the back of the office, and a woman in her late twenties rounded a corner, nearly bumping into them.

She looked out from behind her laptop. "Oops! Oh hey Gary, who's your friend?"

"Hey, Mariel!" smiled Gary. "This is my friend Jay."

Mariel placed her laptop down on a desk, removed both of her headphones, and extended her hand. "Jay! Nice to meet you."

"Nice to meet you, too," said Jay as he shook her hand.

Mariel's gaze shot back to Gary. "I hear you finally got a real job!" She let out a playful laugh, as Gary looked unsure if she was joking.

Like clockwork when he talked to girls, Gary's face turned red and he let out a nervous laugh. "Haha... very funny... Yeah after the coding Bootcamp, I got hired at Livu."

"Nice! Mobile?"

"Yup, it's just a six-month trial run with an interview at the end for a full-time gig."

"Yeah?" she said as a challenge. "Well you're still a youngin', so you'd better deliver some serious value to make sure you lock it in."

"You know how I roll!" said Gary.

Mariel laughed, turned, and pointed to one of the glass conference rooms at the corner of the office. "Your Dad is finishing up with on-boarding a new client, and I think your Mom is out grabbing dinner for everyone."

"Okay cool, thanks Mariel," said Gary. As she walked away, he breathed a sigh of relief, and then turned to Jay. "So what do you think?"

"Yeah, she's pretty hot."

"No! About the offices" said Gary, holding up his arms.

"Oh! I told you, man, this is amazing! I mean, I don't know why I couldn't picture it before I came here... this is legit."

"Right?" said Gary. "C'mon let's grab a drink." He walked over to a kitchen that was open to the rest of the room, opened the fridge, and grabbed Jay a bottle of something green. "Pull up a stool, here you go."

Jay looked around, still taken aback. "Yeah this office is incredible man. What's this?" Jay looked at the green liquid in the bottle.

"Kombucha! And it's delicious," said Gary as he pulled up a stool and sat at the counter.

Jay took a sip and shrugged. "Not bad. So what made you decide to do that Bootcamp? I mean you were thinking about going to college for awhile?"

"Yeah" nodded Gary. "I just analyzed college and the Bootcamp as an investment, and ran the opportunity costs."

"What'd you find?" asked Jay.

"Well, I added up tuition at the best schools I could get into, like P&C. When I add in the opportunity cost of time, and what I could make working someplace else... I'd be down a quarter million dollars..."

Jay coughed on his drink. "What? No way it's that much... is it?"

Gary nodded. "Oh yeah! And just compare it to the Bootcamp. It cost me about $10,000, and in four years, I'm headed towards being up around $250,000-$400,000."

"Are you serious?"

Gary nodded proudly. "And it's work I like, for a company that's reforming education, and I can do it from anywhere."

Jay couldn't understand why Gary had been so modest about all this before. He shook his head as they sat there,

"Why didn't you alert me to all of this before now? Gavin spends 80 hours a week filling out Excel spreadsheets and

PowerPoint's... for people he hates! Why would my parents or I pay P&C for that?"

"Shhh..." Gary looked around. "It's a good point, but you're making a scene, and they haven't paid... yet!"

Jay whispered. "Well then, why didn't you tell me this before?"

"I didn't say much before because I thought you'd only believe it when you ran the numbers... or saw it firsthand! Besides, you'll be able to see it for yourself next month when we visit P&C. Run the numbers yourself and take em' to the admissions office when we go. See what they think." Gary broke into a hysterical laugh that filled the oversized kitchen.

Jay turned to Gary, his mind now racing. "Did your parents pay for the Bootcamp that got your job at Livu?"

"Ohhhhh! No, no, no!" Gary held up his hands and pointed to his chest. "I had to take a loan out to pay for that Bootcamp, all 10 G's of it. I'm paying it back right now, and the second I get hired full time at Livu, that loan will be the best investment I've ever made."

"If your parents have plenty of money, why didn't they pay for you?"

"Because they knew if I didn't pay for it, I wouldn't value it. You've been moping around about how your parents can't pay for P&C, but that might be the best thing that ever happened to you. Because they can't afford it, you've been forced to treat this choice as an investment."

Jay paced back and forth in the kitchen. "This changes everything... I never knew, man... I didn't know there was this much of a difference!"

Gary raised his Kombucha towards Jay. "Let's just toast to you not being afraid to look at reality. Most people are too scared to analyze if their college purchase is an investment."

"Gotcha, well good call on coming here, and thanks for saying something!"

Jay finished his drink, still marveling at the office. "So your parents built all this without college degrees?"

"Yeah! They taught themselves programming, did some consulting work, and eventually started getting job offers when people realized what skills they had."

"And they dropped out of college?!"

"Yeah, the second they had a better option on the table. They both realized that when you have skills that are in high enough demand, you have better options than you'd get from a degree."

Jay downed the rest of his Kombucha. "Yeah... I guess that makes sense. I always thought having money was bad, but I guess your parents are proof you can make it and not let it... go to your head."

"They say it just makes you more of who you are," said Gary. He and Jay both looked up as the door of the conference room swung open, and Gary's dad walked out.

9

MEETING THE TEAM

"I wasn't ready to start a company for a long time. I had to find myself and suffer through horrible bosses... then I was ready."
–Suze Weinstein, Oxen Co-Founder

"Hey guys!" Gary's dad, John walked out of the office and grabbed a water from the fridge. He took a long sip, and then patted Gary on the back. "Good day at school?"

"I'll be out of there soon," said Gary as he stayed tapping on his laptop.

John was an older, and much taller version of Gary. He was still skinny, but his height suggested that an eventual growth spurt for Gary might not be out of the question. Maybe Gary actually was going to hit that growth spurt he always talked about.

Gary had his laptop open, and was working on his assignment for Livu. He looked over to Jay and his Dad with a frown. "Sorry guys, I really want to talk, but I have to buckle down and finish this assignment."

"Duty calls," said Gary's dad. "We'll leave you alone."

John looked at Jay with a smile. "So Gary says you're still not sure about what to do after high school?"

"Yeah," said Jay. "I was supposed to apply to P&C. But... after checking out tuition and everything... I don't know if it makes sense. I guess I'm trying to figure out what it is that I want to do after college. Then maybe I'll be able to figure out the best... and cheapest way to get there."

John took another long sip of water. "That makes perfect sense to me. If more students took some time to think about it, there wouldn't be a trillion plus dollars in student debt." John shook his head as if debt was terrifying. Jay couldn't blame him.

Jay looked around the office. "Thanks for letting me stop by. This place is amazing! I always saw you and Suze working on computers at the house... but I had no idea what you were up to. I couldn't imagine all this."

"Thanks!" said John, looking proudly at the office. "When I first got started, I couldn't imagine it either. I was just learning something that I knew people would pay me for."

He finished his water and motioned to the office. "Want to meet everybody? Ask some questions?"

Jay looked worried. "Ahh... I don't know... I wouldn't want to interrupt them."

"Well, what's still unclear in your mind?"

"I guess what exactly does everyone do at a startup... or technology company?"

John thought for a moment. "There are really only 4 types of jobs in the new economy. You can think of them as BEDS: Business, Engineering, Design, and Science. We have members of our team working in each of these roles. If you go talk to any other company, they will most likely be hiring for those roles too."

Jay nodded eagerly, and hopped off the stool in the kitchen. "Gary has been telling me I should look into learning UX/UI. I used to draw and paint a bunch. Do you have any designers here?"

John and Jay walked out of the kitchen and started their tour. John paused, looked thoughtful for a moment and then answered. "We have two designers here, and learning UX/UI isn't a bad idea. With some elbow grease you can learn enough to be employable in a few months. I know for certain we're not the only company who will snatch you up if you learn user interface design!"

"Seriously?"

"Sure" said John. "We can't hire good designers and developers fast enough."

Jay took out his notebook, and then looked up. "Okay, I'm ready now."

John ushered Jay around the office and pointed out things as they walked. "The three desks over there are for our business development team. They handle marketing, what some people call "growth hacking," and sales. They're the ones who make the business grow and keep track of our results. That's them on a client call now." John pointed to a guy and girl wearing headphones, huddled over a microphone inside a glass conference room. They walked away and John pointed to another group of desks,

"This second area is for engineering, which is led by Mariel."

"Yeah, we met her coming in," said Jay.

"She does similar things to what Gary does, only way more

since she's been doing it for years. She makes sure our product works, is secure, and that we ship updates on time."

They passed Mariel's desk, and went on to a far corner. "Then you have design and data science roles. I'm handling a lot of the data science and sales now, but eventually, we'll hire that out."

John walked over to two desks in the middle of the room, and pointed to a man who was probably in his early thirties with jet black hair, a bright blue t-shirt and jeans, and was sketching in a notebook. "That's Micah, our lead UX/UI designer." John held up his phone with the Oxen application opened. "He's what makes our product look great and easy to use."

Jay nodded. "Yeah, Gary keeps reminding me how good I used to be in Art. He says design might come natural to me... so what's Micah's day look like here?"

"Why don't you ask him?"

"I wouldn't want—"

John laughed. "Micah! Got a second?"

Micah looked up from his sketchpad and nodded.

John and Jay walked over to Micah who was now up and stretching from his chair.

John motioned to Jay. "This is Jay. He's a friend of Gary's looking into what he wants to do after high school. Maybe you can give him an overview of UX/UI, and what it is that you do here?"

Micah smiled, nodded again, and just like Mariel, shook Jay's hand. "Sure thing, boss. Nice to meet you Jay!"

"You too," said Jay, shaking his hand.

John turned away. "And I think my wife is back, gotta help her bring dinner in!" He walked over to the door and Jay was left standing with Micah.

Jay started peppering Micah with questions, and got a crash course in UX/UI design. Micah showed him his designs on the computer, and described how and why he arranged everything the way he did. They walked over to a massive bulletin board where Micah had pinned his product design sketches and mockups. He explained to Jay how these rough looking outlines were going to become a new, updated version of OXEN's current application.

Micah humored all of Jay's questions, and filled him in on things that he never would have thought to ask. Micah had graduated from a design program in college, but when he got out, he discovered that no one wanted to hire him. He was only able to find a job after spending a few months learning the type and style of design that startups were looking for. He also spent a few years freelancing, living and traveling wherever he wanted while he worked. Micah had lived everywhere from a ski-town in Colorado, to a brief stint in Key West, Florida. It turned out that he got his current job by doing freelance work for John and Suze. They were surprised with his talent and level of care (for a freelancer), so when they needed to hire a designer, he was a natural fit.

Micah and Jay talked for a few minutes longer, and he left Jay with a list of books, skills, and competencies that he would need to learn if he wanted to jump into UX/UI. He handed Jay his business card while saying, "If you have anymore questions, just email me. There's no reason you can't get a full-time gig before senior year is up."

"Thanks," said Jay. "Even without college?"

"Sure," said Micah, as if it was the most normal thing in the world. "For any of these jobs, you just need a portfolio of work that acts as proof. Then, just give something of value to the company before you ask for anything. Works every time."

"And that's it? It's that easy?" Jay wondered.

Micah grinned as he started cleaning up his desk. "It's that easy, and it's that hard. It's easy because yes, that's all you need to do. But... it's hard because you're have to learn *how* to learn on your own. Now THAT is what's tough."

"I'll remember that," said Jay as he slid the business card and Micah's written recommendations in his notebook.

Micah closed his laptop and pointed to the kitchen area. "C'mon, looks like dinner is served!"

10

STARTUP SUNSET

"Why would we stay in college when we were getting better offers to leave?"
–Suze Weinstein

Jay was about to ask Micah more questions, but he and everyone else in the office erupted into a cheer over dinner. Suze and John held up the bags of food they'd brought, and called everybody into the open kitchen to eat.

They both walked back to the kitchen where everyone was congregating over dinner.

Gary's Mom, Suze stood in the back, talking to everyone. She waved. "Jay! Great to see you! I got enough Thai food to feed an army, so I hope you're hungry!"

"It smells great, thanks!" said Jay as he walked in and stood by Gary.

Gary's dad had arranged the half dozen Thai dishes on the countertops with serving spoons. He handed Jay and Gary plates. "Dig in, everyone!"

Gary and Jay dug into the food, and everyone ate in the kitchen. John and Suze invited Jay to sit in on their mandatory family dinner, and they all talked as they ate.

"So, uh... Mr. And Mrs. Weinstein... um... Gary and I were talking, and I didn't realize you guys had built and sold your business and everything. I was checking out UX/UI design and just wanted to see if you thought that'd be a good thing to learn?"

John and Suze nodded fervently, excitedly blurting out, "Oh, yeah! Good designers and developers have their pick of where to work now. Have you already started learning?"

Jay felt a rush of relief as he found that asking them questions wasn't that hard. "Not yet, but I was thinking about buying a laptop and starting to teach myself."

Suze smiled. "Now is the time to start. Don't wait until you're out of school."

"Gary told me that you both dropped out of college?" Jay asked.

John and Suze smiled proudly, and John spoke up. "Well, we did, but we didn't drop out until we had something better lined up."

"What do you mean?" asked Jay.

"Well, we went to college because, generally speaking, it was a decent place to figure out what you wanted to do. But once we started teaching ourselves to code, we got job offers that were too good to pass up. So we dropped out, worked for a few years, had a couple ideas for companies, and eventually we built one up and sold it."

"And that seems like it paid off," said Jay, as he glanced around the office surrounding them.

"It did," said Suze. "But if we didn't know what we wanted to do, or if we hadn't gotten those job offers, we would have stayed in college until we did. You can always apply, get accepted, and then learn skills on the side. When you learn enough skills and advertise them, you'll get job offers. Just see how many job offers you get while in college, if you don't have skills!" Suze laughed and took a drink of her water. "If what people learned in college was valuable, they'd get job offers midway through. Employers would be going after them left and right."

Gary's dad nodded. "She's right. The days of finding an amazing job without skills have ended. We're living in an economy that is purely results-based."

Jay looked up from the mountain of Thai food on his plate. It was the best dinner he'd had in weeks. He looked at Gary's parents and smiled. "Hey, thanks again for dinner. This is awesome."

"It's our pleasure," answered Suze.

Jay looked at the sunset to his left as it fell on the trees in the forest, and then looked around again at the brand new office they sat in. This place felt like heaven compared to home and school. This was a place he wanted to work at. This was something that would be worth putting in the work to learn the skills he needed. From what Micah showed him, his job seemed fun, and in stark contrast to the suit and tie office work that most adults he knew did.

In fact, as Jay watched everyone else at dinner, he noticed that they all seemed similar to Micah and Mariel. They were interesting people who were all... really nice. None of this seemed like work, but at the same time it seemed challenging enough to be worth doing.

After dinner, Gary went right back to furiously coding. As Jay walked over by him, he seemed overwhelmed.

"Is that Swifty still bugging you?" asked Jay.

Gary cracked a smile. "It's *Swift*, and yeah, it's not a walk in the park...yet. Did you meet everybody?"

"Just about," said Jay, tapping his notebook. "Micah filled me in on UX/UI stuff, and even gave me some things to start learning."

"Nice!" nodded Gary. "All this technical stuff is easier than you might think. Most people overestimate how hard it is and never get started."

"Yeah, now I guess I have to get started."

"You used to crush it at art, you'd make a great UX/UI designer," said Gary, nodding approvingly.

"Thanks, but do you really think it's that easy?"

"Yes, but getting started and building the habit of practicing it is the ridiculously hard part. Just look up some tutorials and get started. You used to always draw when we were younger. All you have to do is draw screens for the products, learn Photoshop, and learn some CSS, and you'll be good!"

"Really?"

"Yeah, really," said Gary in exasperation.

"But I don't have a laptop...or Photoshop," said Jay.

Gary threw up his hands and pointed to his laptop.

"Why don't you get them and learn!"

"I don't have any money!"

"Then get your lazy butt logged on to Drivr and start getting PAID!"

Jay started to get defensive. "I don't have a car anymore, remember? My mom needs it for work."

"You're full of excuses, man, and here I am, ready to help. Submit an application to drive for Drivr, and you can use my car."

Jay's eyes widened. "Are you serious?!"

"Yeah, dude, I'm serious. I'm always ready to help, but you never ask."

"Well... I didn't know asking was an option until now."

Gary looked straight-faced. "There's always an option. Double check the insurance stuff, but just get approved for Drivr, and you can use my whip. There's no way I can keep up with work, school, and Drivr. The best investment of my time right now is to become a great engineer."

"This is awesome!" said Jay, staying barely seated.

Gary spun his laptop around in front of him. "Don't be lazy. Do it now."

Jay looked at everyone else in the kitchen getting seconds, or laughing and talking. "But everybody else is..."

"They've been busting their asses for years!"

"I know, but–"

"DO IT NOW!" Gary practically yelled, and Jay cringed. "Fine, I'm doing it now!"

He filled out the application for Drivr. Gary put his headphones back on and finished the code he was writing for the day.

A half hour later, Jay submitted his application.

Gary came over to check on him. "Done! For today at least." He let out a sigh of relief, and grabbed another plate of food. He looked over at what Jay was writing up. "Did you finish your Drivr application?"

"Yep!" Jay paused for a moment, and felt awkward about getting help from his friend. "Well, how can I pay you back for letting me use your car?"

Gary thought for a moment, and then pointed at Jay with a smile. "Buy me gas, and teach yourself UX/UI. If you build up some skills, I can help you get a job... or better yet, we can start building stuff... or even start a company together!"

"Start a company together? Doing what?"

"Anything we want. Hundreds of people need tech stuff built. Every business in town needs some sort of technology and is probably getting ripped off by paying some jerks to build it for them right now. I'm learning a lot of the engineering, sure, but if I had a good designer, then we could get moving. But...you're gonna need a laptop, software, and skills first... so hustle up some cash and get them!"

Jay stood up and took his empty plate to the dishwasher. "I'm on it," he answered. "But before we get paid, you might want to wipe that sauce off your chin."

Jay had never thought about just how many choices he had. Why not apply to P&C to keep his parents happy, and then race to learn a skill like UX/UI design that was in crazy high demand? Once he landed a job or created a better alternative to college, his parents would have no choice but to support him... Right? It made perfect sense. And if he blazed his own trail, maybe Gavin would even start to respect him. Now *that* would be a miracle.

PART II

11

PROVE IT

"Get my attention with results. Prove it, and then I'll listen."
–Alan Pencha

The weeks had flown by since Jay had visited Gary's parents' company. It had been a serious wake-up call for him. He knew they were smart and hardworking, but seeing the results of that firsthand was startling. They had gone from no degrees, to working at home, to building a startup... that made money!

From the looks of it, and what Gary casually pointed out, both John and Suze no longer had to work, but they both chose to anyway. Now that was a place where Jay wanted to be... doing something you wanted to do, even after you didn't have to do it anymore.

Within a few days of visiting the company, he got approved to work for Drivr. Once Jay's insurance was approved, Gary handed him the keys to his car. At first he wasn't sure that Gary would actually let him drive it, but then he discovered how overworked Gary was with Livu and school. After that, it was easy for Jay to pick up the slack and drive them to and from school. This gave Gary plenty of "chauffeur" material for jokes. His favorite was that he was a former childhood movie star, hiding out in their small town and staging a comeback. A year ago, Jay wouldn't have been able to laugh about the fact he was driving his best friend around town, but now with money coming in from Drivr, he lightened up and laughed.

He was making good money and saw a path towards a serious career as a designer. It was a path that didn't carry any of the debt and four-year time suck Gavin had undertaken.

After just a handful of good reviews on Drivr, Jay became flooded with requests. He had thought that the town where he lived would be slow, but between happy hours, weekends, and the new city center, there was a steady stream of customers.

Gary's parents passed the advice along to Jay to treat his Drivr work just like his own business. Jay saw what they had achieved so far and decided to trust their advice. He treated every customer who stepped into his car like royalty. Naturally, his customers loved this. He acted as a psychologist for the drunks after happy hours, and even as an impromptu couple's counselor. He decided that learning how to break up the occasional fight with a joke, or story, would be useful later.

The five-star ratings began to pour in.

The amount of money he started to make added up. Soon he would have enough for some of the basic "capital" equipment that Micah had recommended to him. If he was going to learn design, he needed a laptop and at least a few software programs. He sent Micah an email asking if he had a used laptop that he might want to sell. Sure enough, he did! After spending a few hundred dollars, Jay was up and running. He bought a few things that Micah recommended: some UX/UI courses, a monthly Photoshop subscription, and a few used used books.

Spending the money he made was hard, but he kept a reminder on his wall of how much a good UX/UI designer could make. Investing in the acquisition of a skill was the best investment he could make. Time was ticking down during his senior year, and he needed to learn...fast.

He had his visit to P&C and to see Gavin coming right up. After that, the holidays would be here. It wouldn't be easy to fit everything in, but he was off to a great start so far.

Jay felt silly for being so excited about it, but this was the first time that he had a glimpse of what the path looked like towards becoming financially independent. It was months away, but he was starting to see the path to get there.

In the meantime, Jay did the grunt work. He chauffeured Gary around, bought him the occasional burrito dinner, and stayed true to his ultimate promise to learn UX/UI. The second he was good enough at design, Gary was adamant that they could start collaborating. He even thought that he could get him a job at Livu. The nights were late, but his progress was stacking up.

If he wasn't at school or working, he was at Gary's house, working together on their laptops. When Gary's parents were around, Jay would help them with whatever they needed, and then ask them a series of rapid-fire questions. He got John and Suze to introduce him to a few more UX/UI designers like Micah. Between Gary's connections at Livu, and the growing number of industry contacts Jay was making... he and Gary were starting to build up a legitimate network.

He worked as much as he could, but was surprised one night when he found himself getting home before 9pm for the first time in weeks.

He parked Gary's car on the street and walked through the cool fall air to his house. Jay whistled as he spun the car keys on his finger. He opened the door and immediately heard... sounds of an argument from the kitchen.

Jay let out a sigh. That's why it's good to stay busy, he thought. He heard his Dad's voice start up again from the kitchen.

"I already sent a resume there! And, stop telling me to apply to places that ask for at least a masters degree!" yelled Alan.

Jay took a deep breath. He didn't want to deal with this tonight. As he walked into the kitchen, he said, "HEY MOM and DAD!" loudly to announce his arrival and hopefully break up the fight. He bounded into the kitchen smiling. "I just had a great day, what's up?" He carefully placed his book bag (now carrying his laptop) on the table and sat down.

"About time you came home for dinner. You've missed dinner for almost the last two weeks!" said Alan.

"Sorry I've been missing dinner. I've been out working," Jay said, as he sat down at the table.

His mother and father both looked up from their plates. "Oh?" questioned Alan. "Did you get a real job yet or are you still doing that Drivr thing?"

Jay was starting to suspect that his Dad didn't think things were real if he couldn't see them. He did his best to smile. "Well, with that Drivr thing, I made $153 tonight!"

Alan squinted his eyes and leaned back in disbelief. "Huh... Well... That's good...I guess that's good news."

"Yeah, it's the best money I can make right now. I used some of my money to buy a used laptop... I'm going to teach myself design."

"That's impressive!" said Debbie, trying to offer encouragement.

Alan was now smirking. "Ahhh... spending your money already. So you're going to be a taxi driver your whole life?"

Jay fought a surge of anger. "No... but it's the closest thing to being entrepreneurial that I can do right now. What I'm doing right now isn't what I'll always be doing!"

Alan held up his hand. "Well... I guess it's good money for you... IF you keep it up."

"Of course I'll keep it up, besides it's only temporary until I teach myself enough UX/UI to get a job... maybe even where Gary works."

Alan sighed. "I don't know anything about those technology jobs."

"Neither did I, that's why I'm learning about it." Jay jumped up and grabbed his laptop from his book bag. He opened it, typed a few things in, and then spun it around to show his parents. "Look, I met a few people working at Gary's parents' company. They make great money, and there is tons of demand for designers and developers." Jay was pointing to the details and job descriptions at various technology companies on his screen.

Alan's eyes popped when he saw the salaries on the screen. He looked quizzically at Jay. "Seventy five to a hundred and twenty thousand dollars a year? You need to be a doctor or lawyer to make that kind of money! You're sure this website is real?"

Jay rolled his eyes and smiled. "Real? Of course it is! I've even emailed a bunch of them and asked what I need to do to get hired. I met one designer in person, and I think I can teach myself enough to get a job by the end of the year. And the worst-case scenario is that I'll go to a Bootcamp during the summer like Gary did. He got hired right away!"

Alan looked overwhelmed. "That's fine for him, but you still need to get into college. And besides, what will you do after your first design job?"

Jay looked at his Dad in frustration... he still wasn't getting it. "Uh... I'll get the next one? I can freelance or start a company with Gary! Join a big company! Join a small one! I dunno! There's a million different things and it's not like the technology industry is going anywhere."

Debbie smiled, adding more food to Jay's plate. "I've never seen you do so much research... about anything!"

Jay laughed. "Yeah I guess I haven't before."

Alan shrugged as he finished his dinner. "I think you'll find you need college to get your foot in the door." He took a sip of his beer and picked up the paper in the kitchen.

"Not in an industry like technology, Dad. All I need to do is prove I have skills." Jay waited for a reaction, but saw his Dad continue to stare at the paper.

After a few seconds, Alan looked up and sighed. "As long as you're living in this house, you need to apply to college. When you have a real job offer, or acceptance letter from P&C, we'll talk."

Jay's face turned red with frustration. "Gary's parents don't even have to work anymore, and they never went to college. Plenty of the team they hired didn't go to college either."

Alan kept staring at the paper. "What's this business they have? I've never seen or heard of it."

"It's a software company. They used to work from home with remote employees, so no, you wouldn't have been able to see an office. But now Oxen has like twenty employees and an incredible office!"

Alan put down the paper, and cocked his head to the side. "What did you say the name of their company was?"

"It's called Oxen. It's a–"

"Oxen?!" interrupted Alan loudly. "Oxen is the reason I got laid off, Jay. What did I tell you about Gary's parents?" Alan grabbed his beer from the counter and started to pace. "I thought I said I don't want to hear another word about Gary's family!"

Jay's heart was in his throat. He had no idea... there was no way Gary's parents had meant for that to happen... All that he managed to say was, "I'm...I'm sorry, Dad... I didn't have any idea."

Debbie took another bite of her dinner and looked at Jay to say, please drop this.

"I'm going outside for a bit," Alan grumbled, as he walked angrily out the back door.

Before Jay could say anything, his mom put her hand up. "Not now."

The door shut, and Jay thought his Mom was going to be angry, but she wasn't. She rubbed her hands on her temples and whispered, "This isn't your fault."

Jay relaxed a bit... "I'm sorry. I didn't kn–"

Debbie interrupted him calmly. "Your father is just freaking out right now. I wasn't born yesterday son. I know Gary's family didn't purposely get rid of your father's job.

They figured out how to get paid for a better way to do something."

"So, you're not mad?"

Debbie almost laughed. "Mad? I haven't seen you so excited about something in years!"

Jay's head spun, was he hearing her right? She usually always sided with his Dad. This was the first time he had heard that he didn't have to do the same things Gavin did. And, it was all because he was excited about something?

"Thanks, Mom! I'm just trying to find a cheaper alternative to P&C."

"I know, and it sounds like you're finding them! But for the time being, until we get the finances in order, don't overwhelm your Dad."

"Okay," nodded Jay.

"But... keep doing whatever it is your doing. When we had the money, it was easy to tell you to follow in your brother's footsteps, and I'm honestly sorry about that. I don't want to force you to do what Gavin is doing, especially if there are better ways now."

"Oh... Thanks, Mom... yeah I'm not sure I want to... I'll keep looking into everything. I'm trying to save you guys money and find something I love."

"Jay, your father and I don't know the first thing about any of this. All we've ever heard is that college is good, and more college is better..." Debbie sighed, looking tired. "But I do know your father. If you can prove that you've found something that makes financial sense... AND you like it, he'll have to consider it. Honestly, I have no idea how we'd ever pay for P&C... again."

Jay listened to his mom silently and carefully... was she

giving him permission to go for this? No way, he thought.

"Besides," Debbie smiled mischievously, "you heard your father. You have to apply to college, but nobody says you have to go..."

A smile crept over Jay's face, too. "Okay Mom, I will," said Jay dutifully. Now he was fired up and ready to get back to work.

Debbie looked Jay in the eyes as she continued. "If you are serious about this, and keep working this hard, I'll help convince your father."

"Are you serious, Mom?" Jay grabbed his book bag, and got ready to sprint upstairs.

Debbie put her finger up and stopped him. "Yes. But, one more thing... keep your promise to go and visit Gavin at P&C. The last few times I talked to him... something sounded off in his voice."

"Okay! Deal!"

"And remember, keep doing what you're doing, but until you prove you have something better lined up than college, not another word to your father. Do you understand?"

"Completely! You won't regret this, Mom!" Jay ran over, kissed her on the head, grabbed his laptop and ran up the stairs to his room. He had design tutorials to finish before he fell asleep.

12

NO SHAME IN MY GAME

"Shame and guilt? No time for 'em, homie."
–Gary Weinstein

The next morning, Jay headed to pick Gary up for school. In only a few weeks, Jay had gone from broke, with no job, to making great money with Drivr. It wasn't glamorous, and most mornings like this one were completely exhausting. However, after working this hard, he found something that had been missing in his life. He was satisfied.

On the way over to Gary's house, Jay practiced pitching a few things out loud that for his 1-on-1 meeting with Mr. Moore. Jay shuddered thinking about his previous 1-on-1 college prep and counseling sessions with Pemberton. He prayed that Mr. Moore's meeting would be the opposite.

Jay pulled up to Gary's house and walked inside, ready for the Weinstein's usual morning routine of hanging out and drinking coffee together before they went their separate ways.

Sometimes John and Suze would help Gary calm down and figure out how he was going to solve the latest coding challenge that Livu had thrown his way. Oftentimes, they were talking about new books they were reading.

There were plenty of mornings where he didn't understand much of what was said, but Jay was sure to smile a lot, take notes, and listen well. The new habit was beginning to take form, and Jay had gone from dreading waking up in the mornings to loving it. Between Drivr, learning UX/UI, and hanging out with Gary's family, the weeks were flying by. By the time he noticed, they only had a few days before he and Gary were scheduled to visit Gavin and P&C.

It was Wednesday morning, and their P&C visit was this weekend. There were still a few hurdles to get over before they left. After they finished their morning coffee and strategy session, they hopped in the car. Gary put on a podcast he loved, and during the first advertisement, Jay turned down the volume.

"So, you ready for your one-on-one today?"

"Yeah," said Gary, groggily. "It'll be the best part of the day."

"Yeah, I'm with you there," replied Jay. "Hey, I don't know how else to say this, but... about the security application that Oxen makes and sells..."

Gary yawned, "Uhhh... yeah, what about it?"

"Yeah...well... umm, I think my Dad's old company might of laid him off because of that. I said the Oxen name last night and he got all angry..."

Gary was now fully awake in the passenger seat, "Ah...really? I'm sorry... So, your dad freaked out?"

"Yeah... but I mean, what would you expect? Right?"

"I wish you would have said something back at the house. I know there was an entire industry selling a service that Oxen replaced." Gary looked beside himself.

"Well, what happened? Maybe I can explain it to my Dad," said Jay.

Gary sat fully up in the seat now, sipping his coffee, "My parents just took an old time security process that big businesses were paying way too much for and made it way better. They automated it, improved the functionality, and then built it into software. I know there are still some companies that try and do it manually... but they've been overcharging for like twenty years!"

Jay shook his head nodding, "I figured... so they found a better way to do it?"

"Yeah, much better. Look man, I'm really sorry," said Gary.

"Don't be," Jay shook his head and thought for a moment. "It's not your parent's fault. Besides, my dad was always complaining about how much he hated his old job. You would think that he would be glad that he now has a chance to find something new."

Jay laughed, and Gary's face went from worried to relieved.

Gary's eyebrows went up behind his glasses. "Wait... seriously? You're not mad?"

Jay stretched back in the driver's seat as he turned into the school parking lot and looked at Gary, "Nope. I can't worry about their problems if they don't want help!"

"Hmmm," said Gary deep in thought, "you should talk to my dad anyways. I'm not sure, but I remember him saying that he tried to hire some enterprise sales reps from some of the older companies in their space. Wasn't that what your dad did?"

"Yeah, it was... do you think he'd want to hire him?"

"Maybe... I'll text him right now. Don't stress about it though, we'll figure something out."

At the rate they were going, Jay believed it. He smiled and looked at Gary. "Thanks for asking him... but anyways... I have more important things to worry about."

"Like?"

"Like Ella transferring to Mr. Moore's class."

"Wait... what? You convinced her to transfer?"

"Yup," Jay grinned and took another sip of coffee as they pulled into a parking spot. "Today is her first day."

They grabbed their coffees, hopped out of the car, and walked toward the school.

"You suave devil, you! Does this mean she likes you now?!" Gary's face looked both serious and constipated.

Jay laughed. "Stop treating this like an engineering problem. If you look like you're calculating probabilities for everything around girls, it's going to come across as psycho!"

"Oh... Well, when you put it that way, of course it sounds weird. Wait, isn't Ella still going to P&C College?"

"Yeah, her parents are alumni and in love with that place. She just got accepted, which is why she transferred. She doesn't need college prep anymore," said Jay.

Gary shook his head, "You're on fire, son."

"Something like that," smirked Jay.

They walked through the school doors, first to their lockers, and then to Mr. Moore's class. When they got inside, they saw they weren't the only early ones. The first thing Jay noticed when he walked through the door was Ella, sitting in the back of the room. They locked eyes, and she smiled, waving him to a seat next to hers.

Ella pulled her hair back and looked over at Jay and Gary as they sat down, "Good morning, boys. I heard this was the last interesting class at this school."

"Oh, you know it, girl," answered Gary.

Jay looked at Gary and rolled his eyes. "That about sums it up."

Ella held up a page full of notes. "So I've been catching up. Jay, do these notes look like a good place to start?"

Jay leaned over to review the notes with Ella before class started. Senior year was getting better every day.

13

1-ON-1

"Harnessing your imagination is the first step towards creating a life worth living."
–Mr. Moore

After class, Gary had his one-on-one scheduled with Mr. Moore. Jay had his right after, so he waited in the hall outside the classroom. Ella hung around for a while to talk with Jay, and then she was off. She said something about going on a trip this weekend, and Jay kicked himself for not asking her where. Maybe it was P&C... or maybe that was just wishful thinking.

Jay worked on his laptop while he waited for Gary's one-on-one to wrap up. He had printed out images of the Oxen application that Micah designed. Now he was practicing how to replicate them in Photoshop. He might as well start practicing exactly what he'd have to do at a startup.

After a few minutes, the door to the classroom swung open and Gary came bursting out of the room. He looked at Jay with his eyes wide.

Jay seized him, "Are... you okay... you look manic?"

"I'm great! Mr. Moore had a bunch of good ideas. Keep doing what you're doing... I've gotta go get started. Meet you after school! We're going to crush it, Homie!" Gary took off jogging down the hall.

"Crush what?" yelled Jay down the hall.

He turned over his shoulder, "Getting us both full-time jobs at Livu!"

"Okay, but don't forget we're visiting P&C this weekend!" yelled Jay behind him.

"Don't *you* forget to hustle!" Gary yelled back as he ran down the hall.

Well, thought Jay, it looked like Mr. Moore's one-on-ones were a bit better than Mr. Pemberton's awkward, passive aggressive counseling sessions.

Jay got up and knocked on the door to Mr. Moore's room.

"Come on in!" yelled Mr. Moore from inside. Jay walked in and Mr. Moore looked up from his desk. "Here, have a seat. Can I get you anything?"

Jay crossed the room as he answered, "Uh...nah, I think I'm all good."

Mr. Moore pulled out the chair for Jay. He turned and reached into a mini-fridge by his desk. "Sure you don't want something? Vodka? Water?"

Jay laughed, "Uh... I guess water."

"Perfect!" Mr. Moore swiveled in his chair, reached in the mini-fridge and came back with an ice-cold mineral water. He cracked the top, placed it in front of Jay and started talking.

"Gary told me you're both collaborating together... you visited his parents startup... AND I think he said you landed a job?"

"Yeah, I guess we have done a lot," nodded Jay, "I'm making some money with Drivr now, but I'm learning design on the side... basically using the money from Drivr to fund learning a skill... like we talked about in class."

Mr. Moore leaned back in his chair, "Brilliant! We have our first class presentation tomorrow, you're going to share all this right?"

Jay looked nervously, "I guess so... I didn't think it was that big of a deal?"

Mr. Moore looked aghast, like Jay was holding out on all of humanity, "It's a huge deal! You're already making money and learning a valuable skill! Plenty of students are working on cool things, but you're getting your hands dirty. This stuff is the real work. If you talk about a smart approach, this is it!"

Jay couldn't help but grin, "I didn't realize it was smart, I just needed money to get a laptop to learn design."

Mr. Moore waved off his comments as nonsense, "That's WAY more intelligent than the students using mommy and daddy's money for college!" He paused, looking worried that he might have offended Jay, "No offense..."

"None taken," laughed Jay.

"So what's your plan for learning design? Maybe study some designers to reverse engineer how they got their jobs? You could start with the designers at a company you want to work at?"

Jay nodded and opened his notebook. "Yeah, I want to learn design so I can work at a technology company... maybe even a startup – anywhere with a mission and great people to work with. I'm not sure where yet, maybe Oxen, or Livu with Gary. I'm still applying to P&C... but I want to have a job offer before the end of senior year. If not, I'll go to college.

"That is smart... and ambitious," said Mr. Moore. "Good way to hedge your bets. Have you reached out directly to any companies or designers yet?"

Jay took a sip of his water before answering, "Yeah! I've met Micah, who works at Oxen, and I've got introductions to a bunch of other UX/UI folks. I've emailed them all, and am finding out what I should learn in order to get a job like they have."

"So what credentials or skills got them their jobs?" asked Mr. Moore.

Jay looked at his notes, "Some of them went to college, and some didn't. All of them said it's overpriced... and most of them said to scrap it the second I can learn on my own."

"Did any say you should go?"

"Yeah, they said the parties were worth it, but I'd rather visit and party at a bunch of schools instead of being confined to one..."

Mr. Moore chuckled, and glanced at Jay as he paused, "Keep going, this is great stuff!"

"So this makes sense?"

"Total sense. Most students don't think about all the options they have when they make a choice after high school. You're considering everything, instead of confining yourself to a single school for all four plus years."

"Okay... just checking." said Jay.

"And if you keep this up... it won't be easy, but I have no doubt you'll land a job offer at a startup by the end of the school year. I'm friends with Gary's parents and between us, Gary, and you, we can help you find a design job."

Jay looked up from his notes, "What's with you all wanting to help?"

"It's a byproduct of being entrepreneurial! What can I say?" said Mr. Moore as he leaped up from his desk. "Speaking of design, there's one more thing I want to print out and show you... anymore questions?"

Jay thought for a moment, and then decided to ask the biggest question on his mind, "I guess the thing I have the hardest time imagining – where this all leads.'"

"That's where having faith that the eighth wonder of the world will come and rescue you!" laughed Mr. Moore.

Jay rolled his eyes, "... I give up... What's that?"

"Compounding interest! It doesn't just happen with money. It happens when you read, do, think, and plan like you are right now. You've figured out how to earn money on your own, now you're learning skills. As long as you keep thinking while you do both things, you can't imagine now where and what they're going to compound into."

"So... how should that make me feel sure about where all this is going?" asked Jay.

"It shouldn't. If you knew exactly where everything was going, life would be miserable."

"Makes sense..."

"Trust in yourself and the path you're on right now: making money while layering one skill on top of the other. The world economy is changing... rapidly. I can't think of a better path then doing what you're doing right now."

"And that's it?"

"It's a foundational part! Maybe you get good at mobile design, then you learn CSS, then you specialize down further into iOS design? Before long, you'll be among a small, skilled, elite, handful of people. After enough skill layering, you won't be competing with anybody else. You'll be in a league of your own."

Jay had an 'aha' moment and leaned his head back. "Now that makes sense... So you're saying that layering skills will combine into something better than I can imagine right now?"

"Bingo," said Mr. Moore as he handed Jay the piece of paper he'd just printed out. "This is an example of a very simple idea compounding with skills... and patience."

Jay looked at the picture on the page. It was some sloppy pen drawing on a yellow legal pad. "Hmm... yeah, no idea what this is!" he said.

"This is one of the first sketches of what became Twitter. Jack Dorsey sketched out this idea back in 2000. He held onto it for six years while he built up his skills and connections. Eventually, when he was at the right employer, where an idea like this could flourish, he and his co-workers built a company around it. By 2008, it started to become recognizable as Twitter."

Jay marveled at the simple sketch. He could create a mock up of that in Photoshop right now, he thought.

"Ah... Okay, I'm starting to get the message."

"Awesome," said Mr. Moore, "Most ideas as worthless unless you're learning every day. Then, they're not so worthless because you can figure out what you need to do in order to turn them into reality."

"So you really believe I can land a job as a designer before the end of my senior year? How should I apply to those places?"

Mr. Moore smiled, "I believe it. As far as applications go, I already filled your co-conspirator in on an idea I had. He's checking with his parents to make sure it would be a good way to catch the attention of a great company. I'm sure he'll fill you in on it... if he hasn't already built it!"

Jay was cheesing from ear to ear, "So, what is it?" Mr. Moore wouldn't budge. He shook his head and put up his hands, "I'm sworn to secrecy, but trust me, I think the two of you will be able to pull it off."

"And, I've gotta talk to Gary to find out?"

"You've gotta talk to him. Alright, time's almost up. Anymore questions?"

"I guess...," said Jay thoughtfully, "I kept thinking any path outside college was wrong because it seems uncertain...I guess that might be a good thing?"

"I think so," said Mr. Moore. "I look at uncertainty like a tax or an investment you have to make upfront. If you can become comfortable in uncertainty, there aren't any limits to what you can accomplish."

"So...feeling uncertainty... or working through it... that's like a skill?"

Mr. Moore chuckled and mimicked a movie character, "Exactly! It might be the ultimate skill."

Jay felt a calmness wash over his mind. "Thanks, Mr. Moore. Yeah, this makes a lot of sense... makes me feel like I can't screw up."

"Keep doing what you're doing, trust yourself, and there's no way to screw up. But ultimately, don't take my word on any of this... go test it all in the real world. Don't listen to anybody that tells you 'you' should do something. Trust, but verify!"

"Okay, so I have one more question."

"Shoot."

"You were in the military. Then you left and started teaching. But you know Gary's parents, so what else do you do?"

The bell rang, and Mr. Moore looked up at the clock. "Now *that* is a question for another day."

14

Transforming the Public Speaking Fear

"This is a rare time in the history of our world where the work you choose has the power to lift humanity."
–Mr. Moore

On Thursday, Mr. Moore's class had their presentations on what type of careers and jobs the students were considering. Jay prepped a little bit, but he had already done the real legwork outside of class. Now, he had something interesting to present.

Like usual, they got to class early, and Jay grabbed a seat next to Ella. Jay tried to keep the thought of presenting in front of her out of his mind, but he still felt a bit terrified.

While they waited for class to start, Jay tried to get Gary to tell him what Mr. Moore's idea had been that was going to help him get a job. All Gary would say was, "I'm working on it" and, "I'll tell you when my part is done." It made Jay irritated, but it also peaked his interest.

Mr. Moore walked into class with his arms full. He placed a box of coffee and a large bag on the front desk. Whatever was inside smelled delicious.

"Good morning, everybody! Up front here, we have some gourmet breakfast sandwiches: egg, tomato, avocado, and bacon. We also have the most popular drug in the western world... COFFEE!"

The class let out a cheer.

"So why the deliciousness?" Mr. Moore asked as he poured himself a cup of the coffee, "Because we're going to start overcoming the most widespread irrational fear the average person has... public speaking. To help do that, we've got to be properly fueled. Everybody help yourself!"

The class slowly filed up to the front of the room, and started helping themselves to the bounty.

The students and Mr. Moore all talked and congregated up front, which helped release the pre-presentation jitters. After the one-on-ones Mr. Moore had with each student, Jay knew everyone had to be feeling confident and prepared. This was the first time in school that he was looking forward to hearing other students' presentations. After a few minutes, Mr. Moore retreated to the whiteboard and looked to the students.

"So... who says public speaking is so important?"

Heads remained down towards the sandwiches and coffee.

"One of many people is Warren Buffet, who cites that his best investment ever was a Dale Carnegie public speaking course. Crushing the fear of public speaking might be the most important thing we can overcome to start preparing for the real world."

Jay and the rest of the class devoured the breakfast sandwiches and drinks that Mr. Moore brought. Jay leaned back in his seat; he was already feeling at ease about presenting.

Mr. Moore laid out the game plan, "Each presenter will walk up to the front of the room, and say their name and a few sentences about what they've been learning. The second you finish your introduction, it is our job to make the presenter feel at ease. Cheering, compliments, accolades; you get all of that just for your introduction. Only after that will you start presenting everything you've been doing and learning to the class. Sound good?"

There were some bits of laughter in the class, but heads nodded. Jay still had butterflies, but he was now feeling more confident.

Mr. Moore finished his coffee and looked at the class, "We are a team. It's not a race to compete for a finite number of A's. The only competition is a personal one each of us has with ourselves. The economy and our entire world is being transformed by technology. If we're going to create and maintain a life worth living, we have to take small risks every single day. Mastering our fears is the most important step."

It sounded good, but Jay's confidence began to wane. His mind started to revolt. He dreaded getting up there and potentially fumbling his words in front of Ella. Was it really going to help if he walked up front, said his name, and then just stood there while everybody clapped?

"Would anybody want to volunteer?" asked Mr. Moore.

Without thinking, Jay put his hand up before Mr. Moore finished his sentence. He didn't want to at all, but might as well take the leap and get this over with.

"Great! Jay will be first!"

Jay walked up in front of the class, "Hello everyone. I'm

figuring out the best way to get a job at a technology company. My goal is to land a job before the end of senior year... I guess this is the part where you all clap?"

"Exactly," said Mr. Moore, as the class broke into cheers. Jay laughed at the ridiculousness of it, but he was starting to loosen up.

After a few moments of applause and feeling silly, everyone quieted down and he jumped into the details, "I'm driving for Drivr to make money. I toured a local technology company, Oxen. They need designers, developers, and sales types. I talked to a lot of people there, and I'm interested to learn design. I've started to learn about user experience and user interface design. Next I'll start teaching myself Photoshop... and yeah... just go from there?"

The class applauded again, this time even more worked up in celebration. Gary stood on his chair to yell and cheer. Ella winked at him, and Jay walked back to his seat feeling relieved. Public speaking was slightly less terrifying.

He flipped open a page in his notebook and got ready to take notes during each of the following presentations.

Danielle, the social media expert, was up next. Instead of spending her time over the years stalking people, she started to learn about the business and advertising side of social media. Now she was starting to plan how she could offer her services to local businesses that had no idea about what to do on social media. She also had found several social media "Chief Editor" positions for big companies and brands. On top of that, she was exchanging emails with a social media agency asking them about their summer internship program.

The staff that ran the program were shocked that she was applying so early and encouraged her to add a few more projects to her portfolio. If she did, they said she'd be a great fit for an internship at either their New York or San Francisco offices. Her research was solid, and she covered the coming transition from SEO to SMO, which would accelerate the demand for social media managerial talent. What Danielle was learning now was very likely to be valuable in the future.

Gary walked to the front of the class, proudly sporting his Livu T-shirt. He went over the Livu mission and talked about education reform (also known as learning). He outlined several companies like Livu, which were building alternatives and supplements to traditional education. Then he talked about how highly valued technical skills like coding, marketing, design, and data analysis were for a startup. He outlined how he got his job at Livu, how it was a 6-month trial, and he was perfectly prepared ready for it after only a 10-week long coding Bootcamp. In a few months his performance would be evaluated, and he had a chance to win a coveted full-time Livu engineering job. He talked about how he and Jay were collaborating and strategizing together to build their network of contacts. Then, he harped on the fact that every single company his parents knew (including Oxen) needed to hire more technical marketers, engineers, designers, or data scientists.

A short and stocky kid named Nassim walked hastily to the front. He and his family had immigrated to America from northern Iraq. Before his family had escaped through Kurdistan, they had witnessed firsthand how fighting terrorism conventionally actually caused it to spread. Everything he'd been through impassioned him to fight terrorism, but in a way that didn't cause it to spread. Nassim had found a large company that used a proprietary technology to comb financial transactions and online data to identify and prevent terror strikes... preemptively. Their clients included the CIA and governments around the world. They desperately needed IT security talent, so Nassim was learning Java, Python, and Ruby to prepare. He'd been collaborating and learning with another classmate, Dean, who he introduced next.

Dean got up and sheepishly thanked Nassim for the introduction. Dean was a tall, skinny soccer player from a military family. Dean had originally thought he wanted to join the Marines, mainly because his older brother spent a decade as one. But after his brother had returned from multiple deployments overseas, he left the military. When Dean's brother heard he might want to join the military, he went ballistic, and for the first time, laid out everything he had endured. From losing friends to not receiving benefits promised to him, to subpar treatment at the VA. He challenged Dean to do the *real* brave thing and prevent a mess like that from happening again. When Dean overheard Nassim talking with Mr. Moore in class, he knew there would be some synergy. After plenty of research, Dean identified one of the root causes of terrorism as illiteracy. When people didn't know how to read, they usually got stuck in poverty and became easy prey for terrorist recruiters. If he worked to help advance global literacy, he'd inevitably help put the power to become economically empowered into many people's hands. There were a few initiatives and companies already working to increase global literacy, so Dean was figuring out how to reverse engineer a job with one of them. They were all interested in hiring more front-end engineers, so both he and his older brother were learning coding to prepare for their next careers.

Tessa, a girl with dark black hair and bright green eyes, shyly walked in front of the class. She had started high school more than a hundred pounds overweight. Over the last few years, that had changed, and she had dropped all the weight. First she cut out soda, then started yoga, and became fascinated with nutrition and diet. Eventually, everything she was learning began to add up, and now she was in great shape. She wanted to help prevent other children from suffering through what she had. Growing up, she thought her family's eating habits were normal. They weren't, and now she was helping her entire family get healthy. Tessa went to high school for half days and spent the other half of her days enrolled at a local community college where she was earning her certification to be a personal trainer. From there, she was going to start a private practice training clients and teaching yoga classes. Along the way, she was going to keep learning everything she could about nutrition and fitness. And just like Jay, she was working on the side for a service delivery company. Tessa delivered healthy, on demand meals through EatUP.

Jonah followed Tessa, strolling past the desks while giving high fives and fist bumps on the way up. He was a laid back, shorter guy, who never scored high on any standardized test.

But Jonah always had something funny to say, and could bring the class to a roaring laugh at any point. Instead of memorizing facts, he said he'd rather be building and making things. His dad was a machinist and had taught Jonah how to weld several years before. Jonah had worked for his dad's company for years, and now he was applying for a scholarship that was specifically designed for trades and skills such as welding. He was going to use the scholarship to pay for his first welding certification. He ended his presentation with a summation of, "In case y'all were wondering, good underwater welders working for good people pull in $1,000 a day. My dad introduced me to some of them, and their jobs aren't going away anytime soon. Robots and technology aren't going to replace their jobs, they're just helping them do more, and do it better. It's like Mr. Moore said about that Deep Blue computer that beat those chess folks... it wasn't the end of chess... but it was the start of regular folks using computers to beat the grandmasters. It's the same in welding and any trade."

Jonah's friend and collaborator, Mike, presented next. He was the complete opposite of Jonah. He was fast-talking, wore glasses, and waved his hands energetically as he spoke. He had become interested in industrial robotics, specifically in how those robots would affect Jonah's dad's business and Jonah's welding career. Mike was thinking about studying engineering in college, but was looking for ways he could break into robotics more quickly. He had found a few industrial robotics companies with open job positions. After sending them cold emails, a handful of them asked him to apply for their summer internships. Mike would go to college, but would also try to jump in and work in the field as much as possible.

Trent galloped to the front, dressed in a plaid shirt and cowboy boots. His family worked for a large farm, and for years he watched his parents struggle to make ends meet. To help them, Trent tried to keep up with changes in farming and learned that the future of farming was in vertical, indoor growing. Along the way, he discovered that a major disaster could wipe out a city's food supply in only a couple days. Those findings prompted him to learn more about vertical farming. He wanted to solve that weakness. He knew the old economics of farming weren't working anymore. He had reached out to a leading company in the vertical farming industry and began learning the skills that they said they were looking for. Trent even offered to proofread the company's blog posts and press releases for free. To his surprise, they had agreed, and now he was getting paid (a small amount) for his work. It was a slow start, but he got to meet everyone at the company. Soon, he said, he'd work his way up the ranks.

A small, tan kid name Horace shuffled papers at his desk before wandering up front. His family owned a building company. They helped build commercial shopping centers, apartment buildings, and even some residential communities. Horace was working with his older siblings (who all worked there), to help his parents develop extra revenue streams. After he had analyzed hundreds of search trends online, he found that there was a huge interest in "tiny homes." These were small, modular homes that sat on people's existing properties. They were inexpensive, and he found that there were a lot of adults who wanted them. They wanted to simplify, whether it was by moving into a smaller home or placing a tiny home on their property. Several people used the tiny homes on their properties as extra income streams, where guests could stay. Horace ran the costs of building the homes by his parents, and they were now figuring out how to sell or build communities of these tiny homes.

Melissa excitedly bounced up from her chair, wearing a shirt from a private space exploration company. She wanted to study propulsion engineering, and there was a single college program she wanted to attend. That program was heavily recruited and canvassed by the two biggest private space exploration companies in America. She'd be happy working for either company, and was applying to both of their summer internship programs. Her goal was to know more than any other applicant by the time she applied. She had ordered all of the first year reading materials from the propulsion engineering program that she wanted to attend. As she read through it, she took notes and crafted articles around them. The idea was that she would learn and share, while leaving a trail of her credentials online. She'd identified the blogs and news sites that the employees at the space exploration companies read. Now, she was hell bent on crafting articles that they couldn't help but read. She figured she could use those articles as the social proof she needed to start building her network with decision makers at both the companies, along with the college where she was applying.

Jay sat in his seat amazed and taking notes. Melissa was definitely going to stand out from the rest of the other applicants, he thought.

The next student was Tiffany, who started off high school thinking that she eventually wanted to work in financial investing. After some research, she discovered there were now many private secondary markets. These marketplaces matched private investors with private companies that needed funding. There were even marketplaces for bitcoin trading. She said that investors in the public markets knew lots about traditional finance, but they didn't know much about these new marketplaces. Tiffany was now in the process of figuring out what skills these companies valued most. Like everyone else, she found technical skills commanded a premium. She scoured the jobs pages on the website of every company she studied. In a spreadsheet, she kept track of which skills were in demand, points of contact, and any requirements that kept reappearing in the job listings.

Kevin's presentation followed Tiffany's, and it was obvious his fear of public speaking was still quite real. He managed to get out a quick and quiet presentation about the "Internet of Things," and how several firms were projecting it would soon be a giant, multi-trillion dollar industry. He hadn't realized it was an option to go to work right after high school, and the thought of that freedom made him visibly ecstatic. His focus now was on the Internet of Things, which included smart homes and connected consumer devices. Kevin was fascinated at how much homeowners could save by using smart appliances. For instance, by using less electricity at peak times of demand, homeowners could save thousands of dollars a year. Or, they could unlock and lock their doors remotely for guests while they were out of town.

After Kevin was Yancey, who jumped up in front of the room, and had clearly had too much coffee. His family was originally from out west, and they had moved east because of his father's job piloting commercial airplanes. Planes, especially small planes, fascinated Yancey. He used to collect model planes, but he eventually became intrigued by drones. He explained that drones were now either being called UAV's or RPAS's (remote piloted aerial systems). The RPAS industry was projected to keep booming, and now was the perfect entry point. He'd shown the research to his parents, and they agreed that if he liked the industry, it made sense to get involved now. On nights and weekends, Yancey was learning how to build, take apart, fix, and modify the hardware and software of as many RPAS's as he could find. He made sure to end his overly-caffeinated presentation by sticking his arms out like a drone, and "flying" back to his desk.

Bethany described her parents as "dogmatic" about higher education. Her mother was an attorney, and her father was a professor with a PhD. It was assumed that she would not only go to college, but that she would earn a graduate degree. There was no charting an alternative to college, but Bethany did have the power to select a relevant major. The number one major she found was computer science. She might leave college after earning her bachelor's degree in computer science, or maybe she would pursue a PhD in deep learning. But for now, she'd major in CS at whichever college had the program with the best placement rate. With some work,

Bethany had convinced her parents that studying computer science offered the "security" that her parents associated with jobs like attorneys and doctors.

Jen was from a family of union workers. They had worked at several manufacturing plants, and over the years, found their jobs increasingly in limbo. There was always talk of their jobs being outsourced overseas, or that robots were going to replace them soon. Jen started investigating to see if any of it was a real possibility, and found that it was. Like many of the other students, when she analyzed the companies building the robots, she found they weren't run by heartless, greedy entrepreneurs. Instead, she found companies that had been started by people who risked their personal fortunes so that people could be freed up to do more important work. The challenging part was articulating this to her parents, but she did pass them every article she read. Along the way, she uncovered that every company in the robotics field was hiring engineers for both software and hardware jobs. With Mr. Moore's help, she reached out to a few robotics companies to learn about their internships, and how she could learn the skills she would need to get hired.

Jay took another sip of coffee and scribbled some notes. The presentations were fascinating. He felt inspired to do more. He glanced over at Ella, who was busily preparing herself to present next. As she walked to the front of the room, he straightened up in his seat.

It turned out that Ella was fascinated with health care and medicine, specifically– consumer blood tests. This wasn't an accidental interest. Her grandfather had been a successful entrepreneur, and he'd been in Ella's life for as long as she could remember. Unfortunately, he had been diagnosed with cancer far too late for doctors to fight it effectively. If her grandfather had taken a simple blood test years before, doctors could have detected and treated it. Ella had found a female entrepreneur who started a company called CheckUp, which was pioneering a new type of consumer blood test. Ella found that most of the job listings on CheckUp's website required a college degree, but after she emailed the hiring manager, she was told, "there are always exceptions." Especially for, "applicants who come referred from a trusted source."

Diana power walked to the front, expelling confidence. She was originally interested in urban planning and architecture, but after some research, she became interested in plumbing. Most cities had infrastructure, plumbing, and sewage systems that were woefully outdated. To the surprise of everyone in the room, Diana laid out the facts that many plumbers made just as much money as doctors. When she turned 16, she began her training as an apprentice. After she finished the training, she went to work for Mr. Regis' (the school janitor) plumbing business. She was already making great money, and when she turned twenty, she'd get her Journey license. After that, she could become a Master Plumber, and start her own business. She planned on starting a commercial plumbing business and eventually expand into doing large scale city infrastructure projects.

After Diana, Ron meandered to the front and laid out his

family's background, which was in petroleum. His grandfather was a successful wildcatter who helped prospect and pioneer some decent size oil and natural gas claims. Ron heard his stories and wanted to study petroleum engineering. There was a growing demand for good engineers, and not enough students were currently majoring in petroleum engineering to meet the demand. Ron made sure to point out that he was interested in all forms of energy generation. While it made sense financially to start in petroleum engineering, he was already looking into things like thorium reactors and fusion.

Denise, a cheerleader who was always dressed to a tee, had been collaborating with Ella on their research. Like Ella, her grandfather died from something that should have been preventable, Alzheimer's. Denise was determined to fight it, because she couldn't bear to see her parents suffer in the same way. Eventually, she wanted to be a mother herself, and she couldn't stand the thought of having her children watch her suffer. She'd began studying fringe research on how Alzheimer's could be prevented or cured. Most of the medical profession was obsessed with studying beta-amyloid plaques for treatment or prevention. After some searching, Denise discovered an opposing position, and a handful of doctors and researchers who had identified sugar and gluten as the root cause of Alzheimer's. Along the way, Denise found several healthcare and medical companies working to preempt or cure age-related diseases. The best way she found to break into that field was to study nutrition science. She had already found a lab that she could work at over the summer.

Madison spoke next. From a very young age, she had watched her father struggle to build his practice as a financial advisor. At first, she wanted to join him. But she soon discovered that every industry that had middlemen collecting fees was going to be rendered obsolete by software. Financial technology, platforms, and Bitcoin (or whatever came after it) were the future of finance. It had been hard to watch her father struggle, but she wasn't going to help him by chaining herself to a sinking industry. She decided that studying Bitcoin and the Blockchain were the most undervalued opportunities in finance. To study them, she began tinkering, setting up a Bitcoin wallet, subscribing to several newsletters, and reading everything she could about crypto-currencies.

The last student was Sanjay. From birth, it was assumed that Sanjay would become a medical doctor. He watched his older brother and all his cousins go into medicine. It took an entire decade before any of them were able to start their own practices. If Sanjay spent the next decade of his life in college, he worried how far medicine would progress without him. Instead of paying to become obsolete, he wanted to work on new medical diagnostic devices. He found a variety of companies building these devices and services, which were replacing the need to go to the doctor's. Like Ella, Timothy, and several other students, Sanjay's parents were forcing him to go to college. He wasn't disappointed that he had to go, but instead of medicine, he would study engineering, and read everything he could about consumer health diagnostic devices. When several of his parents doctor friends visited his house, he made sure to ask them questions. One of them was candid, telling Sanjay that in twenty years, most of modern medicine would be viewed as institutionalized superstition. He challenged Sanjay to join those who were building the next generation of preventative and diagnostic technologies.

Jay couldn't take notes fast enough. He scribbled in his notebook and listened to the last two presentations. One student was studying how to build better batteries, and another was studying 3D animation and game design.

In a single class period, the entire class had grown more at ease with public speaking. Jay found a new sense of camaraderie forming as they learned about each other. Now it didn't seem outlandish for him to think about skipping college in favor of learning valuable skills. In fact, after hearing about so many students finding companies who were desperate to hire technical talent, it made perfect sense. As class wrapped up, he grabbed his books and headed outside with Gary.

15

LANDING A DATE

"It's like clockwork; every time I push past fear, there's a reward."
–Jay Pencha

After the class and his presentation, Jay breathed a sigh of relief. He wondered if Ella winked because he was cute, in a puppy dog way. Was she just messing with him, or did she actually like him?

Gary assured him that they had both done well, but Jay almost couldn't believe it. As he and Gary talked about their visit to P&C, he felt someone push him in the back. He turned and Ella was standing next to him,

"Great job up there! You too, Gary."

"Thanks... I thought I sucked, but you had an awesome presentation, Ella!" said Jay.

Gary made a face and looked at them. "Don't worry. You both sucked!" Gary howled with laughter.

"That's hilarious, Mr. Engineer. I didn't know you could code, Gary?" asked Ella.

"You didn't? I thought my sexy body gave it away," Gary said retorted, giggling.

Jay rolled his eyes, but was impressed with Gary's ability to laugh at his own jokes for an extended period of time. "Yeah... Gary's figure is a blessing and a curse," joked Jay.

Ella adjusted the books she was holding and they all laughed. "So aren't you two going to visit P&C this weekend?"

Jay felt a rush of excitement but tried not to show it. He mentioned it briefly in a text message... maybe Ella had remembered. "Yeah, we're both going this weekend. The game plan is to visit the campus, hang out with Gavin and his friends..."

"Do you really think you'll still apply?" Ella asked.

"Yeah, I'm still going to apply there and to some safety schools. Besides, I want to see what P&C alumni are like firsthand," said Jay.

Ella looked amazed. "Trust me. You're not missing anything. You should still apply because if you don't go, I'll be the only person from our high school who got accepted."

"Didn't Conor get accepted?" asked Jay. He immediately regretted his question.

"Yea, but I meant you should apply so there is somebody at P&C I want to hang out with."

"Ahh... Gotcha," said Jay, relieved.

"You should text me when you get there... maybe we can meet up?"

"Yea," said Jay. "I guess we could all go grab dinner or something?"

Ella pushed Jay's shoulder. "I was thinking along the lines of you taking me to dinner."

"Ohhh," said Jay. "I got you, yeah... yeah that sounds great! Well, would you like to have dinner with me sometime that weekend?"

"I'd love to," said Ella.

"Don't worry you two, I'll keep Jay's brother and friends entertained. You two have fun! Unless..." he looked thoughtful for a moment. "Ella, do you have any lady friends that need entertainment?" Gary's eyebrows darted up and down.

Ella stifled a laugh. "Hmmm... I'm not sure what you're proposing. Off the top of my head, nobody comes to mind. I don't think you're old enough to be interesting for the P&C Cougar Alumni."

"I'm not old enough?" said Gary defensively.

Ella giggled. "Of age for the divorced and drunk P&C Cougar Alumni. Who'd you think I meant?"

"Now you're talking!" said Gary, clapping his hands and rubbing them together.

Jay leaned over to Ella. "You can't be serious."

Ella turned and gave Jay a hug. "Half joking. When you two get to P&C, text me and we'll go out. Somebody has to save me from my parents and the P&C Alumni."

Jay's insides lit up. He nodded dumbly and only managed to eek out, "They can't be that bad! But, I will."

Ella stepped back and waved. "Bye Gary, see you this weekend Jay!"

"I'll text you when we get there!" said Jay. As she walked away, he turned, locking eyes with Gary who he knew had something to say about it.

Gary punched Jay in the shoulder. "Now *that* is how I want my co-founder to act right there. Ella likes you!"

A huge smile filled Jay's face. "Yea... yea... I guess she does."

16

Mini Road Trip

"When I learned there was a way out of school... I started racing for that door."
–Gary Weinstein

Too good to be true. The phrase swam through Jay's mind as he woke up. He took a deep breath and looked up at the ceiling. It was Friday, and he and Gary were skipping school to go visit Gavin.

Jay's life was finally starting to get interesting. He had thought for years that he was obligated to be exactly like his brother. Now he was going to visit Gavin, but he didn't feel inadequate. With every dollar he made, he was earning his freedom. He was buying himself even more power and options to create a path... and a life, that he wanted. He still wanted to visit P&C and see what Gavin's co-workers and friends were like in person. But now he knew they weren't his only option.

He checked his phone and saw it was 4:34 am. For the first time in years, he'd woken up before his alarm clock on a school day, and felt great!

Now he had a sense of urgency. He was an explorer. He was an investor on a mission to discover if P&C and Gavin's job were the utopias that Gavin claimed them to be. And Jay was getting to go out with Ella and hang out with Gary, so no matter what, the trip would be worth it.

He jumped out of bed and grabbed the things he had packed for his trip the night before. Preparing for things was becoming way easier when he was the one who chose them. Procrastination only came into play when others forced him to do things. He grabbed a few extra things he needed, threw them in a bag, and got his books for school.

Jay tiptoed quietly down the steps; he grabbed his jacket from the hall closet, set everything by the door, and walked into the kitchen. He'd be gone before his parents were up, but first, he was going to make them breakfast.

He hard-boiled six eggs, steamed some kale, cooked up a couple sausages, and got the bread out for toast. In a few minutes, delicious smells wafted through the kitchen. Jay put on coffee and ate his breakfast in a hurry. He finished eating, cleaned everything up and checked his phone, seeing that it was almost 5:00.

Jay's parents would be up soon, so he wrote a quick note and slid the corner of it under his dad's breakfast plate.

Have a great day, Mom and Dad. Going to visit Gavin all weekend. Enjoy breakfast!

Jay grabbed his coffee mug, walked to the front door and grabbed his bag. He opened and shut the door quietly, slipping out of the house into the fall morning. The sun was just rising, and the drive to Gary's house was dotted with the colors of the changing trees.

Gary's parents were out of town on a business trip for the weekend. As Jay pulled up, he heard music blasting from inside the house. When Jay walked in, he found Gary dancing in his boxers, half muttering and half rapping along to one of his favorite songs. Jay shouted over the music, "I'M HERE!"

Gary whipped his head around, waved, and tapped something on his phone. At once, the volume on the speakers throughout the house decreased. "Hey! Glad you said something. I was about to start rocking out."

Jay set the keys on the island in the kitchen and pulled up a stool. "Yeah, I wanted to give you a heads up before you got any weirder. Put on your clothes and let's go!"

Jay pulled out his notebook and wrote down some ideas, thoughts, and a few early morning sketches while Gary ran around the house, rapping to himself as he packed for their trip.

Halfway through writing his ideas for the day, Jay thought about texting Ella, who by now was already at P&C for the alumni weekend. What would he ask her to do? He wrote down a couple ideas – dinner, movie, coffee, walk around downtown... any of them sounded good to him! He figured he couldn't lose by taking her out to dinner and walking around downtown. After a few minutes of filling two of his notebook pages with notes and design scribbles, Jay left the kitchen and walked into Gary's bedroom. He stuck his head in. "What's taking you so long, man?"

Gary looked up over a pile of clothes on his bed and answered, "I'm coming! Have to make sure I have the right gear for the trip."

"Right. Well, hurry up! I need to get there early in case Ella wants to hang out."

Gary stuffed one more shirt into his backpack. "Do you think Ella is going to introduce me to the P&C cougars?"

"Uh... I wouldn't get your hopes up... C'mon, let's go!"

Gary slid his laptop into his bag and threw it on his shoulders. "Done! Let's go!" he shouted.

In minutes, Gary and Jay were headed out of town. To their left and right, they watched the bleary-eyed early morning commuters start to emerge on the roads. Before they got on the highway to P&C, they passed the high school. Jay laid on the horn and Gary waved out the window to everyone walking inside. There were few things better than being out of school while everyone else was stuck inside.

Jay merged onto the highway, and they settled in for the quick hour-long drive. Within seconds, Jay was trying to get answers from Gary about the idea that was supposedly going to help him land a job at Livu.

Gary wouldn't spill any details. He only said that it would be ready for him soon. He did, however, let him in on the research he'd done for Jay's dad. Gary's parents were looking to hire an enterprise sales rep. They needed someone with a lot of experience who could eventually lead their sales team. Jay and Gary talked for a while about it, and Jay filed it away in his head. He doubted his dad would even humor that now... but maybe later. The time flew by, and soon they started passing the signs for P&C College.

"I think we're like 15 minutes away," said Jay. "Can you text my brother on my phone since I'm driving?"

"Yeah, sure," said Gary. He tapped on Jay's phone for a second, and then looked over. "Just did. Done!"

"Thanks," said Jay. "So you're excited about touring

P&C?"

"Yeah, well... maybe not touring P&C... but I'm excited to see where Gavin works, meet some people, you know... that kind of stuff. Plus, I want to see firsthand what goes on during these campus tours."

Jay raised an eyebrow watching Gary get a mischievous smile. "Okay... as long as you don't get us kicked out."

"I won't. But, I am going to ask honest questions."

Jay rolled his eyes. "Yeah, well, nothing too over the top."

"I would never!"

Jay's phone buzzed. "Hey, see if that was Gavin."

Gary grabbed Jay's phone and read the message. "He says... he has to work late. There is a key under the doormat. We can get pizza. There is beer in the fridge. Make ourselves at home." Gary looked up from the phone. "Nice, let's park and go up!"

Jay pulled into the parking garage underneath the building where Gavin lived. He and Gary grabbed their things and walked out into the crisp fall day.

"We're scheduled for a morning P&C tour tomorrow," said Jay. "But we've still got all day today, why don't we check out the town?"

"Done. Let's go," said Gary.

The two friends spent the day driving around the college town, watching parties unfold at the apartment complexes, and caught a glimpse at some of the campus. They grabbed lunch, walked around the town, and when the sun started to set, they headed back to Gavin's place.

Jay grabbed the hidden key, opened the door, and they made themselves at home. Gavin was still working, so they were on their own. Gary found the best pizza place in town, and they ordered the Friday Feast. While they waited for their food to be delivered, they sat on Gavin's balcony and worked. After a few minutes, Jay felt Gary staring at him.

"Are you ready to see my master plan to help you land a job?" asked Gary.

Jay set his laptop down and leaned back in his chair. "Yeah! It's about time!"

"So Livu is all about teaching and building creativity, right?"

"Right."

"They have a ton of people applying for jobs, they need more customers, and they can't hire good people fast enough."

"Yesss... and?"

Gary spun his laptop around. "THIS is how I get a full-time gig, and how *you* get your foot in the door."

Jay looked at Gary's screen. It looked like a rudimentary app framework for an application called, "Creativity Quiz." He glanced over the screens, none of which had designs on them, but he instantly got the gist of it.

"You want to launch this... as a way to send them real customers?

Gary's face lit up. "Yeah! We both give them something of value above and beyond what they're expecting. We give before we get. It's way better than a resume. This will get *you* noticed, and *me* promoted!"

"Genius!" said Jay. "But you'd better have somebody make some good looking screens for the app."

"Exactly," said Gary. "I need a UX/UI designer to get this app looking beauuuutiful!"

Jay's head flooded with ideas, and he started sketching.

"Say no more... well actually... do say more so I know what to draw."

Gary and Jay huddled over the sketches and the laptop, and within minutes the two friends were working away on their first product. As they worked on the balcony in the fall air, Jay noticed this didn't feel like work. He vaguely remembered it was a Friday night, but the realization that this could get him a full-time job filled him with energy.

After a half hour, a knock on the front door signaled their Friday Feast had arrived. Gary sprinted to the door in his socks, sliding across the wood floor. He tipped the driver, and he and Jay spread the feast out in the kitchen.

"Now this... is a good reward for learning Photoshop," Jay's mouth watered, and he turned to Gary. "I'm glad you came up, man. This would have sucked on my own."

"Don't get all emotional on me son." Gary cleared his throat and took on a mock parental voice. "You know I don't approve of you looking at risky insurance products like college!"

"Shut up!" laughed Jay. He looked down at his phone buzzing on the table and tapped the text message. "Just got a text from Gavin. He says he won't be back till late, he "has to go drinking with the boss" ...riiiiight," said Jay.

"No worries. I'm tired anyway. Let's just crash after we feast," said Gary as he took a massive bite of pizza.

"Sounds good to me," said Jay, as he loaded his plate.

After dinner, Gary pulled out the living room futon, and Jay pulled out the couch. Before he fell asleep, Jay checked his phone. No message from Ella. He wanted to text her but figured he'd wait until tomorrow. With his stomach filled with pizza and entrepreneurial visions of getting hired at Livu floating through his thoughts, Jay drifted off to sleep.

17

VISITING P&C COLLEGE

"If a degree from P&C is so enlightening, then why don't they let more people buy one?"
–Gary Weinstein

The next morning, they woke up to Gavin's blaring alarm clock.

Jay stumbled into Gavin's room and turned it off. "Jeez, it's Saturday, what gives?" asked Jay.

Gavin mumbled something and rolled over.

"Good to see you too," said Jay.

Gavin leaned up in bed. "Yeah... good... to see you, bro."

"We've got to head out for the campus tour in a minute," said Jay.

"My head is killing me," said Gavin. His face looked puffy as he sat up in his bed, sporting a five o'clock shadow and huge dark circles under his eyes.

Gary leaned his head in the room. "Hey Gavin! You're

finally up."

"Ah.... *Gary*... Yes. I'm awake."

"Man... you don't look so good," said Gary.

"Shut up. I'm hung over and just came off an eighty-hour work week."

"The drinking last night probably made it worse, huh?" asked Gary.

"Shut up Gary."

Jay shot Gary a look that said drop it. "So, aren't you coming with us on the tour?"

Gavin rubbed his face. "I was, but I need to go into the office to get work done. You two have fun. Besides, I need my energy to go out tonight..."

"Okay, well we're gonna head out in a second." Jay walked into the kitchen. Gary was already brewing coffee and eating leftover pizza. Gavin stumbled out a few minutes later, wearing clothes for work. He poured himself a cup of coffee that Gary had made, still rubbing his temples from the hangover.

"Jay, make sure you're ready to go out tonight after the tour. My boss will be there. He's the one with the S600 I keep telling you about."

"Gary and I will be ready, assuming you're there this time. What's the S600 again?" asked Jay.

Gavin shook his head and chuckled. "It's a CAR worth almost as much as mom and dad's house."

"Oh... Right." Jay couldn't help but feel defensive about their parents. They didn't care about what type of cars they drove. In fact, it was that lack of interest in status symbols that paid for Gavin's college.

Gavin leaned his head back, finished his cup of coffee, and

grabbed his keys and sunglasses before walking out the door. "See you two tonight. Have fun on the tour."

Jay and Gary finished getting ready. They walked down to the parking garage and headed off to P&C. With their guest-parking pass in hand, they set out to find the rest of the tour group. The fall air was getting colder, and Jay and Gary both zipped up their jackets as they walked.

"I can't believe we come to visit, and Gavin keeps ditching us," said Jay.

"Yeah, I guess he thinks it's a given that you'll come here," asserted Gary.

"I guess so." Jay squinted, looking around the campus. "Do you see the tour group anywhere?"

They both looked around an empty campus. The only people awake and walking around seemed to be in the same state as Gavin, hung over. Jay guessed everyone else was still sleeping it off. On the other hand, the campus was gorgeous. The trees had all changed colors, and they matched the ornate red brick buildings. Jay and Gary both marveled at how many massive buildings were completely empty. They both were starting to understand why tuition was so expensive. Gary grabbed his arm and pointed off in the distance.

"That's gotta be our group! C'mon!"

Jay and Gary jogged to make sure they arrived in time. They walked up to a huddled group of parents, students, and a tour guide with a bright P&C sweater in the middle. Jay pulled out his phone and texted Ella a picture of the campus. "You're missing out."

"If you could please put your phone away and direct your attention up here, we'll get started on the tour!" The tour guides nasally voice startled Jay, and he pocketed his phone.

Gary rolled his eyes and whispered, "This is lame already."

Jay laughed. "Just act normal until we get out of here. Who knows, we might run into Ella on campus too?"

Gary looked at him like he was crazy. "Stop wishing for stuff and finalize your plans to go out with her tonight."

"We're supposed to go out with Gavin."

"Screw that. He ditched us yesterday and today. Meanwhile, Ella is trying to hang out with you!"

The nasally voice piped up again. "Please keep the conversations down while we get started."

Jay and Gary paused and looked around to find that the entire group was staring at them.

Jay and Gary gave an apologetic smile. "Sorry," said Jay.

The tour guide resumed his whiny pitch, and they started their walk around campus.

As they walked, he talked a lot about the buildings and history, but of course there was no mention of why P&C was valuable to students. He was tall and spoke loudly, but he wasn't saying much except rattling off facts about the University's prestige. He hadn't even talked to anyone in the group to discover why they were all there. It was painfully boring, but at least when he got home, he could tell his parents that he had done the tour.

Midway through the tour, Gary became fidgety, then bored out of his mind. Eventually, he raised his hand to start asking questions. The tour guide ignored his hand for a while, but eventually Gary waved it so hard that the tour guide was forced to answer his question.

"Uh... I think there is a question... You in the back." The guide pointed to Gary. The group turned their heads, and Jay cringed.

"Hello everyone! What a nice day we have for this tour, huh?" Several parents nodded their heads. Gary continued, masking his voice in a preppy sounding tone. "I am a young man who's interested in attending P&C. But I'm just wondering what your job placement for students is like? I'd like to know what I'd be buying, or what type of return on investment I'll be getting for my tuition money?"

The tour guide looked at Gary like he was crazy; "With *your* money?" he smirked.

"Yes with my money. What kind of ROI are you producing at this institution?"

The guide started to flounder, and then stammered in front of the group. "There isn't a value you can put on a real liberal arts education from a college like P&C."

Most of the group looked irritated at Gary for asking the question, but Jay noticed a few parents who looked like they wanted a real answer. But, after a long pause, none of them spoke up."

"You've answered my question perfectly. Thank you," said Gary.

The guide went back to talking, and the parents went back to listening. In moments, everyone was enamored by the guide's pitch for P&C's new gymnasium. In a minute, both students and parents were entranced in the descriptions of comforts and amenities of P&C.

Gary whispered to Jay, "Look at these people, man! They don't realize you're allowed to ask questions when somebody tries to sell you something. They want you to feel guilty and unworthy until you buy the degree. It's the same business model that the Catholic Church implemented to sell indulgences!" Gary had spoken too loudly, and once again, several parents turned their heads.

Jay's eyes met the gaze of a middle age woman who looked furious. She was staring at Gary like she was going to hit him, and leaned over in his ear, whispering angrily,

"Excuse me, young man, but MY family is Catholic."

"Wonderful!" said Gary, beaming as if he'd found a new friend. "I was just telling my friend... the P&C business model... it's like the Church in the 1500's!" Gary patted her shoulder and winked. "It's like, how are we gonna get out of economic purgatory? The school knows... degrees!"

The lady stepped back from Gary in horror, and her husband stepped in front of her protectively.

"Is there another question back there?" asked the tour guide.

"Not at the moment, good sir!" shouted Gary before Jay could elbow him in the ribs. Jay was embarrassed, but also was trying to not laugh out loud. Gary had no filter. But part of what he was saying made sense in a disturbing way.

As they walked by the dorms, Gary kept watching the other parents like a kid at a zoo. He tapped Jay's shoulder. "Dude what did I tell you? This is what fundamentalism looks like! You're not allowed to question anything otherwise they threaten you with hell!"

Jay put his finger over his lips, but Gary wouldn't shut up.

"Oh *Lawd* forgive us sinners!" laughed Gary.

The tour guide paused, and his nasally voice grew louder. "Is there a problem back there you two?"

"I apologize, sir! Please forgive my friend here." Gary pointed to Jay.

"As I was saying!" The tour guide ushered everyone into

the academic advising building. Gary, true to form, peppered the staff with ROI related questions and got no satisfactory answers. He asked them why all of their alumni who maintained ties with the university were either hiring managers, recruiters, real estate agents, or financial advisors. They didn't have an answer, and the scary part was, none of the parents understood why this should terrify them. Gary explained the alumni that stayed connected only wanted access to students, but nobody got it.

After a few more minutes of walking, Jay decided he had had enough. Might as well leave before Gary got them kicked out. The two drifted away from the group and walked around.

"Yeah, you've made your point about all this. I guess I'm just bummed Ella will be going here and I won't."

Gary shrugged. "I think it will be way more fun for you to visit Ella with cash and an awesome job working at a growing startup. You'd still be able to party or hang out with Ella without paying whatever they're charging. Plus if you really want P&C info, just read the books for the classes on your own."

"Yea, I guess you're right," said Jay. "There's no reason I can't hang out or visit Ella."

"Of course not. Besides, at the rate you're going you'll land a job right after I get a full-time offer."

"Good point. Speaking of Ella..." Jay pulled out his phone and texted her, "I'm pinning down our plans for dinner right now."

"That's my man right there," said Gary.

As they walked back to the car, Gary texted with his co-workers in a group chat while Jay texted Ella. Jay told her he'd pick her up at seven. Now, they had time to grab a late lunch, and go to wherever Gavin's happy hour with the boss would be. Jay figured that afterwards, he'd have time to go meet Ella.

They reached the car, and Gary and Jay drove back to Gavin's apartment.

"You sure you don't want to see any other buildings?" asked Gary.

"Nah," said Jay. "You've made your points."

"Now, let's get ready to party!" said Gary.

Jay rolled his eyes. "*You're* going to party? With Gavin's Wall Street bro's?"

"C'mon, don't judge 'em till you meet 'em. We'll make it fun," said Gary.

Jay wasn't sure about that.

18

GAVIN'S LIFESTYLE

"Do I like my job? What kind of question is that? I like making money!"
–Gavin Pencha

Gary and Jay worked on their Creativity Quiz app while they waited in Gavin's apartment. He was running late at work, and finally texted Jay with his boss's address.

Jay looked up at Gary. "Okay, we're supposed to meet Gavin at his bosses place now."

Gary closed his laptop and hopped out of the chair. "Then let's go! I've gotta put on some fly gear first."

"Sounds good... just no anti-college or anti-Wall Street outbursts around Gavin's friends."

"I would never... almost ready!" said Gary, as he rushed into the bathroom with his bag. He re-emerged a few minutes later wearing a polo shirt. He had taken off his glasses and put in contacts, and attempted to style his hair.

Jay looked at Gary's new look. "Well, now you do look more like a P&C student."

"When in Rome. Let's roll!" said Gary as he hurried out the door. Jay laughed and followed, locking Gavin's door behind them.

They got into the car and drove to Gavin's boss's condo. They pulled up next to a massive tower near the waterfront area of town. Judging by the look of it, the condo building had to be twenty stories high at least.

Jay parked the car in the first open parking spot they found. As they walked up, it was clear that this was one of the nicest buildings in town, if not *the* nicest.

"Gavin says it's on the fifteenth floor," said Jay, tapping the elevator button.

Gary adjusted his hair while looking at the reflection in the elevator doors. "Wow! This guy is rolling hard! We're going to be able to see the whole campus and the waterfront from up here!"

As they came out on the fifteenth floor, Gavin was waiting for them with a smile on his face and a drink in his hand.

"Wait until you see this place... the view is insane!" He motioned them to follow him, and after a short walk down the hallway, they heard voices and music coming from an open door. Gavin ushered Jay and Gary inside and shut the door behind them.

Insane was a good way to describe it. Jay marveled at the condo. Dark hardwood floors stretched through an open kitchen and massive living room with a central fireplace. The open living space was surrounded with beautiful floor to ceiling windows. Past the windows, Jay could see the P&C campus and the waterfront area. He swung his head around and discovered that the high ceilings gave way to a loft upstairs.

Jay recognized several of the guys he saw from Gavin's drinking pictures. They were all standing at a bar outside on a large covered balcony.

"Wow." Jay said to Gavin. "This is amazing."

"You think!?" Gavin said. His eyes were already red from drinking. "Now you're starting to see some of the perks from going to P&C, huh?" asked Gavin in a mocking tone.

"This place is sick!" said Gary with a smile.

As they walked through the condo, the tallest guy on the balcony walked back inside and bellowed out. "This must be the little brother and his friend. I'm Brio." A huge guy with dark, thinning hair and a gut walked over and nodded to both Jay and Gary. They nodded back, and he motioned to a huge painting hanging on the wall.

"It's a Pollock," said Brio arrogantly, as he took a sip of his cocktail.

Jay wasn't sure what to say except, "It's nice... Thanks for having us over, this place is epic!"

Brio shrugged. "It's okay for now– one of the perks of working where Gavin and I do. So, you two toured P&C today?"

"Yes, we did," said Gary.

Brio finished his cocktail. "After the P&C tour, we have a tradition. It's called getting wasted."

"Oh... okay," said Jay, unsure if Brio was joking or not.

Brio motioned to his condo with his hands. "This is where your brother will be after just a few more years! Help yourself at the bar," and Brio spun around, heading back to the group of guys outside.

Gavin patted Jay and Gary on the back. "Come get something to drink."

"Okay," said Gary.

"I can't, have to drive later," said Jay.

"We're taking a Drivr to the happy hour spot," said Gavin quickly.

Jay nodded and held firm. "I know, but I have a date afterward. I want to drive."

"What?" said Gavin angrily. "You're already bailing on us?"

Jay turned to him. "No I'm not bailing! You're the one that's changed plans twice since we've been here."

Gavin looked at Jay like he was a child. "The things I do for you... I don't know why sometimes." Gavin looked frustrated, then walked away and rejoined the group on the balcony.

Jay fought the urge to say anything else, and Gary passed him a bottle of water that he had grabbed from the bar. All the guys had beers or cocktails in their hands, and Gary decided it was a good idea to get a wine glass. He tapped his wine glass to the side of Jay's plastic water bottle.

"Cheers! Pinkies up!"

Jay couldn't stay serious looking at Gary's face. They laughed and walked outside with the rest of the group. They marveled at the view; the late afternoon sun crept lazily across the sky, and the balcony towered above the entire city.

"Cheers means cheer up," said Gary.

"Yeah I know, I can't help but feel like something's off with Gavin," said Jay.

"Yeah, it's called being drunk! If I had to spend eighty hours a week in a suit, working for Brio... I'd have to get drunk a lot."

Jay chuckled at Gary's joke, even though it was sad. Gavin,

Brio, and the rest of the guys out there were oblivious to them, as they took another round of shots.

Brio started yelling above the group, and then raised his shot glass. "To Saturdays after pay day, top-shelf booze, and strippers at night!"

The group around Brio did some mix of cheering, and Jay and Gary halfheartedly toasted their glasses. Jay took a swig from his water and looked at Gavin. "You guys go to a strip club... every Saturday?"

"Yea, it's what we do on Saturday nights. But, I mean not till later. Brio can get you two in you know."

Brio shouted to the group again. "Fill them up one more time, and then we're going out!" He poured the rest of whatever liquor they were drinking into each of the guys' shot glasses. The group downed them, along with Gavin.

Jay looked over at Gary, who was staring out at the sunset in another world. The sky was an orangish hue, and the view over the water and city lights was amazing.

If this is what Gavin has been doing every weekend since he left home, it was no surprise he was different. Jay felt distant, but he also felt the growing desire to prove how much further he could get than Gavin's five year P&C plan. After all, the only reason Jay's parents thought Gavin had achieved anything was because of his salary, and the fact that they recognized the name of his company.

Gavin shook his head after the next group shot and walked over to them. "Isn't this place sick?!" He slapped his hands on Jay and Gary's shoulders.

Gary smiled at Gavin. "Yea this spot is pretty dope."

"We're getting ready to go, just called a Drivr. Since you're not riding with us, do you know where we're going?" asked Gavin.

Jay shook his head. "I can find it. What's the place?"

"We're going to Marin's. If you think Brio's condo is nice, wait till you see this. If we were driving, you'd see Brio's S600," said Gavin.

"I'm sure it's awesome. We'll meet you there."

Brio, Gavin, and the rest of the group stood around the bar arguing about something sports related. Slowly, they headed inside, grabbing jackets, finishing beers, taking more shots, and making bathroom runs.

As they did, Gary and Jay quietly snuck out of the condo. As the door shut behind them, Gary spoke up first.

"You're right. They're idiots. Did you see all of Brio's disciples cycling through the bathroom?"

"Uh... not really why?"

"Probably drugs," shrugged Gary. "Watch for it when we get to Marin's. Wall Street and the Ivy Leagues at their best."

Jay shook his head in frustration. "Yeah I'm starting to see that. No way I'm going to P&C so I can work eighty-hour weeks with Gavin... If any of them liked what they did, they wouldn't be getting wasted all the time."

"True story. Hey, sometimes we all have to see it to believe it," said Gary.

Gary and Jay drove to Marin's bar. As they pulled up, it looked a lot like Brio's. It had an ultra modern exterior, and was in the nicest part of town. It was still early, yet already bursting with a line out the door. Green vines covered the walls outside, running along the entrance and all the way to a red brick patio on the side.

After a few minutes of waiting outside, a Drivr car with Gavin and the gang showed up. Brio led the crew to the front of the line. After a quick conversation with the hostess and bouncer, they all were ushered inside and up to a table in the back. The music was loud, and the inside was dark.

The group got to their table, sat down, and a server started taking drink orders.

After a few minutes, the server reached Jay and Gary. She looked Gary up and down. "Does your mother know where you're at little boy?"

Gary smiled at her and raised an eyebrow. "Uh... Yes... yes, she does, Ma'am."

Brio leaned over. "It's okay Tiffany, put it on my tab."

"So what'll you boys have to drink?" asked Tiffany.

"Hmm... Whiskey... yeah I only drink that," said Gary.

"You... want whiskey on the rocks?" asked Tiffany.

"Yeah, it's been a long one. My friend here will have water since he has a date later."

"Thanks for ordering for me, Gary." said Jay. "Yea water's fine, thank you."

"Perfect," Tiffany said, as she walked away.

Gavin leaned over the table and shouted to Jay, "You gotta have at least one drink with us man."

"I already told you, I can't. I'm driving and taking Ella out." Jay waited, but he doubted Gavin could even hear him over the noise.

Brio downed his first whiskey and leaned over to Jay and Gary. He was clearly tipsy. "Taking a girl out instead of partying on Saturdays? You want some knowledge about girls, Jay? Hit it and quit it. Hit. And quit."

Brio paused for effect as if he'd said something prophetic.

Then he turned to Gavin and talked as if Jay wasn't even there. "Your brother just needs to learn man... that's it... then, he'll drop the attitude and start having a good time."

Jay studied Brio and Gavin for a moment. Brio was far down the ladder of intelligence, but seemed to have a massively inflated ego. Jay knew Gavin was twice as smart, but couldn't figure out why on earth he'd want to fight for Brio's approval. Was this type of stuff supposed to impress him? Intimidate him? Or, were they like this all the time?

Tiffany arrived with another round of drinks. "Here you go!" She handed Jay his lemon water and gave Gary his whiskey. "The biggest stud here gets the biggest whiskey!"

Gary's face turned bright red as he smiled back. "Thank you very much!"

Jay laughed and leaned over, "Is she flirting with you?"

"It's my new look... and biceps, " said Gary, as he held up his skinny arms. He took a sip of the whiskey and coughed. "Ugh... what IS this?"

Jay laughed. "Whiskey."

In a few more minutes, both Gary and Jay started to grow antsy. There wasn't any conversation, just yelling about sports, drinking, the strip club, or whose turn it was to buy shots.

Gary watched it all as if he was at the zoo, observing some weird rituals taking place. Jay looked over and snapped his fingers in front of Gary's face. "Hey! Don't stare at them, look around a little bit, too."

Gary laughed and nodded. "Oh yeah, good idea. But I think they're all too drunk to notice." He leaned over to Jay. "My parents used to tell me about this stuff, but I didn't believe it. You know, until I went to public school, I didn't know there were so many people who got drunk all the time and hated their jobs."

"Well here they are in the flesh," said Jay.

"Yeah, in their natural habitat too!"

Jay glanced at his phone.

"I'm supposed to go meet Ella in a minute... but do you think Gavin is going to be alright? I don't know if I should leave him."

Gary looked over. Sure enough, Gavin's head was already bobbing.

"I can keep an eye on Gavin and them. Why don't you roll out, Jay?"

Jay looked around at the table and decided Gary was right. He wasn't missing any opportunities by leaving early. He doubted he could stand a single day of working for a guy like Brio. Sitting before him was a group of guys fanatically crazed about making more money, who didn't care about how that happened.

Jay waved his hands to get Gavin's attention. He held up his phone and motioned to the door. "I've got to head out now!" he yelled.

Gavin got up and walked over to Jay. "What'd you say?"

"Hey, I have to meet Ella now."

"You...you scared to drink... or scared to go to the strip club?" asked Gavin.

That made Jay's blood boil. He looked into Gavin's glazed eyes. "No. But I am scared of spending my weekends getting wasted with a bunch of guys who make trips to the bathroom together." Jay was proud of his comeback, but Gavin might be too wasted to understand.

Gavin leaned on the table and put a finger in Jay's face.

"Hah...you're the one... thinking this technology stuff you like...you think this stuff... is gonna get you where P&C can? I thought you weren't... weren't a nerd like Gary."

"Gary and I are figuring out how to make things... which is very different from figuring out how to skim money off everyone's retirement savings."

Gavin took a sip of his beer and glared at Jay. "Don't want my help? Fine. You're stupid AND ungrateful." Gavin walked back and slid into his seat.

Part of Jay hated Gavin, and part of him felt bad for him. He couldn't figure out who his brother was anymore. It wasn't just booze, Adderall, and whatever else he was doing... Gavin was doing all this to himself so he didn't have to think. Getting in a pit like that terrified Jay more than anything else.

Jay waved goodbye to everyone at the table. They were all either too drunk to notice or too focused on trying to get Gary to listen to their horrible business ideas that, which "needed a coder to build."

Jay leaned in and patted Gary on the shoulder.

"Hey, I'm out of here. I'm serious, you don't have to stay. I mean, be careful around these guys... okay?"

Gary gave him a thumb's up. "Make sure you get to your date on time! I'll keep an eye on them... and Gavin. He turned back to the group to field more questions about their "billion dollar" app ideas that none of them were able to clearly articulate.

Jay turned and walked out of Marin's through the tightly packed crowd by the bar. The music was obnoxious. Could these people even hear each other over here? Could anybody explain why they were here, he wondered? Did their jobs suck to the point where they didn't know what to spend their money on except $15 drinks and drugs? He wasn't sure and didn't care.

He quickened his pace as he approached the door. He kept moving past a bouncer who (rightfully so) glared at him like he shouldn't have been in there. Nothing was going to stop him from a chance to hang out with Ella.

19

THE DATE

"My grandfather's biggest regret? Probably that he failed to prevent the wealth he created from ruining my parents."
–Ella Johnson

Jay stepped out of the dim blue bar lighting to a gorgeous setting sun. Everyone at Marin's seemed too preoccupied to notice.

He walked to the car and shivered in the night air. The thought of getting trapped in whatever game those guys were playing was terrifying. If this was the end result that P&C had waiting for their graduates, he didn't want any part of it.

He kept up his brisk walk to the car and relaxed in the seat.

He glanced down at his phone and smiled when he saw the new message from Ella:

"Waiting...Where are you? I'm sure hanging out with your brother's Wall Street friends is soo cool. >:D I thought we were going on a date!"

So it was an official date! Jay pumped his fist in the air as he texted back.

"We are, they're lame. What's the address?"

He watched her typing bubble appear and the address popped up. He tapped it into his phone and texted back. "Enroute now. Be there in 10!" He made sure his directions were coming through the car's Bluetooth speakers, and drove off.

Ten minutes later, Jay was in front of what looked like a mansion. The Victorian style home lay on sprawling grounds, and he saw a string of luxury sedans and SUV's parked on the streets leading up to it. He pulled up along the side of the road as close as he could get and parked the car. He hoped Ella would meet him outside, but cringed when her text said,

"Come around the side of the house. We're all outside. My parents want to meet you before we go anywhere."

Jay texted back, "Okay, on my way."

He took a deep breath and looked in the car mirror. If he knew he was going to be in front of a bunch of P&C alumni, he would have dressed up a bit more. He got out of the car and shook the nervousness out of his limbs.

Jay turned into the massive open gate and walked along a lighted pathway until he arrived at a huge backyard. The scene looked like it was out of a movie. Rows of lights hung from trees, a tent was set up, and there were even a few waiters walking around with trays of food and drinks. He scanned a few groups of people, but he didn't see Ella. From the looks of it, he was underdressed, but it looked like he might be the most sober. He spotted the largest group under a tent and headed towards them. As he approached, a figure moved out of the larger crowd ahead.

It was Ella.

He'd never seen her dressed up like this before. She had

curled her hair, put on makeup that made her eyes pop, and was wearing a red sundress.

He smiled and gave her a hug.

"Wow. You look great!"

She laughed. "Thanks, so you do. Meet my parents and then get me out of here!"

"Sure thing," said Jay, as Ella took his hand and led him through the crowd. They walked up to a man and woman standing by a well-lit section of the bar. "Dad... Mom... This is Jay."

A tall man with gray hair turned around. "Jay, you said? Jay, I'm Ella's father, Mr. Jordan."

"Nice to meet you, sir." Jay shook his hand and felt a crushing grip.

"And this is my mom," said Ella.

"Hello Jay," said Mrs. Jordan flatly.

Mr. Jordan's eyebrows were curved sharply downward as he sized Jay up. "So you're here to visit P&C? You didn't get in early like Ella?"

"That's right. No, I didn't. I haven't applied yet," said Jay.

"You think you'll get in?" asked Mr. Jordan. His eyebrows raised even more now as if he had caught Jay in some sort lie.

Ella sighed and jumped in. "Not everybody is staking their entire existence on going to P&C Dad... We're getting ready to leave for dinner."

"I have a few plans, applying to P&C was just one of them," said Jay.

By now, Mrs. Jordan had turned around to the bar and Mr. Jordan acted as if Jay hadn't said anything. He just stared at Ella, looking perplexed. "What's wrong with the food here?"

"Nothing, Mr. Jordan, I thought we'd go out to dinner and

walk along the waterfront downtown," ventured Jay.

"I trust you're not drinking and driving?" asked Mr. Jordan.

"No, no, of course not," said Jay.

"Well then, have Ella back here before 11:00 pm," he said curtly.

"Okay, we'll be back before then. It was nice to meet you Mr. and Mrs. Jordan."

Jay thought they'd respond, but instead they both nodded and turned back to the bar.

"Bye!" said Ella as she grabbed Jay's arm and turned him around. As they walked away from the party, she leaned over and whispered, "Oh my god, I'm sorry! Just keep walking. They'll be passed out before 11:00 pm."

The fall breeze made Ella's sundress flutter as they walked. She looked beautiful, and Jay wondered how he looked to her. Next time he'd splurge on a nicer outfit.

Wow, it looks like the party is raging pretty hard over there" said Jay, as he nodded his head towards several guys laughing and stumbling around the yard.

"Ahhh yes. I think they're all alcoholics. Which makes having a single glass of red wine very easy," she laughed, smiling at him.

Jay noticed several of the rowdy crowd begin to drift towards them as they walked. One of them pointed and walked over. He looked at Ella and then looked at the group of guys staring at them. One started to yell Ella's name.

Ella leaned over to Jay. "Good Lord... I told you to keep walking!"

Jay recognized the next yell and turned around. It was her

ex-boyfriend, Conor Trajan. He eyed Jay up, the same as he always did in school. Then, he looked to Ella.

"Hey Ella, all of us are going to Marin's in a bit. You should come with."

"We're leaving," she said.

Jay leaned his head in front of Conor, who was staring at Ella. "Marin's was alright. I just came from there."

"How did you get in, Jay? I didn't know you... partied."

"My friend knows the owner. But, like Ella said, we're leaving. Have fun at Marin's!"

Ella clamped onto Jay's arm a bit more firmly this time as she led them away. "Okay hotshot, now I'm serious. Keep walking. I guess you are a party animal, getting into Marin's on a Saturday night. Do you have a fake ID?"

Jay laughed. "Yea right. No fake ID, it was just my brother's boss. You're sure your fans won't mind you leaving?" asked Jay. He gestured back to the crowd that had assembled around Conor. Ella glanced back at them and shook her head,

"Ugh. Spoiled trust fund babies. Those creeps have been stalking me all night," she said.

Jay took her hand as they walked away. "I think they'd get along well with Gavin's friends."

"Hah! Probably right. So where are you taking me?" Ella had a bounce in her step as they walked to Gary's car.

"Surprise, a spot downtown I picked out."

As they walked closer to the car, Jay's attention snapped up, and he jumped ahead to Ella's door and opened it.

"Woah..." Ella stepped back and put her phone down. "This is getting classy!"

"I guess P&C is rubbing off on me," said Jay.

"I doubt that. But thank you." Ella got into the car, and Jay shut the door behind her.

When they pulled up to the restaurant, Jay crossed his fingers. He thought since Ella's family was always visiting, she would have come here once or twice before.

"Ever been here?" he asked.

"You'd think so, but no," said Ella. "I've wanted to stop here ever since I was a little girl. My parents always said it was too dumpy to stop at, so we never did. But, now I am!"

Jay parked, and Ella was out of the door and laughing before he could walk around to open it for her. She waved him off. "Nice try, I got the door this time."

Jay laughed and took her hand as they walked into the restaurant. This restaurant and bar were the opposite of Marin's. The place was brightly lit, with a relaxed crowd. The bar was well laid out, but not the main attraction. Old reclaimed farm wood lined the walls, and the place was filled with couples.

They sat down at their table, and within a few minutes they both decided on the same salad. After they had ordered, Ella sparked up the conversation again.

"So, are you still going to apply to P&C? Cause I might lose my mind if I'm the only one from our school going here."

"I'll still apply, but I don't know if I want to go anymore. The more I learn about technology, the more I think I can't afford to take a four-year break from it... if that makes sense?"

"Yeah it does, I'd miss you... but I kinda understand."

"Why's that?" wondered Jay.

"Just from seeing how well you and Gary work together.

Plus, your UX/UI sketches all look great. You'll be a designer at a great company in no time," she said.

Jay took a sip of his water on the table and asked, "When have you seen my drawings?"

"Well, during Mr. Moore's class when I get bored."

Jay started to feel nervous. "You've been looking at me draw them?"

"Well yeah, duh! You're sketching out screens and product ideas, right? So, what are you and Gary cooking up?"

"Nothing major, just a few ideas I'm working on. I have to get my portfolio up to speed first."

"Well keep it up, because they look great. I can't wait to see what you and Gary build."

"Thanks, we're working on an idea," he said.

After dinner, Jay grabbed the check, and they walked slowly out the front door.

"Want to go walk along the water for a bit?" he asked.

"That sounds perfect," she said.

Jay slipped his arm around Ella as they walked out the door. Step one complete, he thought. They talked and walked along the waterfront for a while. They talked about everything, from Jay's brother, to all the research Ella had done around the company CheckUp. They were doing the work that could have saved her Grandfather's life. Jay had never talked this deeply about anything with her... he needed to do more of it.

After talking outside for an hour, Ella checked her phone. "Hey it is almost 10:30, and I had an amazing time tonight. Thanks for taking me out," she said while turning to him.

"Yeah of course," said Jay.

If he didn't try to kiss her now, Gary would rip on him for

the rest of the year. Jay leaned in and kissed her. Ella kissed him back, and Jay did his best to not jump up and shout. They walked back to the car, and headed back in time for Ella's curfew.

They made it just in time, as he pulled back up to the mansion.

As Jay pulled up to drop Ella off, he fumbled on what to say. He ended up with, "I had a great time."

She giggled and grabbed her purse. "I think that's what I'm supposed to say," she laughed.

"You're right... but it's true," he said.

"It's okay if you're nervous," said Ella.

"What?" asked Jay. He felt his face turning red in the dark car.

"You already did once. You don't have to be scared a second time," she said, looking into his eyes.

He tried to think of some clever way to act like she wasn't reading his mind, but before he knew it, Ella was in front of his face.

"Hi!" she said and kissed him. She leaned back and opened the car door. "Your turn next time. Night, thanks for dinner!"

"Good Night! Anytime!"

Jay took a deep breath and waited until Ella opened the front door and walked inside. He watched her father come out and stare at him. He waved to her Dad, who nodded, and then walked back inside.

Jay leaned back in the seat of the car and let out a burst of excitement.

"YESSSSS!"

20

BACK TO REALITY

"If your intentions are good, don't let haters stop you from speaking up."
–Gary Weinstein

Jay's next move was to unleash a fury of texts to Gary. This was the best night of his entire year! Well... so far. He sat smiling stupidly to himself in the car for a few minutes. He had kissed Ella Jordan. Not once... but twice!

He turned on some music and headed to pick up Gary and Gavin. Jay wondered where they were. Probably still at Marin's. There was no way Gary would go to the strip club with them. Jay saw a text and pulled to the side of the neighborhood to check it.

His stomach sank as he looked at the phone. "That's awesome man... hate to burst your bubble, but get over to Marin's. Fast."

"What's wrong, is everything okay?" Jay typed back.

"Yeah, it's alright, I just need help carrying Gavin out. He's okay, but just wasted. His "friends" left w/o him."

"Ok, I'm enroute."

Jay shook his head and drove back to Marin's.

He found Gary outside the restaurant, with Gavin's arm draped over his shoulder. Getting Gavin to the car was a struggle, but they did, and eventually got him to bed at his apartment.

Gary and Jay hung out on Gavin's balcony for a few minutes, recounting the night. Gary filled Jay in on what he missed: more shots and more trips to the bathroom. Gavin had only made one trip and faded early. The rest of the group tried to drag them to a strip club until they discovered that Gavin couldn't walk on his own. Brio and the gang quickly pawned him off on Gary and left.

Jay could barely believe it. "Thanks for looking out for him."

"No problem," said Gary. "I'm just glad you got to go out with Ella."

"Yeah, at least there's that," Jay said with a smile.

Gary stretched out on the futon and went to sleep. Jay decided he needed to stay up and make sure Gavin didn't throw up in his sleep or anything crazy. Jay slid to the floor in Gavin's room and pulled out his phone to read a book.

After a few hours, Gavin woke up, stumbled to the bathroom, and drank a glass of water. He mumbled that he was fine, and then got back in his bed. Finally, Jay was able to fall asleep.

When he and Gary woke up in the morning, Jay's first thought was that drinking was one item on a laundry list of Gavin's problems. Gary made them breakfast while Jay decided to see how deep Gavin's issues ran.

He didn't care about appearances anymore, or about getting caught snooping. He started searching through his brother's drawers. It didn't take long before he found the first bottles of pills. He instantly recognized Gavin's go-to choice from high school– Adderall. But there were a few more bottles he didn't recognize. Gary walked around the apartment, nervously helping Jay do Google searches to ID these new pills. The closest match they found was opiates... or basically synthetic heroin.

"Good lord!" Jay blurted out in frustration.

"Yeah, this isn't good," said Gary.

He sat down at the counter wondering what to do as Gary pushed a plateful of scrambled eggs in front of him. They ate in silence.

After breakfast, Jay glanced in Gavin's room. He was still snoring loudly. "You know, I kind of figured something had been wrong with Gavin for awhile."

"Are you going to say something to your parents?" asked Gary.

"Definitely. First I'm going to get rid of these," said Jay, as he took the pill bottles into the bathroom. He emptied them in the toilet and flushed. In a juvenile way, he felt vindicated for every single time in the past when people told him to be more like his brother. But on the other hand, Jay felt horrible that his brother was drugging himself. Maybe this would give Gavin a wake up call.

He and Gary poked their heads in Gavin's room and said bye. Gavin woke up briefly, walked them out, and that was the end of their visit.

Gary and Jay didn't talk much on the ride home. After he

dropped Gary off, Jay dreaded the drive home and facing his parents. What was he supposed to say? Would Gavin hate him for saying anything? What if he overdosed on something before Jay could speak up? Jay shook his head. Of course he was going to tell his parents, they'd have to believe him... right?

They didn't.

The conversation between Jay and his parents was awkward at best. When Jay tried to convince them Gavin was drinking too much and taking pills, they went on the defense. From there, they just grew irritated, and Jay saw himself fighting a losing battle. Alan and Debbie both said they'd call Gavin tomorrow to check in, and they'd drive up and see him some weekend. They thanked Jay for speaking up... but they didn't take it seriously.

21

FALLING

"As the work got harder, finishing it became more rewarding."
–Jay Pencha

Back at home, Jay's parents contacted Gavin, and he appeared to be fine. He fought to convince his parents that Gavin needed help, but after a certain point, there was no more he could do. They didn't want to hear it, so he ignored them, and focused on his work.

Fall led to Thanksgiving, which quickly led to Christmas. When Gavin came home for the holidays, Jay seemed to be the only one worried about the massive dark circles under his eyes. Jay did his best to stay open and show his brother that he could talk with him, but it didn't work. The conversations were all superficial. Jay could tell Gavin was angry, and so once again, he went back to focusing on improving himself.

The more he learned, the more his classes at school bored him. Mr. Moore's class was the only one that was bearable.

To keep his parents and Pemberton happy, Jay applied to P&C and a few obligatory safety schools. His senior year was ticking by, but he still had time to land a job before graduation.

When he first heard it, the concept of not needing college seemed far-fetched. But as he met more people working in technology, he found that it was increasingly common. Jay got into the habit of sending cold emails to any designer he wanted to meet. Sometimes, he'd even email CEO's of companies. He asked their opinions on college, what skills they suggest he learn, and if they would hire him. It felt silly, but sometimes they responded with detailed answers, and some even invited him to keep in touch or apply when he was ready.

To make sure he improved his design skills, Jay toned down the amount of time he spent working for Drivr. Sacrificing that income allowed him to invest his time into learning every skill he'd need to make way more money later.

On nights after school, he either hung out at Ella's, worked at Gary's or they'd both go in to the Oxen offices. Sometimes Jay would shadow Micah, or one of the other talented designers.

By the time early February arrived, Jay's portfolio was filling with his projects, mock-ups, and sketches. Gary was approaching the end of his six-month trial work period, and soon, he'd be heading out to the Livu offices in Silicon Valley to interview for a full-time mobile developer position. The position came complete with a large salary and even stock options.

He and Gary found the time to launch their Creativity Quiz

app and were working on adding some features for an updated version. The biggest features they were working on where the social invites, but also to promote Livu in the app. They ran their numbers and thought they'd be able to send the Livu website a few hundred visitors per day. Jay wanted to have this finished, but he also realized his time was ticking down. He decided to send in his resume and portfolio to Livu. Instead of telling Gary, he decided to keep it a secret, and hopefully... landing the job would be a surprise.

Behind the scenes, Jay talked to Gary's dad when he got a chance. Oxen was still looking for an enterprise sales rep, and there was a job if his dad would be willing to apply. But in the meantime, Jay knew his dad would never listen to him until he landed a job of his own. He learned everything he could about the position, filing it away for later.

Euphoria was the best word to describe how Jay felt after the long days of working, planning, and learning. Somehow, when you put everything you had into something you cared about, the exhaustion felt good. In his entire life, he had never felt anything quite like it. He had pushed himself hard...almost to the breaking point. There were many nights where he wanted to take the easy path, work for Drivr, go to college, and party like everyone else. But he knew if he gave in, he would always regret not testing his limits.

But that feeling of euphoria from charting his course couldn't last forever. Gavin came home early to visit for their mom's birthday weekend. He was in rough shape. In front of their parents, Gavin attributed his disheveled look to his long hours at work. When Gavin brought up his recent pay raise, the questions completely stopped.

The brother Jay remembered from their childhood was gone. That person bursting with energy and ideas had vanished. He'd been replaced with a cynical, highly functioning addict. The thoughts turned in his mind, and eventually, he'd run into Gavin alone.

Jay slipped through the door after a night of working at Gary's house. He was hoping Gavin would be asleep in his old room. Unfortunately, when Jay went to raid the kitchen, there was Gavin, seated in front of the TV watching a movie. In front of him sat a bottle of liquor, a chaser, and a glass with ice.

"Hey, what's up," Jay said, as he put his things down and grabbed a snack.

"What's up, bro! Haven't seen you in awhile."

"Yeah it has been awhile," said Jay. "I've been busy." He grabbed leftovers in the kitchen and started eating.

You don't want to talk to your older brother anymore?" said Gavin. He poured himself another mixed drink.

"That's not it. I'm building something with Gary. Just have to make sure it's good to go."

Gavin laughed. "Mom and dad said you're still trying to get a job... as a designer? Is that right?"

"That's right." Jay tried to show zero emotion, but it didn't work.

Gavin sipped his drink loudly. "You'll never make as much as we do in finance. Mom and Dad say you spend all the money you make buying books or computer stuff."

"I'm not so sure about that... and what's wrong with buying what I need to learn?"

"You're dumping it down the drain. You haven't even got

accepted to a decent college yet, and you think you know everything!"

Jay scooted his chair out from under the counter and cleaned up his food. "I'm just trying to learn... there are lots of things I'm exploring."

"You might want to try and get realistic," said Gavin, as he took another sip.

Jay fought the urge to punch Gavin in the face. He knew he was on the right path. If this path made people who were sick like Gavin uncomfortable, then maybe it was a good sign.

Jay looked at Gavin's sunken eyes in the dim light of the kitchen. He leered at Jay and took another big gulp. Jay smirked back. "I know you're drunk right now, and it's not a good time to talk."

He walked out of the kitchen to Gavin's irritated voice. "Lighten up! You'll wish you listened!"

Jay walked upstairs furiously and closed the door to his room. He would get realistic, he thought.

22

FINISHING THE UPDATE

"Sometimes you've got to scheme your way out."
–Gary Weinstein

Jay woke up early on Friday. He heard from his parents that Gavin had some errands to run later in the morning.

He went downstairs, made his breakfast, and left coffee out for his parents. He threw sandals on, ran outside, and moved Gary's car down the street. His parents and Gavin had to think that he had already left for school. When Jay got back to his room, he opened his laptop.

Get realistic... the phrase burned in his mind. Gavin was right. Jay did need to get realistic about the right things. And the most important thing right now was to wake up his parents to the fact that Gavin was an addict. If nobody spoke up, he was going to kill himself with alcohol and pills.

Jay remembered one of the things Mr. Moore had taught the class. Several students were facing rejections, or people who told them to, "get realistic" about their ambitions. Translated, Mr. Moore explained that "get realistic" was usually code for "your ambition makes my laziness noticeable," or "if you can do it, then I can do it, but I don't want to think about that."

Thinking about the psychology and philosophy behind Gavin's words took the anger out of Jay's mind. It allowed him to separate the comments from the person, who was still his brother.

And, this brother needed desperately to be saved.

In the meantime, he had an app update to design. The current Creativity Quiz app was getting a few hundred downloads a day. Jay thought they could do much better, and even could start promoting Livu within the app. Jay fired up Photoshop, and within minutes he was working hard on an update. If Gary was on schedule, he should be adding the social component to the app, where users could challenge their friends to play against them.

As he worked, Jay kept an eye out the window.

First he watched his mom leave for work, followed by his dad for an interview. Finally, after another hour, Gavin walked out to his car, and left to run errands. Jay was patient for a few minutes to make sure he was really gone. Then, he ran downstairs to Gavin's basement room. After some light searching, he found several full Aspirin bottles that didn't contain Aspirin. He hid them in a kitchen drawer, and then rushed to go pick up Gary and get to school in time for Mr. Moore's class.

They got to school late and got off with a written warning.

Success, thought Jay. He had hidden Gavin's pills, and when his parents got home from work, he'd confront them with the cold hard truth... and the facts. There was no way they could ignore the truth now.

The rest of that Friday flew by. Mr. Moore's class was great, and he was thrilled that Gary was closing in on a full-time offer. After a bit of convincing, Mr. Moore had Jay and Gary get up in front of the class and talk about what they were up to. They got to demo their app to the entire class, but Jay was adamant the entire time to make sure they knew an update was coming soon.

Mr. Moore encouraged the class to follow Gary and Jay's example of building something, or completing a project that they could point to. That project would act as the dynamic resume that employers needed to see. Gary explained how eventually they'd use the app to send visitors to Livu, and Jay would cite that fact when he applied. Mr. Moore loved the idea, and told them to go for it. He said the future of the new economy was all about living by the golden rule. Reaching out to Livu after sending them value was a great way to 'do unto others.'

The praise from Mr. Moore felt good, but Jay was still waiting to for the ultimate praise... a job offer from Livu.

After school, they jumped right into finishing and rolling out the app update. Finally, Gary put the finishing touches on his end, and they clicked *submit* in the App Store. Jay and Gary celebrated with some Thai takeout, and both of them already had ideas for the next version. Hanging out at Gary's was a blast... until Jay remembered he still had to confront his parents at home. He dutifully said goodbye to his co-conspirator, and drove home. He didn't know how he'd bring it up to his parents, but he could figure it out later. For now, he had to get home, and hopefully... Gavin would already be asleep.

23

ADDICTION'S FACE

"I've never met anyone who says, 'let me show you everything alcohol helped me do'... unless they were selling it."
–Mr. Moore

Jay opened the front door, and it appeared quiet. Maybe he got lucky and everyone really was asleep. He tiptoed inside towards the kitchen. He stopped and paused. He could get a snack tomorrow. He didn't want to chance running into Gavin again.

Before he could turn around, a voice came from the living room. "I can see you in the mirror, idiot!"

Damn it, thought Jay. He walked into the kitchen and nodded to Gavin in the living room.

"Thought you were sleeping... didn't want to wake you up. I'm going to grab a snack." Jay walked into the kitchen, and Gavin got up and followed. He smelled like alcohol.

Gavin pulled up a stool at the kitchen island and watched Jay get food out of the fridge. "You don't have to avoid me."

"I'm not. I didn't want to wake you up," Jay tried to ignore Gavin, who with his drink of choice in hand, sat there and stared.

Jay pulled out some leftovers from the fridge, made himself a plate, and put it in the microwave. While his food heated, Jay glanced over at the living room where Gavin had been sitting. A shot glass sat by a bottle of liquor on the coffee table. Most of the bottle was gone.

"You just get home from driving your taxi?" asked Gavin, sarcastically.

Jay's heart sank. He didn't want to argue with his brother when he was sober, let alone drunk and confrontational.

"I didn't drive tonight. I was at Gary's."

"Nerding around?"

"No, we're just working on a side project that's going to help me get hired at a sick job."

"Good luck getting hired without the best college, bro. I hope your new job is less embarrassing than driving your little taxi around." Gavin took a long sip and put his drink down. The smell hit Jay's nose and the thought of cheap vodka made him nauseous.

"I'm sorry that anything entrepreneurial embarrasses you."

Gavin shot Jay an angry look and shook his head. "Mmmhhhmm... Still learning all the wrong things."

"I'm learning so mom and dad won't have to pay for P&C... or any other college."

Gavin laughed louder and glared at him. "Jay, you can't even help yourself. I saw your rejection letter from P&C. You couldn't even go there if you wanted to!"

"I'm starting to see that rejection letter as a good thing." said Jay.

"You know what's even funnier?" asked Gavin.

Jay stared silently and didn't answer.

Gavin smirked. "I guess I'm supposed to congratulate you on getting accepted into SSU though! Do you know what my company thinks about graduates from colleges like that?"

"Shut up–"

"That they're a joke!" hissed Gavin, moving his head down in front of Jay's eyes. "After SSU, you'll be unemployed in the basement with mom and dad!"

"I'm not going to SSU, I'm going to land a job before I graduate," said Jay calmly.

Gavin smirked. "Where at? Gonna get a job at Livu?"

Jay's head spun... Gavin must have found the letters from P&C and SSU in his room... but how did he know that Jay had applied to Livu? There was no way Gavin could know before him... unless... "Are you reading my emails?!"

"I did... but only because I got bored looking for something that's mine. You're still using your same password, huh?"

"Checking my email is a childish thing to do" said Jay, as he grabbed his empty plate, put it in the dishwasher, and started to walk towards the steps and his room.

Jay stayed stoic and moved to walk around Gavin, but Gavin stepped in front of him.

He stared into his brother's glassy eyes. "You're drunk. Get out of my way."

"I'm not that drunk... yet." Jay tried to go around him, and Gavin pushed him in the chest and slurred, "You're going to wish you listened to me."

Jay batted Gavin's hand away. Gavin laughed and widened

his eyes. "Gonna slap me? I guess that's what angry nerds do."

"Why are you *so* angry?"

"Because YOU..." He tapped his finger into Jay's chest. "...Took something that is mine."

"I don't think you need them," said Jay calmly.

Gavin snapped. "I let you off the hook when you visited. The pills you flushed cost me a couple thousand dollars. That's not going to happen again!"

Gavin's eyes and nostrils flared as he pushed Jay again with both hands, knocking him off his balance to the floor. He moved towards him, but in an instant Jay was back up in his face. "Mom and Dad have them."

Gavin's eyes narrowed and he grabbed the front of Jay's shirt, pulling him forward. "WHERE ARE THEY?"

Jay was six years younger than Gavin, a couple inches shorter, and about twenty pounds lighter. He might be drunk, but Jay looked in his eyes, and saw a madman. He stayed calm, but realized Gavin was about to get violent.

"I told you, Mom and Dad have them Gavin."

Before he had time to think, Gavin reared his arm back and smacked Jay in the side of the head, pushing him against the kitchen wall. Stars filled his vision. No other choice, thought Jay.

As Gavin went to get in his face again, Jay thrust his head forward into the bridge of Gavin's nose. His brother let out a gurgling sound and staggered backward. Jay took the opening and dove into Gavin's midsection, knocking him to the ground. Gavin's first punch caught Jay in the jaw, and he wrestled to stop the next one. He barely heard a crash in the living room as they knocked over something. Gavin hit him again, but Jay rolled on top of him, adrenaline surging. He leaned back, dodging Gavin's next swing and punched him in the face. Gavin crumpled back, and his hands shot up to his face. He rolled over, his nose now gushing blood. Jay pushed himself off of him.

A massive breath filled Jay's lungs and he stood up, panting. "What the hell is wrong with you?"

In the next moment, Jay's parents were downstairs.

"BOYS! What's going on down there!?" yelled Alan from the steps.

By the time their parents rounded the corner, Jay was pacing back and forth, and Gavin laid holding his face on the ground.

Alan and Debbie came running into the living room. "Oh my God." What happened?! Jay, what did you do?!" wailed Debbie.

Gavin started to get to his feet, and Alan stepped in between the two of them. "What is wrong with you two?" He turned to Jay. "Back up! What's the problem here?"

Before he could think twice, Jay muttered, "Shut up."

"WHAT did you say?" roared Alan, who stepped in front of Jay.

Jay's hands were shaking, mixed with his brothers blood and his own.

"Were you both drinking?" asked Debbie.

"Drinking?" said Jay. "No, that's Gavin."

Alan stepped back in front of Jay's face again. "You'd better think carefully about what you say this time... what happened?"

"Shut up and believe me, Gavin's an addict!"

"You'd better–" Alan snarled and stepped towards Jay, but Gavin's voice interrupted.

"Jay's mad he didn't get into P&C or his designer thing."

"You didn't get into P&C?" asked Debbie and Alan at the same time.

Jay couldn't believe it. "Oh my god. You both are still obsessed with that. NO. I didn't get into P&C, and I'M NOT TRYING TO!"

Jay turned around, reached into a kitchen drawer, grabbed Gavin's pills, and tossed the bottles onto the kitchen table. He pointed to the pills and the liquor bottle that was now spilled on the carpet.

"Wake up, Gavin is an addict!"

Debbie was crying as she knelt over Gavin. She handed him tissues for his nose, which was, thanks to the alcohol and Jay's fists, bleeding all over the place.

Jay grabbed a handful of paper towels and dabbed the blood from his lip.

"I'm not coming back here until Gavin goes to rehab. I don't want it on my conscious anymore..."

Alan rubbed his temples. "Are you telling the truth– "

Jay cut him off. "I have been the whole time!"

Alan stepped closer to Jay. "What the hell are you talking about?"

Tears filled Jay's eyes from anger and frustration, but he stood his ground. "Come on Dad... you know Gavin's not okay. Why would I make any of this stuff up?"

Debbie and Alan both had tears in their eyes, and Debbie had a towel, blotting Gavin's face.

Jay saw his father's face go from angry to confused, and he

backed away from Jay.

"Do you think attacking your brother is going to solve anything?" said Alan to Jay. His was voice cracking, and Debbie was crying.

Jay wiped the trickle of blood from under his nose, and then looked at his parents. "All I did was defend myself from someone who can't function without those," he pointed to the bag and bottle on the table.

"That someone is your brother, young man. No matter what, you need to care about him!" said Alan, who now, along with Debbie, had tears streaming down his face.

Jay felt himself crying. He knew his parents were fighting through the denial. He pointed to Gavin, whose eyes were still filled with anger. "I don't know who that person is... and I'm the one who was worried about where he was going from the beginning."

Jay turned, walked out of the house, and slammed the door behind him.

24

A (REAL) OPEN DOOR POLICY

"Anything worth achieving feels impossible along the way.
If it didn't, it wouldn't be worth doing."
–Mr. Moore

Jay dabbed his face with his hand and glanced at it under the garage light. He was still bleeding. He sighed and wiped his hand on the front of his jeans. He needed to leave before he said or did something that he would regret.

As he got into Gary's car, he saw his hands were still shaking with adrenaline. Where was he going to go? At first he just assumed he'd go to Gary's. But how could he let Gary or his parents see him like this? He looked ridiculous.

The path that everyone else wanted to push him towards led to a dark place. Gavin was proof. And the person he got into a fight with inside the house wasn't the brother he had known growing up. All these years Jay had known that jumping through the hoops of academia was the wrong path for Gavin. He punched the steering wheel in anger.

Jay felt stupid for even getting into this situation. He didn't want anyone to see him like this, but he needed help. He needed to talk to someone who understood him. Maybe I can talk to Mr. Moore, thought Jay. He thought back to the class syllabus, where Mr. Moore had listed a 24/7 open door policy.

He opened up the app that the class used for messaging and sent one to Mr. Moore,

"The 24/7 Open Door policy... is it real, or just one of those things teachers say?"

Jay leaned his head back in the car. It was starting to throb. He saw his breath in front of him as he dabbed at his face with his hands. The blood had stopped.

Jay's hands were still shaking as his phone buzzed. There was a new message from Mr. Moore in the class messaging app.

"It's real. What's up? You okay?"

"What do you know," thought Jay. Maybe this guy was serious about everything he taught.

"Yeah, I'm fine. Need to talk."

"Sure. Come on over."

"Now?"

"Sure, why not? I'll be outside on the porch."

Jay watched as an address came in. He recognized where it was, and started driving. In a few minutes, he pulled up in front of Mr. Moore's house. It was in a nice section of town, and the outside lights were still on. He got out of the car slowly, still shaken up from the fight. On the front porch, Mr. Moore sat wearing a jacket and holding a Kindle. He hadn't looked up yet.

Jay sighed. Should he even be here? He immediately thought about leaving. What was he going to say? Was he just going to complain about everything?

"Hey, don't be a creeper out there! Come on up!"

Mr. Moore's voice startled him. Too late now, he thought.

"What's up? You sure you're okay?" Mr. Moore put his book down and walked down the porch steps, squinting to try and see him.

Jay waved and walked into the light. "Yeah, I'm alright."

"What happened? You didn't kill anybody, did you?" said Mr. Moore, as he motioned to Jay's shirt and face.

Jay laughed for a second. "No, no, it was a... it was a bad fight with my brother. He was wasted... being an idiot. I was trying to cool down and didn't know where else to go."

"Having students visit you at 10pm and covered in blood sounds like a recipe for a promotion!" laughed Mr. Moore. He opened the door to the house and motioned Jay inside.

Jay chuckled nervously, feeling the pain in his jaw. "Yeah, sorry it's a spur of the moment thing. I haven't been drinking or anything. Just the fight with Gavin."

"Well either way, it's alright. C'mon in." Mr. Moore stuck his head in the door and yelled, "Heather, can you put some tea on and grab some towels?" He turned to Jay. "living with your parents comes in handy."

Without thinking, Jay asked, "You live with your parents?"

Mr. Moore laughed. "Only joking. Heather's my wife. C'mon in!"

They walked into a well-lit kitchen where two laptops sat open on the table and something smelled delicious.

"You lucked out, and you have perfect timing. We're night

owls and we've got a batch of cookies getting ready to come out of the oven."

Heather came in and introduced herself to Jay, and politely declined to shake his hand until he cleaned up. She had set out some towels, alcohol, and band aids in the bathroom for Jay. In a few minutes, he washed up, put some alcohol on the cuts on his face, and organized himself the best he could.

When he returned to the kitchen, he found a steaming mug of tea on the table and a plate full of fresh cookies. Over cookies and mint tea, Jay filled Mr. Moore in on everything that had happened. He vented and decided to just let everything out. When he finally realized he'd been the only one talking and that they had both finished the tea and cookies, he paused.

"Sorry. I guess you didn't want to hear all that."

"No! I think all of this pushback, drama, and crazy circumstances are good."

"What?"

"Yeah! It signals you're doing interesting things, you have courage, and you're standing up for what you think is right. Sometimes that means you take a few punches, and I guess you just took the literal ones tonight."

Jay laughed. "Yeah... I guess. I just thought before graduation I'd be able to land a job at a technology company... or at least a startup. I've been preparing all year... I just thought it would work. I feel like an idiot for not putting in enough effort applying to colleges. I mean, I got rejected by Livu... I just feel stupid."

"You should feel stupid."

"What?" Jay looked up from his tea.

"You should feel stupid! You've only applied to Livu once!

ONCE! But for everything else that you have done so far, you should be proud. You've busted your ass this whole year. That's nothing to feel stupid about."

"Well I don't feel very smart about my decisions right now, that's for sure..."

"Of course it doesn't tonight, that's alright. Realize how far you've come!"

Jay shrugged, he still felt confused. "I have no idea what to do."

"Have patience. Have faith in yourself and keep making daily improvements."

"That's it?" asked Jay.

"That's always it!" said Mr. Moore, as he grabbed the last cookie on the plate and took a bite. "Oh! And reapply to Livu. Reach out to the CEO and tell him about the app you created. Don't take no for an answer."

"You think that's all I need to do?"

"Yeah! Don't stop what you're doing, that's for sure. You might have saved your brother's life! Now *that* requires courage, and sometimes courage will lead you to a fight. The only dumb move you can make would be to slow down now."

Jay nodded and sipped his tea. "Yeah, I guess it would be pretty dumb to stop following through now, or not apply to Livu again."

"Very dumb. Most places will say no to everyone the first time! Hiring is one of their biggest expenses. It's a huge risk for them. Plus you're younger. You're going to have to prove to them how bad you want the opportunity and how much value you can bring to them."

Jay nodded solemnly. "Thanks. I'm guessing the bill for this counseling session will be in the mail?"

"Counseling session? OHHHH NO. Are you calling me a SHRINK?" Mr. Moore feigned anger.

"No, no... you know what I mean," laughed Jay.

Mr. Moore let out a deep laugh. "Life is one big long mental game. The mental game is everything, and to win, you've got to strategize with others. It's not counseling. It's strategy."

Jay laughed. "Well, then thanks for the strategy session."

"Anytime. Remember that only the best are humble enough to seek strategy. The people who stay dumb are the people who think that getting help signals that they're weak. Seeking strategy and wisdom is a sign of high intelligence."

"Thanks," said Jay.

Mr. Moore poured them both the rest of the tea. "Isn't Gary supposed to fly out to Livu for his full-time interview soon?"

"Uh yeah, why do you ask?"

"Well if I were you, I'd tighten up my design portfolio and fly out there with him. Get a meeting with the highest person you can at Livu and tell them why you want to work there. Heck, get as many meetings with startups or CEO's as you can. You're already delivering traffic to Livu with your app. That is valuable! Don't be afraid to tell them... and preferably, tell them in person!"

Jay finished his cookie and stood up, "You're right. I've got to go get started!"

"Good! Make sure you tell your parents where you're at to let them know you're okay," Mr Moore said.

"I will, and thanks for the cookies, tea, and strategy. I think I'll head over to Gary's and spend the night."

"Great idea. Your parents probably need some time to get to the bottom of everything with Gavin. I'm sure they'll do what's best and get him some help."

Jay and Mr. Moore walked out of his house, and they passed shelves of books. Jay pointed to them. "You and Gary's parents both read all the time."

"I don't know anybody seeking wisdom who doesn't."

"I'm starting to see that," said Jay, as he stepped out on the porch.

Mr. Moore's face turned serious for a moment. "Jay, keep doing what you're doing. You're so close to landing a job... all your efforts are going to pay off... okay?"

"I will," said Jay. "In fact, I think I'll get started on reapplying tonight at Gary's."

Mr. Moore laughed. "Sleep first."

Jay rolled his head. "Fine, sleep first. But after that I'm submitting an update to our app and reapplying to Livu. Plus, I've got to start planning so I can go out to Silicon Valley with Gary and meet the Livu team in person!"

"Now THAT sounds like a plan."

"Thanks, Mr. Moore, see you in class."

"Anytime."

It was after midnight, and his face hurt like crazy, but Jay had a bounce in his step. Go out to Silicon Valley with Gary, meet the Livu team in person and reapply. Now that was a bold idea. He'd never been out West before. Maybe now was the time to see firsthand why Gary called it the *Promised Land*. He drove over to the Weinstein's and thought about it the whole way.

25

WAKING UP

*"You know the ingredients, now bake the cake. Take it to
the hosts, and let them cut it. If it's good, you might get a big
slice."*
–John Weinstein

Jay stayed at Gary's house for the next week. He talked
with his parents only enough to confirm that he was okay and
that Gavin was okay. His parents had been in denial, but that
night had finally made them see the reality of things.

Jay's parents apologized profusely, which was a first. But
the most challenging part was thinking about all the years
where Jay had heard, "be more like your brother." He was
glad Gavin was getting help, but he needed a few more days
to cool down. His parents filled him in on what had happened.

Gavin insisted that Jay had started the fight. He was fine,
and had just been drinking too much that one night. He said
the pills were both Adderall and Ritalin, but that was
obviously a lie. Jay's parents asked him to take a few days off
from work to stay at the house. They wanted to prove to

themselves that Gavin was perfectly fine without the pills and booze. In just two days, Gavin cracked. He started acting erratically, demanding to go back to his place and back to work. On day three, he was found manically searching through the house for the pills they had taken from him. Eventually, Gavin broke down and Jay's parents could no longer deny what Jay had known for years... something wasn't right. Arrangements at a rehab center were made, and Gavin (to Jay's surprise) insisted on going.

It was horrible, yet a relief, at the same time. Jay had held his ground, and now it felt like a tremendous weight being lifted from his shoulders. He didn't care about being right. He just felt relief that he no longer had to watch Gavin fall apart.

Debbie and Alan wanted Jay to come home, but Jay wasn't ready yet.

Gary's house provided the sanctuary that he needed before he would head home. He had a few late night conversations with Gary, and Gary's mom and dad.

The rest of the time, he was either working with Gary or texting back and forth with Ella. Jay got to see her at school, and they hung out at her house a few times after school. They'd go for walks, watch movies, or work side by side. Just like Gary and his parents, Ella wasn't afraid to give Jay advice. She reminded him that as far as parents go, his had been remarkably receptive. It had taken a single fight with his brother to wake his parents up, while her parents seemed content to live in denial about many things. Ella's grandfather had been the last risk taker in the family, and now her parents seemed fine with letting his wealth sit, live lavishly off the interest, and brush everything else under the rug. Rehab stints were the norm for Ella's extended family. She even guessed that her parents would eventually, "make the rounds."

From this perspective, Jay's situation didn't look so bad. Ella encouraged him to go home. Not only did his parents need him now, but they would need him even more so after Gavin got out of rehab.

With just a few months left at school, it was down to the wire. At Gary's house, they kept up a crazy work tempo. In the mornings, it was Jay's duty to wake Gary up. Occasionally this meant he had to drag him out of bed to make sure they both ran or got a workout in. Gary would be hostile, whiny, and protest during the first five minutes. Jay would force him to workout or run with him. Like clockwork, after every single workout, Gary apologized for his pre-workout behavior. Then, he'd make Jay promise to keep making him workout.

During school, he and Gary got whatever work done that they could. Afterwards, they rushed home and poured themselves into coding or design. Most nights, Gary was busy with work for Livu, but he could occasionally tinker with side projects. Jay poured himself into practice building as many screens and user experience and interfaces as possible. Midway through the week, the two of them finished an update to their Creativity Quiz app. Gary added the ability to challenge your friends, and Jay tweaked the on boarding process. The new goal of the app was to provide them with a fun quiz game, but suggest that if they really wanted to boost their creativity, they go checkout Livu. Before Jay resubmitted his application to Livu, he wanted to literally be delivering them value. He knew if he gave first, and then ask to receive, his chances were much better at getting hired. He and Gary eventually finished the app update, submitted it, and within a few days it got approved and went live in the App Store.

Overnight, their daily downloads increased, and now over 4% of their users would take Jay's recommendation to go checkout the Livu site.

This was huge. Not just for Jay, but also for Gary. After all, he would be interviewing soon to go from a temporary employee to full-time. Now, their Creativity Quiz app was delivering Livu a steady stream of new customers. This was the best way they could think of to signal their competence above and beyond what was expected of them. Now, reapplying (this time with Gary's help) was a no-brainer. Jay not only had a great portfolio piece, but their app would put him above many of the other applicants. This was the karmic way to get what you wanted.

Gary was thrilled. Their app had now passed ten thousand daily active users, which wasn't massive, but it was big enough to send Livu some amazing new customers.

Now both of Gary's parents were certain that Jay should reapply. Jay wasn't completely confident, but he changed his mind after getting harassed to reapply over every single Weinstein family dinner. All three Weinstein's couldn't believe that anyone on earth would stop trying after they heard a few "no's."

Like Mr. Moore, both Suze and John suggested that Jay not only reapply, but that he should go to San Francisco with Gary and meet the Livu team in person. They told Jay that he could meet the folks at Livu, but also set up appointments at other companies and startups. After non-stop nagging from Gary, Jay caved and said that he'd buy a plane ticket and come with him.

The first step was to land Jay an interview. The Weinstein's had a motto that when you wanted something done, you go to the top. In that spirit, Jay and Gary crafted an email to send to the CEO of Livu, Ryan Parker.

Ryan had founded the company a few years ago, and now it was growing steadily. Gary already knew him, and thought he would love to hire Jay if they made it easy for him to say yes. So, Gary wrote an email saying he was looking forward to the interview. He cited their app, and introduced Jay as the app's designer. On top of that, he pointed out that it was Jay's designs inside the app that were responsible for sending 400-500 people a day to the Livu website. At the end of the email, Gary casually mentioned that Jay would be coming out with him to SF.

After proofreading the short email for almost a half hour, they finally hit send. Minutes later, a response came back from Ryan.

Hi Gary,

You've done great work here so far. Looking forward to seeing you next week! Re: The CQ app. Some one on our team pointed the Creativity Quiz app out to me the other day. It's great to meet the builders!

Re: Jay. We're always hiring and would love to meet him. Bring him by the offices when you get here.

Thank you both for sending us some traffic!
Best,
Ryan Parker
Founder, Livu

Gary waved Jay over and showed him the email. Jay

couldn't believe it. "They told me no!"

"Dude, some random person told you no! Ryan's the one in charge who understands giving before you get."

Jay's face lit up. "Awesome... thanks man! I can't believe this."

"Believe it homie. Now go home. Buy your plane ticket. We're going to California!"

"Done," said Jay. "Looks like we're both going to California!"

"That's my BOY!" shouted Gary.

Jay grabbed his things and drove home. After his week of camping out at Gary's, it felt amazing to come home with a victory. His parents had demanded he prove this path was better, and now he was closing in on it. Now Jay felt even more of a drive to follow through and prove that his path was the right one for him.

There was no way Gavin's rehab would be cheap. This meant that asking his parents to pay for any college or training would be out of the question. Sure, they might still offer it, but he wasn't going to let them. Besides, if he kept up what he was doing now, he'd land the Livu job. What would he do if he didn't get the job? He thought about the worst-case scenarios, and they really weren't that bad. He'd get a job at some other startup, and could freelance on the side. As he considered this possibility, he started to realize that there was no, "worst case", there was only opportunity. No matter what, he'd still be light years ahead of his friends who would be stuck at college or a random job they hated.

As he hopped in the car, he remembered that the biggest thing he could do to help his family was to land this job.

Proving that he could be successful on his own without driving his parents into debt for college made sense to him. His mind turned to Gavin, and he remembered what Mr. Moore had told him... "You can only help those you care about by first helping yourself."

Jay gripped the steering wheel confidently as he drove, and put down the windows in the car. The cool, refreshing spring air instantly filled the car. He didn't imagine that senior year would be like this, but it no longer mattered. His senior year was becoming interesting, and for the first time in his life, Jay was becoming something. He felt more alive than ever, and couldn't wait for his trip to California with Gary. He was taking risks and doing awesome things. At this rate, he couldn't imagine what his life would be like in a couple years. As he drove, he noticed that the trees, flowers, and everything around him were starting to bud. He felt grateful for it all. Soon, he would be traveling across the entire country to chase an opportunity.

Now that he was writing a better script, his life was turning into a much better movie.

PART III

26

HOW LEADERSHIP
FEELS

*"Getting into a fight with Gavin was one of the best things
that ever happened to me."*
–Jay Pencha

Jay was worried that the first night back home would be awkward, but it wasn't. He and his parents had a heartfelt conversation, sharing tears, hugs, and apologies. He did his best to listen, accept their apologies, and move on without holding any anger. Of course, this was easier said than done. He decided that for now, he could pretend he was over it until it eventually became natural.

Debbie and Alan seemed terrified about Gavin. The prospect of the rehab center being able to help appeased them a bit, but they seemed more fearful than relieved. Gavin's rehab center was a decent place, a few hours from home. These first few months would be the hardest, and it would be a long road ahead. But it was a good starting point.

On a deeper level, Jay had no idea if Gavin could get clean in rehab. He feared that the brother he knew for years might no longer exist. He did his best to suspend disbelief. If he could change himself... then anyone could. Even Gavin. After a long night of catching up with his parents, he headed to his room to get some sleep. This entire process had been draining. Thoughts spun in his mind, and it took him awhile to fall asleep.

The next morning, Jay opened his eyes before his alarm sounded. He took several deep breaths, thinking about the prior night. Thoughts of worry surfaced, but he chose not to entertain them. He was disappointed that he got in a fight with Gavin, but he told himself that it might have saved Gavin's life.

The fight with Gavin had sparked a newfound intensity in his life. He was no longer a passenger watching things happen. While he was vulnerable and stood up for what he believed, he discovered how this attracted people to him who wanted to help.

While he lay in bed, he did some quick research on his laptop. The cost of Gavin's rehab program was staggering. There was no way his parents could handle paying anything more: whether that was college, living expenses, or anything else. He couldn't ask them too do that with a clean conscience. He remembered what he had learned from Gary's parents and what Mr. Moore repeated over and over, "You don't value things you don't pay for." He saw what happened the first time Gavin was handed his P&C tuition and prayed it wouldn't be the case for his rehab program.

Jay knew he had to keep moving and continue to step out

on his own, like he was already doing. He had to get out in the real world and start leading by example. If he didn't, he ran the risk of watching his family crumble from the weight of Gavin's debts. There were no more alternatives. He had to step up and become self-sufficient, no matter what. Before the warmth of his blankets was too great, he threw them off and hopped out of bed.

His feet hit the cold wood floors of his room. He stretched his arms and legs, shaking his feet all around. He started to go through a series of exercises that he had learned. He saw a picture at Gary's house of the five Tibetans, a type of ancient morning exercise routine. Jay had snapped a picture of them on his phone, and then sketched the routine out and taped it to his bulletin board.

As he started to go through the exercise, he heard a series of voices in his head criticizing him. The most consistent one he heard was Gavin's voice, always ready to criticize him, "You're doing yoga? Hah!" Jay had heard that voice for years, and still played in his head. Anytime he took a risk, felt ambition, or tried something new, he heard that voice of criticism. He decided to use that critical voice as a compass to point towards what he should explore.

He watched the imagined voice of his brother's criticism along with his own and laughed. Laughing helped belittle the voices. When he realized how ridiculous it was to use his imagination to punish himself, he could get on with what was important.

He finished his morning workout routine drenched in sweat. He had read about the benefits of cold water immersion, so while in the shower, he cranked up the cold water handle. Before he could think, he turned the hot water handle completely off. In an instant, he was gasping for air, silently mouthing a string of expletives. After thirty seconds, he bolted out of the shower and grabbed his towel. Now, he was fully alert. He got dressed and sat down at the desk in his room.

Jay fought the urge to check his phone, and instead started reading a book that Gary's mom and dad recommended to him. He hated reading his textbooks for school, but the non-fiction book that Gary's parents had recommended was nothing like the school textbooks. It was the life story of a successful inventor, and Jay devoured it. He read for thirty minutes, and then pulled out a 4x6 note card. He wrote down his victories. He had completed his yoga and exercise practice, stretched his willpower by enduring a cold water shower, and upgraded his mental operating system through reading. He was ready to tackle the day.

He picked out his three most important tasks that he wanted to accomplish. He knew that if he completed these, it would move him towards his end goal of landing a job at a technology startup.

He looked at the note card and wrote down the three tasks:
• Research plane tickets to Cali, get on the same flight as Gary
• Plan for meeting with Ryan, the CEO of Livu
• Write down companies and designers (outside of Livu) to meet with while out in Cali

He glanced at the list, fought the urge to do nothing, and got started. The reading, exercise, and ice cold shower crystallized Jay's thinking. After two hours, a few texts back and forth with Gary, some online research, and additional reading, he was finished all three tasks. As he got up and stretched again, his Mom's voice sounded from downstairs,

"Jay! Breakfast is ready!"

Jay walked to his door and opened it. "Sounds good, mom, be right down!"

As he hopped down the final step in the staircase, he heard both his Mom and Dad laughing. He hadn't heard that in a long, long time.

"Hey guys, good morning!"

Both his parents were beaming, sitting at the table.

"Your father and I are proud of you, Jay," said Debbie, her eyes tearing up. Alan's eyes were on the verge of tears too, and his voice cracked as he put his arm around his son,

"We're thankful for you pointing out what we couldn't see, Jay. You saved Gavin's life."

"Thanks, guys. I appreciate that. "

"So, what have you been up to at Gary's?" asked Debbie, as she set Jay's plate down in front of him.

"A bunch!" said Jay. "In fact, if it's okay with you both... I was thinking about going out to California with Gary. I emailed the CEO of Livu, where Gary works, and he wants to meet me."

"Hmmm," said Alan, taking a sip of coffee. "Is Livu the place that turned you down the first time?"

Debbie held her breath, waiting for the usual argumentative banter, but it never came.

"That's the one," said Jay. "I know I can get the job this time if I show up in person and meet them. Gary and I are sending them a few hundred new customers every day, so now's the time to reapply. Even if Livu does say no again, that's okay because I now have a portfolio of work. And, from all my research, I realized there are tons of companies desperate to hire great designers."

Alan's eyes widened. "Then I think you should go out there! You know, I don't understand a lot of this tech stuff... But I do know that if you were sending me a few leads a day at my old job, I'd have no choice but to hire you... on the spot!"

Jay knew he was getting through to his parents now. He smiled and nodded. "Thanks, Dad."

"You bet. So, you're serious that you don't want your mom and I to pay for your college?"

Debbie looked over, her face worried. "You know we can always take out a loan to pay for it Jay, even if you want to go to SSU. We just want to make sure you aren't making the no-college decision solely because of our recent financial troubles."

"Well... that's one part of it. But, I've also run the numbers on the cost of college. It's not something I would buy on my own, so I don't think I should make anybody else buy it for me. The first few hundred bucks that I made, I bought myself the laptop and software to teach myself design. And I've gotten a ton of use out of both of them! I'm just starting to think that people won't value anything if they get it for free."

"Amen to that," smiled Debbie. Alan wondered if he and Debbie should have Gavin pay them back for the rehab treatment. He'll bring that up another day, he thought.

Jay added his last point. "Besides, the worst part would be going there for four to five years and falling behind in technology. Change and innovation are happening really quickly right now. If I don't keep learning what's valuable, by the time I get out of college, it'll only be worse."

"Okay, well know we want to help out. We're not sure how to, but let us know what we can do." said Debbie.

Alan nodded. "We do. All this is new to us...we just want the best for you... and for Gavin."

"Thanks," said Jay as he finished his breakfast. "First things first, and that means getting ready for the California trip to land this job at Livu!"

"That's the spirit," said Alan. His eyes seemed to sparkle, like he was excited, instead of his usual morning overwhelm. He looked at Jay proudly. "You're really stepping it up. Thanks for keeping us in the loop with everything. The more you do, the more it keeps our minds at ease."

"Yeah, of course, Dad. Don't worry. I have my last 1-on-1 meeting with Mr. Moore today. We're going to prep for the meeting I might have with Ryan, so I'll be good by the time I get out to California."

Debbie had tears in her eyes as she cleaned up breakfast and gave Jay a hug. "Well you'd better get ready, and get your ticket for California before I try to stop you! And you'd better keep us in the loop...with everything!" Her voice was a mix of half joking, and half trying not to cry.

"Mom... I always will!" said Jay, as he patted her back.

"And text Gavin when you get a chance..."

"I will, Mom."

"And Jay?

"Yeah?"

"We love you and we're proud of you."

"I know!" Jay gave his parents a hug and then rushed over to Gary's house to pick him up for school. He hadn't heard those words directly in a long time.

27

THE EIGHTH WONDER
OF THE WORLD

*"You've got to search before you can find. Sometimes that
means taking a cross country flight."*
–Gary Weinstein

After a month of hustle, Jay had a ton to talk about with
Mr. Moore during his final 1-on-1 meeting. They talked about
everything from Gavin, to what he and Gary had been up to,
and especially the exciting prospect of his trip to California.
As they moved towards the end of the meeting, Mr. Moore
leaned back in his chair and laughed,

"You're doing everything!"

"What do you mean?" asked Jay.

"You're reading, learning, taking risks, reaching out to
CEO's... you've been earning this opportunity all year. Now,
it's time to seize it!"

Mr. Moore was right. Jay didn't even realize that most of
the year had flown by. If he had known he could get this far in
a single year, he would have started a long time ago. He

invested in himself all year, and the return on that investment was now being realized.

He showed Mr. Moore the Creativity Quiz app that he and Gary had built. Mr. Moore looked at it carefully, along with their download numbers and user usage that Jay had printed out from an analytics service. "This is amazing, Jay. I can't believe you're sending Livu a few hundred daily visitors. Now that you've done this part, if Livu doesn't hire you, somebody else will snatch you up. Any final prep you're doing for the interview?"

Jay glanced at his notepad. "Yeah, I've been asking Gary's parents for advice and help, which has been really beneficial. I've learned everything I can about Livu. And, before we leave for California, a designer I know from Oxen agreed to go to lunch with me to help practice for the interview."

"Perfect," said Mr. Moore, still glancing through the app.

"So, you really think I'm ready?" beamed Jay.

Mr. Moore looked up and nodded. "Yes. Everything you've done is what the other 99% of people don't want to do. The last piece of the equation is to follow through on your plans. Have a couple of ideas for Livu about how your designs can improve their bottom line and help them make more of a profit. Remember, it cost an employer a crazy amount of money to hire anybody, usually about twice their salary, so layout how you're going to help them make more than that. And, make sure to listen well and care about them before you expect them to care about you."

Jay scribbled a few bullets down in his notebook.

Mr. Moore continued, "Remember to stress the point that if

you were able to increase conversions in your own app now, you can start learning how you can do that across all their websites, apps, and social media. If you convert their potential customers into actual customers, that would help them make a lot of money."

Jay kept scribbling. "Yeah I never thought about it from that angle. That's a really good idea."

"If you do those things, prepare, and present yourself with confidence, I have no doubt you'll get a job offer." Mr. Moore looked up at the clock. "Time's up. Senior year is counting down. The goal you set is within your reach... Go get it!"

Jay jumped up, and he and Mr. Moore shook hands.

As Jay walked out of the room, he felt a mixture of excitement and nervousness about going the trip to California.

He walked down the hall to meet up with Gary. He was spending the night there, and they'd be flying out tomorrow to SFO on a red eye flight. Jay glanced around as he walked. These halls had been his temporary holding cell for the last four years. A part of him was going to miss it, and a part of him was thrilled to finally be free. He passed Pemberton's college prep class and shuddered. Pemberton's loud, monotone voice echoed in the halls around him as he droned on about the required courses for the first year of college. Jay glanced inside, and saw row after row of students taking the advice seriously, as if any of it would help them in the real world. He shook his head.

Outside of a few professions and certifications, those students were all taking the risk of paying for obsolescence. Jay's eyes were open to what he could accomplish in only a few months. He could barely imagine how far he could get during the five years that the average student spent in college.

Jay breathed a sigh of relief that he had transferred out of that class.

28

A STOWAWAY

"When I can't imagine a solution... it's usually a job for Gary Weinstein."
–Jay Pencha

After school was over, Gary and Jay headed over to Gary's house. They put the windows down as Jay drove. With any luck, this would be one of the last times he chauffeured them around. They talked about the trip, and started to plan where they'd live if they both got the job out there. A job and apartment of their own... Jay liked the sound of that.

"So, you ran the trip by your parents?" asked Gary.

"Yeah, they're actually all for it," said Jay. "They just told me to be safe, and good luck meeting the CEO of Livu!"

Gary put his hands together and talked to Jay like he was a puppy, "Such a big day for my little Jaybird! This is his first trip outside the nest, huh?"

"Shut up..." Jay pushed Gary's shoulder. "It's *your* first trip without your parents, too!"

"True... true... this is a big trip for G-Bird too," Gary said sternly.

A few minutes into their conversation, Jay remember what he'd been forgetting as they planned out their California trip.

"Oh crap," said Jay, taking off his sunglasses and rubbing his eyes.

"What? What's up?" asked Gary, sitting up in his seat.

"I totally forgot that I promised Ella I would hang out with her this weekend."

"Can't you just reschedule?"

"I don't want to look like a jerk... I mean we just started talking and hanging out. But, I guess I have too," said Jay. He groaned and grabbed his phone to text Ella the bad news. A few seconds later, Jay's phone started to ring. It was Ella, and without thinking, he answered it.

"It's fine," said Jay, speaking into the phone. He paused, listening to what Ella was saying.

As she talked, Jay's eyes flashed from excited, to worried. "Yeah! I mean I'd love that, but wouldn't your parents freak out?" He paused and listened. "Are you sure?"

"I know, but I don't want them to find out and get pissed off," said Jay.

Gary eyed Jay suspiciously while he was talking and driving. By now, he'd heard enough of the call and decided to make an executive decision.

Mid sentence, Gary snatched the phone from Jay's hands, and covered up the phone's mouthpiece.

"Dude! What the hell?" said Jay.

Gary pointed a menacing finger at Jay and snapped,

"You'll thank me later. Now, shut up and drive, chauffeur!"

Irritated, Jay looked back to the road. Gary had better know what he was doing.

He took his finger off the speaker, and in an instant, Gary Weinstein's voice transformed into an over the top polite and professional voice. "Hello, Ella. Gary Weinstein here... Oh?... Oh yeah... that's a good point. No, I don't know any other Gary's either."

"So, anyways, I apologize for Jay. He was trying to talk and drive at the same time. Can you believe that?"

"I know. Neither can I. That's why I snatched the phone...Yeah, I'll tell him he's stupid for you..."

"So, thanks for expressing interest in our Silicon Valley tour! We'd be honored to have you join us!"

Jay leaned over and hissed, "I don't want to mess things up or make her parents mad!"

Gary listened and nodded. "Sure! We're on flight number 1334, and there might still be tickets."

Jay was still freaking out, mouthing something about Ella's parents. Gary turned away to avoid Jay's worried face and kept talking. "Ella, sorry, could you hold on for one second?" Gary covered up the speaker on the phone and turned to Jay.

"*What* is wrong with your game?"

Jay looked offended. "What!? I just don't want– "

"A fine shorty who you're *supposed* to be talking to is trying to fly across the country with you... and you're too scared to let her! WHAT THE HELL IS WRONG WITH YOU?"

Gary said it all so fast that Jay had no choice but to crack a smile.

Gary shook his head back and forth, uncovered the receiver and kept talking. "Ella? No, sorry about that. Nothing's up, we'd love to have you join us! Yep, it's flight 1334 to SFO, that's it!"

"Yeah, flying out at 5:00 in the morning... No, we couldn't have picked a better time. It's the cheapest one."

"They still have seats? Perfect!"

"Okay, nice... Oh wow! You already got your ticket? That was fast. I'll tell Jay. No worries. He was just being salty... Mhhmm yeah... I guess we'll pick you around 2:30 am tomorrow morning? Awesome. Peace."

Gary ended the call, and sighed. "Maybe you need to peep my game, Romeo."

Jay's smile spread across his face... "Okay... bravo, Weinstein."

"That's what best friends are for, but you'd better check yourself next time!"

29

CROSS COUNTRY FLIGHT

"My parents love money... as long as someone else takes the risks to create it."
–Ella Johnson

They pulled up to Gary's house in the early afternoon. As he and Gary rushed inside, they finalized their game plan for the night. They needed to finish prepping for their interviews, do a five-mile run, and eat a massive dinner. They figured if they got a long enough run in, they'd be able to fall asleep early so they could easily wake up the next day for their 5 am flight.

Jay prepped with Gary's parents for his interview, followed by Gary. Afterwards, they stepped out in the late afternoon spring sun, and started their five-mile run. Towards the end, Gary starting walking, panting and swearing until Jay called him the "typical engineer." True to form, Gary started jogging again in anger, and then thanked Jay when they finished.

Back at Gary's house, they hydrated and ate a massive Italian dinner including baked seven layer lasagna, and a salad overflowing with veggies and feta cheese. They devoured it and were soon poised to enter a carbohydrate coma. They both checked to make sure they had everything they needed packed. Then, they shuffled into Gary's room, Jay folded out the futon he slept on, and Gary collapsed on his bed. Within minutes, they were both snoring.

Their self-induced hibernation ended abruptly at 2:30 am on Friday morning.

Jay bolted upright on the futon to blaring music... where was he... what was that *noise*... was that Prince?

It was Gary's phone and custom alarm. "Gary! So...loud...too early... for this music!" Jay shuffled around in the dark trying to find the phone.

Gary swiped his phone to turn off his alarm.

"Prince?" said Jay incredulously. "I was expecting rap. When did you start waking up to the 80's?"

Gary stumbled out of bed and put on his glasses. "Don't hate "

Jay cut him off. "C'mon, we've got to go in a minute!"

They both got ready, hit the bathroom, and remerged a few minutes later.

Jay shook himself to wake up. They dragged themselves out and into the kitchen. After a quick snack and drink, they did one last equipment check.

Jay patted Gary's back as they walked out the door. "I won't tell anyone at Livu you wake up to Prince."

Gary chased him to the car, and they drove to pick up Ella.

On their way over, Ella texted Jay to remind him to not pull up in the front of the house. She didn't want her parents waking up and freaking out. As Jay approached the road to her development, he rolled down the windows and Gary peered out along the road. Between both of their squinted eyes, eventually they spotted her waving and walking towards them.

"Gooooood morning, boys!"

Jay felt butterflies in his stomach. They were going to hang out for an entire weekend! "Hey!"

"Hey, Ella," said Gary, groggily.

She put her carry-on luggage into the back seat and hopped in.

"I'm can't believe it's 2:30 am and we're flying to Silicon Valley."

"*Promised Land,*" corrected Gary.

Jay laughed and rolled his eyes. "I can't believe your parents think you're at a P&C preparatory weekend."

The three of them burst out laughing, and Ella leaned in between the seats. "The sad part is, they're fine with me going to the booze soaked P&C social gatherings... but the tough sell would be letting me go across the country so I can meet one of my heroes, and tour her company!"

"Who's that?" inquired Gary.

Ella perked up in her seat. "Angela Hobbs, at CheckUp."

"Oh nice! Her company is replacing doctors' visits right?" asked Gary.

Ella seemed surprised that anyone else knew about it. "Yup, quarterly blood diagnostics paint a much better picture than the usual routine at the doctors. I'm meeting some CheckUp connections I made. They invited me to tour the company, and I might even get to meet Angela!"

"I hope you get to," said Jay, looking over as he drove. "Isn't she a P&C drop out?"

"Yes she is!" said Ella, proudly. "She dropped out her sophomore year."

"So, your parents should be excited about you going to visit her, right? They wouldn't get mad about you traveling with us?" wondered Jay aloud.

"Ohhh no," said Ella. "Anything that makes them have to think causes problems. They might like Angela's story because she's a billionaire now. But that's the only reason. They would freak out about me flying out to...," she looked over at Gary, "...the *Promised Land* with two heathens who aren't going to a brand name college."

Gary rocked back and forth in the passenger seat, laughing like a little kid. "That's SO us!"

Jay's smile widened as he glanced over at Ella. She was still leaning forward between the center consoles. "I'll admit that going straight to work for CheckUp does *sound* exciting. Tempting for me to skip P&C all together."

"Why don't you?" asked Gary.

"I'd rather study the best and learn from them," she said. "Angela beat them at their own game. She went to P&C, took advantage of their brand name, and the second she was ready, she dropped out. If you drop out of P&C after you get a better offer, all the adults think you're even more of a genius." Ella turned to Gary and Jay. "But don't tell anyone my evil plan."

"I would never... that's does sound smart," said Jay. "Your parents aren't going to see that coming."

"No they won't," said Ella beaming. "But by the time they hear about it, I'll have built a compelling enough case."

Gary smiled and looked at Jay and Ella. "It's like, wake up and smell the Flynn Effect, ya know!" He burst out laughing at his own joke.

Another one of Gary's jokes that Jay didn't get the first time around.

Ella let out a giggle and then looked at Jay who seemed confused. "IQ's go up every generation," hinted Ella.

"Ahhh... that's right," said Jay, nodding like he had just remembered.

Ella patted Jay on the shoulder. "I think you take for granted that everybody's parents are like yours or Gary's. Anything that my parents don't understand, they instantly fear or hate it– end of discussion. But no more talk about that... it's pilgrimage time!"

Gary bounced up in his seat. "Damn right!" he said, as he put on his Cali playlist. His normal rap music piped through the speakers. Jay cracked the windows and they got on the interstate for the airport.

At 3:45 sharp, Jay, Ella, and Gary pulled up to the airport parking. They had to drive around twice until they found the right parking lot.

They snapped a picture of their parking spot, locked the car, and started jogging behind Ella to the terminal.

She turned to them. "Move it! We only have like an hour left! You'd better both get your butts moving!"

Jay looked at Gary and they both burst into laughter as they jogged. By the time they checked in and made it through security, both of their legs felt like Jello from their run the night before. Right when they got to their gate, the flight started boarding. They squeezed into the three seats that they managed to get together. In minutes, Gary had his blackout mask on and was snoozing.

Ella leaned her head on Jay's shoulder and fell asleep.

30

THE PROMISED LAND

"Welcome to the promised land, where creating value is all we know!"
–Gary Weinstein

After takeoff, Jay eventually dozed off. He woke up a few times during the flight. He and Ella got up, walked around, and listened to the crying baby up front. As they stood at the back of the plane stretching, they chatted about her CheckUp research. Jay had no idea how much she had read about health care. She didn't just know a little bit. It sounded like she knew everything about the changes coming, new technologies, and how CheckUp's business model worked. He was impressed. She peppered him with mock interview questions, forcing him to address her as CEO (for practice).

Back at their seats, they talked a bit more and made sure to take a video of Gary's awkwardly loud snoring. Before they knew it, the fasten seatbelt sign illuminated, and the voice of the captain sounded over the intercom. They were approaching SFO. After a bit of turbulence on the way down, the plane landed smoothly, and Jay turned on his phone. There was a single message from Mr. Moore:

Jay,

Have fun and be safe on your trip! What you're doing now separates the men from the boys. Boys talk, argue, debate, and keep themselves distracted with things that don't matter. If they stay busy enough with that crap, they never have to achieve anything that matters.

Men go out, see the world, discover the injustices, and then take action to create a better life for themselves and others. They create things that they know will make the world a better place. They take prudent risks, and they're not afraid of doing the real work.

You're in the latter group. What you're doing is the real work. Remember, courage and confidence first. Everything else will follow. Crush it!
-Mr. Moore

Jay started tapping to respond, and then stopped himself. The best way to respond was to come back with a job at Livu. In fact, the best way he could thank everyone, including his parents, Gary's parents, Gary, Ella, and inspire Gavin, was by landing this job.

The plane reached the terminal, and eventually, all the passengers unloaded and walked off. None of them were old enough for a rental car. Jay and Ella assumed that they would take a train into the city. When they started to walk down to the train station, Gary waved them off. His skinny arm pointed in another direction and he started walking. "Follow me, you two!"

"Okay..." said Jay, reluctantly.

They walked through the parking lot while Gary kept his head down looking at his phone. He glanced up occasionally, and then pointed to a sedan. "Bingo!" He lay on the ground, fished around underneath the car, and came up with a key. He unlocked the trunk while Jay and Ella eyed him suspiciously.

"Don't worry, it's a co-worker's. I helped them with a project. They owe me!"

They hopped in, and Gary took over as their tour guide. He was proud to show off his experience and knowledge. He drove while pointing out landmarks and notable technology companies. Ella and Jay's faces remained pressed to the window. Neither of them had been to California before, and they were wide-awake now. They stopped to grab tacos for lunch, and then drove through the city until they reached their Airbnb spot. The place they rented was a small cottage in someone's back yard, near the Presidio and the Golden Gate Bridge. It was small, but it was on a hill, and the view was breathtaking.

They unloaded their stuff, and Gary pulled out his notebook and cleared his throat. "Your attention, please. Our itinerary is as follows: Jay and I are headed to the Livu offices today, and I believe Ella is going to tour the CheckUp offices... is this correct?"

Jay and Ella played along and nodded.

"Very good," continued Gary. "Saturday, we have some touristy things lined up, and Sunday, our flight leaves in the late afternoon."

"Yes, thank you, Mom," said Ella, jokingly. "I'd better head out to CheckUp... I'll take a Drivr there, and maybe we can all meet for dinner?"

"Perfect!" Jay said. "Good luck, even though you don't need it."

"Thanks," said Ella. After a few minutes of sprucing up, they parted ways. After one final look in the mirror, Jay took a deep breath, grabbed his laptop that contained his portfolio of work, and he and Gary drove over to the Livu offices for Gary's interview. Jay knew this was his chance to make something happen.

31

MEETING THE CEO

"Master yourself, and gain mastery in whatever you choose."
–Ryan Parker, CEO and Founder of Livu

Gary parked on the street, while Jay marveled at the building.

"It's at the top?" asked Jay.

"Yup," said Gary, nodding with a grin. "It's a loft office and wait till you see it. It's on point!"

Gary opened the door for him, and they walked through the Livu lobby. The Oxen offices were amazing, but this was on another level. The setup was similar; open floor plans, raised desks, employees working all over, and a group of people playing ping-pong. The ceilings were massive, and Jay saw a ring of conference rooms and offices at the end of the open space. The Livu offices opened up onto a rooftop garden area that overlooked the city. In the distance, you could even see the Bay.

Gary tugged his sleeve and pointed to a hallway at the far end of the open space. "That's where we're going, just stay close, and Ryan will have to make time to meet you."

Jay nodded, and they walked towards the hallway. Gary waved to a few people, but otherwise, everyone seemed occupied. As they walked through the hallway, they came out into another open space. This one, like the last, had access to the rooftop garden, and Jay watched people outside. Some were working, and others were throwing a Frisbee around.

Gary led him to a stand-up desk and waved to the young, thirty-something employee behind it. The man wore a plain white t-shirt and jeans. He looked like a coder, designer, or data scientist, thought Jay. He turned and waved to Gary.

"Hey Gary, great to see you in person again. It's been what... six months?"

"Yeah, it has! I emailed you right after you came and talked to our Bootcamp class."

"Ahhh... that's right," said Ryan smiling. You were the youngest guy in there! Awesome, well let's go chat about your first six months here."

Holy crap thought Jay, this was Ryan... the Livu CEO. He couldn't be more than thirty-three, thought Jay.

Gary motioned to Jay. "Sure... but before I forget, I wanted you to meet my friend Jay. He's the guy who designed the Creativity Quiz app."

Jay looked Ryan in the eyes, smiled, and extended his hand. "Hi Ryan, great to meet you!"

"Ohhh... yeah that's right. Great to meet you too, Jay! Glad you could make it." Ryan looked busy as he ushered Gary into a conference room. As he did, he leaned over his shoulder. "Jay, let's chat after Gary and I talk. In the meantime, make yourself at home."

"Sure thing!" said Jay. Gary and Ryan walked into the

glass conference room, and Jay found a seat in the open area. He brushed up on a few of his notes, and a Livu employee, Navair, brought him a cup of tea. He accepted the gift, and struck up a conversation with the engineer. After they'd been talking for awhile, Jay started suddenly received a string of texts from Gary.

"Something came up, Ryan has to head out, don't miss this chance to talk with him. Walk and follow him if you have to!"

A sinking feeling crept up in Jay's stomach. Would the interview fall through? He hopped out of his seat in time to see Ryan walking briskly out of the conference room, and he started to walk with him.

"Jay, sorry man. Something came up with one of our engineers. I've got to head out right now to meet him. Look, nobody your age reaches out in the way you and Gary did." Ryan was walking briskly around the office as he grabbed different things and left a note on a desk. Jay tried to keep up with him. He stopped at another desk, grabbed a few things, and then turned to Jay. "Gary says you all are in town for the weekend? Why don't you come out with us on the Bay tomorrow? We're taking the boat out. Paddle boarding, fishing, kayaking, drones, you name it... it'll be fun!"

Jay's worry turned to instant elation. "That sounds great, I'd love to come."

Ryan looked absent-minded as he rushed around. He texted on his phone and glanced back up.

"Oh! Gary said your girlfriend is here visiting CheckUp?"

"Yeah, she is," said Jay.

"Cool. Feel free to bring her, too."

"Okay, awesome! I was hoping to get a chance to go over my portfolio with you?"

Ryan laughed. "Already looked at it!" He kept walking out, and Jay tried to keep up. "That Creativity Quiz app that you and Gary cooked up has been sending us hundreds of visitors a day to our site... thanks!"

"Out of the hundreds of thousands of daily visitors you probably already have," Jay said, jokingly.

Ryan's eyebrows squinted, and he turned serious. "Intentions matter. It's the best value-add job application I've seen all year!"

Ryan's assistant rushed to meet him, apologized to Jay for interrupting, and handed him a phone. Ryan took it, covered up the speaker, and turned to Jay. "Meet us tomorrow morning at 8am at the Fort Mason Center Marina. Bring sunscreen and water, and dress in swimsuits of course."

"Okay, great... sounds good!"

And with that, Ryan took the phone call, started talking quickly, and he and his assistant walked out of the Livu office.

Jay sighed as he stood there, feeling a buzz of emotions. He didn't get to prove himself in an interview, and didn't receive a job offer yet... But he did get an invite to hang out. That had to count for something he thought.

The rest of the day, he and Gary hung around the offices. Since nobody seemed to mind Jay there, he opened his laptop and got to work. Gary introduced him to the two designers at Livu, and Jay asked them if they needed any help. At first, they seemed hesitant until he assured them he was serious. After Gary showed them the app Jay had already designed, they shrugged. Within minutes, they offloaded a project onto Jay. This was it, he thought. Do what others won't. While

Gary went off to start working, Jay jumped into helping out the design team.

Towards the end of the day, they drove back to their Airbnb spot and Gary tried to console Jay.

"Don't worry, an invite to hang out is huge! Ryan's just ridiculously busy!"

Jay nodded, but didn't say much.

When they got to their cottage, Ella wasn't back yet. Jay grabbed the hidden key and opened the door. Gary was still trying to cheer him up, but it wasn't working. Jet lagged and exhausted, he stretched out on the bed.

"That's it... you'll feel better after a nap," laughed Gary.

Jay groaned and rubbed his face. "Shut up..." He rolled back over and tried to fall asleep. He wondered how Ella's visit at CheckUp was going. He hoped she made her connections, but didn't want to check up on her.

Slowly, from jet lag, worry, excitement, and nervousness, he started to bat his eyes. Eventually he stopped fighting it and let the all mighty nap overtake him.

32

SUNSET OVER THE GOLDEN GATE

"After I found the person I'd be proud to work for,
everything else was easy to figure out."
–Ella Johnson

Jay's eye snapped open in front of Ella's. He blinked twice, and his eyes adjusted, meeting her green eyes. He smiled. She put a finger to her lips and whispered, "Shhh... Gary's still napping."

Ella took his hand and led him outside.

Outside, she had two tea's sitting for them on the table. They both sipped them, and Jay slowly woke up. It was late afternoon, and a warm breeze blew through the patio outside the cottage. Before he could talk, Ella spoke up. "I got your text. Going out on the boat tomorrow sounds amazing."

"Great, how was your trip to CheckUp? I didn't want to bother you while you were there. Did you get to meet the CEO... uh... Angela, right?"

"It was incredible! No, Angela was on a business trip.

But... their head of marketing showed me around the offices, I met a few of the VP's, and even one of Angela's co-founders."

"Wow," said Jay. "That's impressive... how did it go? Don't they have a few thousand people working there now?"

"Yeah, they do. We talked for a while and they asked me a bunch of questions. They all encouraged me to apply," she said proudly.

"That's incredible! With no portfolio?"

"Yup, no portfolio. They loved the fact that I got accepted into P&C and knew so much about their business. They said that hardly anybody took advantage of their tours or bothered to learn what they actually did."

Jay held up his tea and toasted it with Ella's. "That," he said with grin, "requires a toast... cheers!"

Ella smiled, brushed her hair back behind her ears and took a sip of her tea. "Cheers! You know, before we started looking into any of this stuff in Mr. Moore's class... I had this image of Silicon Valley. I assumed it was super nerdy, but it's not. They're way ahead of the curve in a lot of ways. There are tons of women in leadership positions at CheckUp," said Ella.

Jay nodded. "I know what you mean. It seems like this place is the biggest meritocracy. It's all about who you are and how you can help. It's so different from my brother's co-workers and... uh... their way of life."

Ella agreed, nodding.

"So, did you run your plan by anyone at CheckUp?" Jay asked.

"Yeah, I did. They all encouraged me to apply even though I'm going to P&C. They offered me an internship now, and a job if I learned some basic data science skills. I might take a page from the Jay Pencha playbook and start teaching myself," said Ella, as she grinned. "Not to blow your head up or anything."

Jay winced. "Oooh no... I didn't even get into P&C! That name still carries some serious weight."

Jay grabbed her hand and tried to pull her up from her chair. "The sun's going to set soon."

Ella shook her head. "Not for a few more minutes?"

Undeterred, Jay lifted her up out of the chair. "C'mon... there's someplace I need to take you."

"Fine... what's the rush? Where are we going?"

They walked out onto the slanted San Francisco street and got into their car. "So? Where are we going?" Ella asked excitedly.

"It's a surprise!" Jay put the car in drive and attempted to hide his smile from her.

In order to pull off his surprise smoothly, Jay had studied a map of San Francisco thoroughly so he'd know where to go. He carefully counted the lights and turned after three of them. Then, he headed two blocks east, turned left. As the car crested the hill, the Golden Gate Bridge appeared in front of them. They were headed straight for it.

"Wow, nice! I wanted to see the bridge," said Ella.

"We are... and we're also going to see the best view of San Fransisco."

As they drove over the bridge, Ella snapped pictures. Jay turned left up a steep and winding road that led to an overlook. After what felt like an endless climb of zigzagging roads, they found a parking spot and hopped out of the car. Instantly, the wind whipped at them from over the hill. Jay took Ella's hand, and they walked into it. Their steps took them along the trail, and by the time the wind gusts stopped, they were at the overlook. He couldn't have planned the timing better if he tried. The sun was setting, and the view was crystal clear.

They stood on the rocky overlook, and the Golden Gate Bridge, the Bay, and the San Francisco skyline spread out before them. From this height, the ships in the ocean below looked tiny. Ella nuzzled into Jay and turned from the wind. As the gusts died down, they looked out at the sprawling view. Slowly, like a thousand fireflies, the lights of San Francisco started to twinkle in the distance.

Ella raised her voice to talk over the wind. "This is breathtaking."

"I'm really glad you came, Ella," said Jay.

She looked up at Jay and they kissed.

Their fingers felt frozen, but they managed to snap a few selfies. The wind was brutal now as Ella clung to him. "F-f-f-freezing!" she whispered. They both laughed and Jay pulled her close for warmth. "I didn't realize it would be so cold!"

Jay pulled her close, and her hair blew up and around his face. He smelled her perfume and felt her cold ears against his neck. He was sure he was in heaven.

Ella looked up at him. "It's a beautiful surprise, but I might freeze to death if we don't get back in the car!"

Another gust of wind cut through Jay's t-shirt, and he nodded in agreement. They sprinted back to the car. For a few minutes, they huddled in the seats, out of breath, and with the heater blowing.

Ella blew on her hands to warm them up. "So, you and Gary are really going to move out here, huh?"

"Yea, we are. If I can talk to Ryan and get a job with Livu, that is."

"You know you can work for a technology company back at home, right?" asked Ella.

"Yeah, but out here there are so many people working on cool things. I feel like there aren't many people at home who love the work they do. Besides... I want to learn what's possible, you know? It's just... everybody has all these imagined limits. Whether it's Mr. Moore... Gary's parents... or Ryan from Livu... it seems like none of them think like most people."

"Well said, my little orator. I suppose I'll let you come out here. But, only on one condition."

"What's that?"

"That you and Gary aren't the only ones who get to go on a road trip."

"What do you mean?"

"Why don't we plan one too? I've never seen the west coast... I want to visit again anyways... What if we took a road trip up and down Route 1?"

Jay's stomach leapt up to his throat, and he tried to play it cool. It didn't work. "Yeah! We definitely should. Why didn't I think of that? When could we do it? You'd really fly out here?"

"Of course," said Ella, like it was obvious. "I don't want to spend all summer at home!"

"Let's do it. I'll pay for your ticket."

"How about I pay for my ticket, and we'll plan and figure out the west coast road trip together? You'll be buying plenty of tickets when you come home to visit your family."

"Sounds perfect," said Jay.

33

THE LIVU LIFESTYLE

"Technology lets you do more with less. It can be used for good or evil. It's our duty to use it for good."
–Ryan Parker

Saturday morning came early. A few rays of sunlight came through the shades in their cottage, and Jay got up first. The mornings here were chilly, and the wood floors were freezing on his feet.

He made coffee, and filled up their water bottles. After a few minutes, Ella woke up, followed by Gary, who whined until Jay put on coffee. He put a cup by Gary's glasses, and like a cat, he slowly stirred. Jay threw on his swimsuit and got ready. Ella came out wearing hers and they sprayed sunscreen on each other.

As she rubbed sunscreen on his back, Gary sat up, drinking his coffee. "Ugh... you're both disgusting."

Jay and Ella looked at each other and laughed.

After a few minutes of getting ready, all three of them hopped in the car for their boat trip on the bay. Ryan had been adamant to bring nothing but swimsuits, sunscreen, and water, so that was all they took. They ate some breakfast along the way, and headed to the Fort Mason Marina. Gary looked at his phone as they pulled up. "Perfect. Ten minutes early."

They climbed out of the car, and Jay had an idea.

"Hey, want to help me run an experiment?"

"Always!" said Gary, perking up.

"What is it?" Ella asked.

Jay thought for a moment as they walked. "Here it is. When we're talking with everybody today, we should find out as much about them as we can. Everything from what they do inside of work, outside of work, where they grew up, etcetera. We want to know what kind of people they are."

"No problem, I can practically read minds," said Gary.

"Sure, but what's the experiment for?" questioned Ella.

"I want to find out who I might be working with. I know what the east coast finance types are like... especially Gavin's friends. Everybody seems completely different at Oxen... and out here... but I want to prove it."

Gary raised a finger. "Everybody I know here has been awesome so far. But remember, they're not going to be your co-workers unless you land this job. You should spend your time talking with Ryan, and me and Ella will get some info for you on everybody else."

"Sounds good to me," said Ella. "I want to make some friends and get some intel anyways."

The three of them headed towards the marina docks. Ella was shivering. "I hope it warms up!"

Gary nodded. "It always does." He pointed to a small white yacht at the end of the Marina. "Thar she blows!"

A group of Livu employees stood around the white, two-story yacht at the end of the pier. The three of them walked up to a cluster of Livu employees. As they approached, Jay noticed Ryan standing in the center, telling a story as twelve Livu employees listened intently. They walked up, and he smiled and stepped out of the group, extending his hand.

"Morning, Gary and Jay!" he said, shaking their hands.

"Morning," they replied.

Jay motioned to Ella. "Ryan, this is my girlfriend, Ella."

"Hi, it's nice to meet you," said Ella, as she shook Ryan's hand.

Ryan smiled and stepped back. "Great to meet you. I think we're about ready to go. We've got a full day planned: check out a few islands in the bay, fish, paddle board, Brian brought a drone to tinker with, and we've got lunch!"

"That sounds great!" said Jay. They stepped out onto the boat from the dock. As they mingled on the open portion of the back deck, Gary went around and introduced Jay and Ella to everyone. Ryan had a breakfast spread waiting for the entire team. Jay noticed one entire table dedicated to juices, coffees, and teas. Next to it was the food, and it was anything but plain. Neatly arranged on the table was everything from smoked salmon, avocados, huevos rancheros, small crepes, and even an assortment of fresh berries. The Livu team members grazed the table, filling up their plates. Jay and Ella looked over the boat in amazement. The two-story cabin was large, and the outside area was just as big. On the back end of the boat, they saw an assortment of paddle boards and kayaks.

"This is legit," whispered Jay.

"Tell me about it," said Ella. "I'm glad we're missing the usual tourist attractions. Good call on getting us invited."

"It's the least I could do," laughed Jay.

By now, Ryan and a few of the Livu team had untied the boat. The yacht wasn't too big, and in minutes they navigated out of the Marina. Soon, the dark blue bay was all around them. They picked up speed, but the boat didn't seem to rock much.

Jay and Ella walked to the bow of the boat and marveled at the view. It was almost like sightseeing, as they leaned on the railing and watched the shore of the city go by off to their left.

"You sure you don't want to come out here too?" asked Jay. He put his arm around her to keep both of them warm.

Ella giggled. "It's tempting after seeing CheckUp yesterday, and now this. I don't know though. Gary said that one company here even offers a scholarship for dropping out of college?"

"Yeah, the Theil Fellowship, I think."

"I'm not ready to move yet. But we'll see! C'mon," she said, grabbing his hand. "Let's see what everybody's doing. Besides, you need to talk to Ryan!"

"Let's do it," said Jay.

They walked past the cabin of the boat back to the open deck area in the back. By now, everyone was warming up, laughing, joking, and hanging out around the table with food and drinks.

Navair, one of the Livu engineers, had a drone sitting on the table. It's casing was off, and he was attempting to teach Gary something about the hardware. Gary tinkered with the pieces, and Navair showed him how the controls worked. Jay and Ella listened in as Navair described the system, and the custom parts he'd built and added. One of them was a swiveling camera for the GoPro, mounted on the drone's base. He was starting to gather footage to put together for a Livu recruiting video. He and Gary bolted on the drone's plastic casing, and took it to the edge of the boat. Navair, who was around twenty years older than Gary, still acted like a kid, and he made the entire crew countdown for liftoff. He tapped a few buttons on the drone's controls, and the drone whirled to life, with all eight propellers spinning. In seconds, it practically jumped into the air, flying up and above the wake of the boat. He handed the controls of the drone over to Gary, and rendered a salute. Gary returned an overly serious salute back and started piloting the drone around. Navair showed him how to control the GoPro feed on the drone, and soon he was filming the boat. The camera system and custom mount that Naviar built seemed to track the boat perfectly.

An hour later, they docked at one of the islands in the bay. Some people laid out to get sun, a few did an impromptu polar bear challenge and jumped into the freezing water, and the rest took out paddle boards or kayaks. After eating a snack and talking with Ryan for a bit, Jay moved to find Ella. She was hanging out with the other girls on the Livu team. When she finished talking, they picked out one of the two-seater kayaks, and after balancing precariously on the edge of the rocking boat, they managed to get in without tipping it. Jay pushed off the yacht, and they were off. The shores of the island were rocky, and seagulls hovered above them as they paddled along. They paddled lightly, and Jay sat in the back to steer them. The water was freezing, but the day was warming up, and the skies were clear blue. As they paddled by a rocky outcropping, Jay tapped Ella's shoulder and pointed to a rock off to their right.

"You've got an admirer," he said. He pointed to a sea lion basking in the sun. The animal's dark eyes and whiskered face looked up briefly, blinked, then grunted and relaxed again.

"Adorable!" said Ella, snapping a picture. "This is already the best weekend ever. You know, it's so great, I'll just let you paddle for awhile."

Jay laughed. "You're right. I couldn't have imagined all this."

They talked, paddled and did a full circle around the island.

When they arrived back to the boat, they carefully boarded from the kayak and hauled it on board. Jay checked his phone. It was noon and he was already starving. Just like at breakfast, Ryan had another amazing lunch spread on the yacht's tables.

Most of the Livu team was back on the boat, eating and laughing. Navair stood in front of the group laughing, and re-enacting something about Gary. When they saw Gary's red face, and that he was soaking wet, they guessed (correctly) that he'd fallen off the paddle board.

After lunch, they pulled up the anchor and headed off to their next stop. Several guys on the team started to fish in the deeper waters. The rest of the team got out a game, and Navair and Gary recharged and tweaked the drone.

While Ella hung out with several of the girls, Jay decided to walk up to the second floor where Ryan was steering the ship.

As he got to the top, he saw Ryan and his assistant, Leanne, standing at a makeshift command center. He steered the boat, and she was working on something on her laptop.

Jay waved and walked up. "This boat is amazing! Thanks again for inviting us out."

"No problem," said Ryan turning the wheel. "It's nice to use it! Most of the time it's rented out, or somebody on the team gets to use it. For once, it's me!" he laughed.

"Only seems fair," laughed Jay. "So Livu is your second company you've started?" asked Jay.

Ryan nodded and squinted behind his sunglasses. "Yes, and no. It says second on my Wikipedia page. But honestly, to get here, I've started probably twenty different ideas I've had. I grew some of the ideas for a while and cut a lot of others off. Most failed, but hey, that's how I am where I am now. Only two official companies though... the last one I sold. And now Livu... Heck, I could do this for another twenty years."

Jay laughed. "That's impressive. So you're not planning on selling this one?"

"Selling? No. Growing? Oh yeah. Reforming education is one of the biggest challenges we have, and most companies out there don't get what's happening. Transforming education into learning is going to be a multi-decade challenge."

"Yeah, that's a massive challenge! I hope Gary and I have helped in a small way," he joked.

"Of course you have... not many people have the patience to give before they ask for something." Ryan looked down at the boat's navigation screen and back to Jay. "Which reminds me, aren't you still in high school?"

Jay felt worried. "Yeah, but I graduate in two months."

"Are you eighteen yet? You're not going to college?"

"Yeah I am. And about college... I taught myself design, I

love reading, and I set out this year to get a job at a technology company before I graduated."

"That's a ballsy move," said Ryan, with a straight face. "It took me two years before I realized it was a scam."

Jay wasn't sure where this was all going, so he nodded politely and listened.

Ryan looked back over at him. "Sorry about cutting out of the office yesterday. I was in a rush, and I'm glad we could catch up today."

"Yeah, no problem."

"So I talked to George yesterday. He's my lead designer. He said you spent the rest of the day finishing one of his projects, and that you started working, finished it, and then asked for the next one? Who does that?"

Jay cringed. He was worried a critique was coming. It didn't.

Ryan only smiled and said, "If there were more people like you and Gary, we'd have no trouble with hiring. All the team members have liked Gary so far... and if you're his best friend... and after yesterday... what do you say? Want to join the team?"

"Of course," Jay said, without even thinking. He paused and blurted out, "Shouldn't we have an interview?"

Ryan put on his sunglasses and laughed "You've already passed my interviews. Welcome aboard! You guys are here until tomorrow right?"

"Thanks! Yeah, we fly out late afternoon."

"Perfect." Ryan pointed to Leanne, who was talking on the phone while walking around the second floor. "Stop by Leanne's place tomorrow morning, and she'll get you and Gary the HR paperwork before you fly out."

"Awesome! I can't wait to get started; everyone seems so great. In fact, it seems like everyone is friends here," said Jay.

Ryan nodded and smiled. He motioned with his hands down at everybody. "Life is way too short to not spend the time working with your best friends. Besides, friendships... relationships... They're only fun if both people are growing. I only hire people who like to learn, and ideally, I love hiring friends in groups of two... or even three."

"Yeah... that makes sense," said Jay.

Jay looked around. Nobody seemed to be drinking, and everybody looked fit and healthy.

"You guys don't drink a lot, do you?"

Ryan shook his head. "Everybody does a little wine on the weekends, but not much. Personally, I'm not a fan. Sometimes somebody will force a glass of wine on me, but not very often. Alcohol always leaves me feeling depressed and there are too many things I want to do. When I built and sold my first company, I learned the value of time. There were a few days were we won major victories. I literally changed the course of my life, and eventually sold that company by making each day count. A single day with a hangover is too high a price."

"Makes sense," said Jay. "Gary was saying you guys travel together, or you're always doing stuff like this?"

Ryan nodded. "Yeah, usually at our off sites."

"Off sites?" asked Jay.

"Yeah, as a group, we'll pick out some place we all want to go. I'll rent out a big house, hire a chef, and we'll go have a workcation. We've been on a couple... We did Mexico, Thailand, and Whistler so far."

"That's incredible. Well everybody at Livu seems great, so

I guess they can get work done anywhere."

"Yeah, we usually work hard for a few hours in the mornings, then go out for the rest of the day. It's amazing what our team can do in a few hours with zero distractions."

"Yeah, everybody seems very driven."

"We all are," smiled Ryan proudly. "We're all on the same page here. The world can be a nasty place, and while we're all here, we're going to make it better. Reforming education is a great place to start to have a positive impact."

"That makes sense to me," said Jay.

"And on a bigger level," continued Ryan, "A better world for all of humanity isn't guaranteed. That doesn't happen unless we build it... unless we will it into existence. Too many people in the world think human evolution and survival are guaranteed!" Ryan shook his head. "We seem to be the only species that lives and works like we've already won those battles."

Right to the point thought Jay. "Is there really anything we can do to fight those? Or ensure that humanity survives?"

Ryan squinted at him behind his glasses. "There always is, and extinction is always looming. I mean, whether it's from behavioral changes, a meteor, war, or a virus... there are always forces working against us. The only way to beat them is to increase human consciousness through learning, becoming more aware, imagining a better future, and then teaming up like this to build it. As a species, our adaptability is predicated on taking what's in our imagination and turning it into technology that others can use. That process is the only way we'll survive as a species."

"Wow. I never thought about it like that," said Jay. What Ryan said made perfect sense. Life wasn't promised or guaranteed. Why on earth would he not invest his time into something rewarding... but also something bigger than himself? Jay looked out over the bay in awe. The afternoon sun painted the clouds orange as it drifted lower in the sky. From the second story, he heard laughter and glanced down at the deck below. The team Ryan had assembled was out lounging on the deck. Several of the guys had caught a few Rockfish that they were beginning to clean them. Jay and Ryan both perked up when they heard a high pitched "Ewwwww" from below.

"One of the girls?" asked Ryan, turning around.

Jay shook his head. "Nope...that was Gary."

They both burst our laughing.

This wasn't what Jay had expected, but he was grateful he'd taken the plunge to come out here. Seeing Gary's parents' company had expanded his view about what was possible. But everything he'd been through since then had increased all of his perspectives and ambitions.

He thought back to all the times he'd procrastinated on college searching, schoolwork, and homework in the past. He'd only done that because he had no idea that a place like Livu existed. If he knew that in only a few months he could train and land a job like this, he would have jumped at the chance years ago.

The prospect of long days didn't phase him, if it meant that he was working with good people, solving big problems, traveling to cool places, and taking time off like this in between. He took another deep breath and felt relieved. He'd done it.

Ryan let his hands off the steering wheel, and motioned to Jay. "Want to steer us to dinner?"

"Sure!" said Jay. He took the wheel, and Ryan pointed out where they were headed on a map. It was a new waterfront spot he wanted to try for dinner. Jay steered the boat while talking with Ryan and Leanne.

After a half hour, they pulled up to the waterfront restaurant Ryan had been raving about. Ryan took back the wheel, and guided in the boat. Everyone slowly hopped off and walked into the restaurant.

Leanne leaned over to Jay and Ella as they walked up and whispered, "Get whatever you want." Jay and Ella nodded politely, and then secretly shot each other an excited smile. The restaurant was brand new, looking right over the Bay. They sat down at a table waiting for them outside.

Gary leaned over to Jay. "Time to get my lobster and filet on!"

Jay chuckled, and looked over the menu. It was mouthwatering. He ended up getting steamed shrimp and a massive Cobb salad. Delicious didn't even begin to describe it.

Ella got oysters and a pasta dish, and Gary got a filet with a lobster tail. After chowing down for a few minutes, Jay leaned into them.

"I got the job offer," he said.

"What! That's so amazing!" said Ella. She kissed him on the cheek, and Jay tried to hide his excitement.

Gary rolled his eyes, "Not at the table, you two."

Jay leaned in to them, "So, I talked to Ryan a bunch. What about you guys? Did you some intel on everybody?"

Gary went first. "Well, most of it I already knew... read, tinker with stuff, build new stuff at work, indoor climbing, mountain biking... every single one of them is an expert in something."

"Solid," said Jay, as he turned to Ella.

"I heard mostly the same stuff... they travel, cook new recipes, play sports... the people at CheckUp did the same things too."

Jay laughed. "This has to be the complete opposite of P&C."

"There are a few nut jobs out here," said Gary, raising his eyebrows. "But there are way more awesome people to make up for it."

Jay looked around at the spread on the table, and the team that sat there. From everything he knew so far, Ryan was a down to earth, great guy. He'd made a lot of money, but was far from letting it corrupt him. He was determined to make life better for everyone around him. The perks of creating technology and joining a great company were becoming crystal clear, thought Jay.

Midway through the dinner, the owner of the restaurant brought Ryan some special dishes to try from the kitchen. Apparently they knew each other, and he brought everyone samples of their deserts, on the house. There wasn't a single look of worry in Ryan's eyes about putting on the day, the dinner, or any of the perks at Livu for his employees. In fact, Jay was starting to notice that Ryan looked like he was having the time of his life.

After dinner and desert, they climbed back on the boat and everyone huddled inside the cabin. It was close quarters, but just enough to be cozy, and not claustrophobic. Most all of the conversations were way above Jay's head, so he did his best to listen. After thirty minutes, they were pulling back in to the

Marina.

They all hopped off the boat and everyone said their goodbyes. It was now after midnight, and once again, the jet lag was starting to catch up with them. Jay looked over at Gary and Ella and saw both of their eyes drooping. All three of them thanked Ryan again, and he waved them off, saying it was his pleasure.

They headed back to their Airbnb spot. On the car ride home, Gary drove, and Jay texted everyone: his parents, Gary's parents, and Mr. Moore. He'd done it. He set out to land a job by the end of his senior year and now he had one. He was about to move across the country with his best friend AND he was about to spend the night with his girlfriend.

Jay gave a silent fist pump in the back of the car and held back from screaming with excitement. Gary and Ella talked back and forth, and he sat there in awe. He'd really done it. Soon enough, they pulled up to their place. It was way after midnight at this point, but nobody seemed to mind.

The night before, Ella and Jay had slept apart. But tonight, she was cuddled up alongside him. In minutes, Gary was snoring on the futon. Jay glanced over, and saw Ella had already drifted off to sleep. He thought about how gracious he was for the day and closed his eyes.

34

WHY GO BACK?

"I don't talk about equity over breakfast."
–Gary Weinstein

Morning light fell through the window onto Jay's face and woke him up. For a split second, he forgot where he was. In an instant, he smiled because he was waking up with Ella. He stretched and got up. By the time he got out of the bathroom, both Gary and Ella were awake. They had planned to go for a run along the ocean today, and judging by the fact that Ella was lacing up her running shoes, maybe they'd follow through with it. She and Jay had to drag Gary out of bed. After some bumbling around, they all were ready to go.

The morning was warmer, which was a relief from yesterday's cold. Jay looked down the streets and saw them filled with fog. The three of them walked a few blocks to Baker Park. After a brief search, they'd found the running trail they wanted to try that overlooked the ocean. As soon as they did, Ella took off in a jog and turned around. "C'mon you weaklings!"

They ran through the forest on a trail that snaked past the ocean. The view was amazing, with the Golden Gate's tips sticking out above the fog. The views were breathtaking, and in minutes, they were all sweating and wide-awake. After they had finished about three miles, they looped back around to the starting point of the trail. Drenched in sweat, they walked back to their Airbnb.

By now, the foggy mist started to lift. They got back and began to pack up. Only a few more hours left in San Francisco.

They stopped by Leanne's house. As Ryan's assistant, she was in charge of the hiring for Livu. She was ready for Jay and Gary, and had all their docs out, ready to sign. They both checked over the pages, but to be certain everything was in order, they sent a picture to Gary's parents. They got a thumbs up from John and Suze after a few minutes and signed the docs. Leanne gave Jay his login information for their group chat channel and a few other company specific logins that he would need. She shook his hand, and that was that. He was now a designer for Livu.

As they got back in the car, Jay was brimming with excitement. "I don't want to leave!"

Gary smiled and nodded. "I've been *trying* to tell you it was the Promised Land... about time you opened up your ears!"

They laughed and Jay felt his stomach growling. "I'm starving. Is it time for breakfast yet?"

"You read my mind," said Ella.

"Let's brunch," said Gary firmly. "And it's on me!"

Gary filled them in on the details of where they were going, and soon they pulled up at a cafe with a huge collection of tables outside.

"This is the spot," said Gary gravely. "I've never brunched so hard!"

They sat down at one of the tables outside and relaxed in the late morning sun. A few bikers sped by them on the streets and tourists were out and about.

"So, Ryan introduced you to the Founder of CheckUp?" Jay asked Ella.

"Yeah, he already gave an email introduction, which will be super helpful. I already had an offer to apply for an internship or job... but it never hurts to go to the top of the food chain," said Ella.

"That's legit," said Jay.

A server from the restaurant walked over, smiled, and handed them menus. "Good morning, what can I start you three out with?"

Gary jumped in. "Good morning, sir. The three of us have been scheming and hustling hard all weekend. We're here to celebrate our conspiracy to change the world!"

Ella put her hands over her face as the server looked at Gary with a blank face. "That's... uh... That's fantastic! What can I start you three out with?"

"We're famished and we need a massive brunch. We'll start with coffees and juice... and sir? I'll take the check when we're done," said Gary, proudly.

"That must have been some kind of offer they gave you," said Jay.

Gary's face blushed, but only slightly this time. "It was a *very* good offer, and let's just say.... breakfast is on me."

After a few minutes, the food arrived, and they feasted on omelets, bacon, hash browns, fresh berries, toast, and coffee.

After the run, they needed the feast, and they all leaned back in their chairs, completely stuffed."

"I've never been so full," said Ella.

"Tell me about it" said Jay.

"Best brunch ever," muttered Gary.

Gary held up his glass, and the three friends toasted orange juice over their empty plates.

"To an extremely successful trip my homies!" Gary yelled.

"Cheers!" said Jay and Ella, as they all clinked their glasses together.

"I guess this means the trip is over," said Gary.

"What do you mean? You two get to come right back out here!" said Ella, laughing.

"Yeah, I can't believe we're getting ready to move," said Jay.

Their weekend trip to San Fransisco was over, but it felt like it had lasted a month. Jay, Ella, and Gary had packed as much activities in as humanly possible. The tradeoff was that they had only logged about four hours of sleep a night. But, as they looked back on their weekend, all three of them agreed that it was worth it.

From the restaurant, they dropped off the car Gary had borrowed, got on the train, and headed to SFO. The three friends dragged themselves through security and collapsed at their gate until it was time to board their plane.

35

BLISS AND HIDDEN PATHS

"As a kid, I always wanted to create stuff. I didn't realize I could do that and get paid."
−Jay Pencha

On the five-hour flight home, the three friends slept as good as economy seating would allow.

The wheels of the plane touched down early Monday morning at JFK airport. Jay drove them home while Gary continued to roll the windows down and shake Jay to keep him awake. Jay dropped Ella off at a safe distance away from her parents house. Then, he swung by Gary's house and thanked him for getting everything going.

As he drove home by himself, Jay put all the windows down in the car to let in the spring air. Only a few weeks left until graduation, he thought. He'd done it. He accomplished what he set out to do, land a design job at a technology company. The realization was finally starting to sink in. He had skills that Ryan Parker and Livu desperately needed. He wasn't in a dime of debt, and he had plenty of options in front of him. At the start of the year, Jay couldn't have imagined what he'd do if he didn't get accepted to P&C. Now, with the feeling of freedom coursing through his veins, he couldn't imagine being forced into another four years of school.

He checked his phone... it was 3:35 am in the morning. He laughed out loud to himself as he pulled up to his house. How on earth was he going to drag himself out of bed in two hours for school? He slowly opened the door to his house and crept into the kitchen.

To his surprise, the kitchen was spotlessly clean. On the table, there was a note from his parents. In his sleepy haze, he read the note:

Dear Jay,

Gavin called us from Rehab. He's doing better. We're proud of you. There's a sick note for you on the table. Take tomorrow off and sleep in! We're proud of you for landing that job. We knew how the world used to work... but more and more, it's starting to look like you're the expert on how the world works now.

We're both impressed. Now, catch up on your sleep, young man!

Love,
Mom and Dad

He almost couldn't believe those words came from his

parents. In that tired moment, Jay relished the thought of sleeping in late. It was funny that as he kept taking action, the support he needed seemed to appear. With each step of the way, he started to realize that the capacities and limits that he thought he had did not exist. Of course, he had limits, but they were somewhere way beyond what he previously thought. He decided there wasn't any better feeling than betting on yourself, and being proven right.

He walked up the stairs and into his room. Moonlight illuminated the walls and covered his desk and bulletin board. He looked proudly at his year-long daily calendar that was covered in check marks. Each one represented a day where he learned something or completed his three most important tasks for the day. As he stared at it proudly, he noticed the older papers and cutouts he'd tacked up years ago. He forgot how old they were, and he walked over to re-examine them.

Like an archeologist, he carefully moved aside the latest things to expose an older piece of paper that caught his eye. As he stared at the paper, he saw his two favorite passages from books that he'd been obsessed with as a kid. The old dusty piece of paper carried his handwriting from years ago. He stood in the silence of his room, bathed in moonlight, and looked at the messages from a younger version of himself. As he read over the first passage that he had written down back in the day, he felt goose bumps wash over him:

Follow your bliss.
If you do follow your bliss,
you put yourself on a kind of track
that has been there all the while waiting for you,
and the life you ought to be living

is the one you are living.
When you can see that,
you begin to meet people
who are in the field of your bliss,
and they open the doors to you.
I say, follow your bliss and don't be afraid,
and doors will open
where you didn't know they were going to be.
If you follow your bliss,
doors will open for you that wouldn't have opened for anyone
else.
–Joseph Campbell

He was starting to realize that his earliest interests as a kid were pulling him. They were guiding him towards his bliss. Jay had so many ideas as a kid. He wanted to be so many different things, but above all, he wanted to create stuff. He wanted to make the world a better place. Now he was. As he moved his gaze to the second handwritten passage, he remembered why it was so important that he hadn't waited to get started:

Still round the corner there may wait
A new road or a secret gate,
And though we pass them by today,
Tomorrow we may come this way
And take the hidden paths that run
Towards the Moon or to the Sun.
–J.R.R. Tolkien

The goose bumps re-emerged, and ran up Jay's arms, and

to his neck. He had the uncanny feeling that he had recognized, found, and opened that secret gate. He thought about how many people were just like him, vaguely aware of the things they loved to do as a child, and then suppressed them. He'd spent years convincing himself that his earliest interests in design and drawing hadn't meant anything and weren't, "realistic."

Jay couldn't help but see everything in his earlier life as purposeful. All his earlier inclinations towards drawing, design, art, business, and helping people was all tied together. They were all attempts he made as a child to follow his bliss.

This was the start of finding and living his life, instead of the life others tried to force him on. They thought they were well intentioned, but only *he* could be the one to uncover the path that was his, and his alone. He was in a euphoric state from a lack of sleep, and the knowing that he'd soon be moving across the country. He'd be taking a road trip with his best friend at a time when most students his age were stuck at home, working hourly wage jobs that they hated.

The only way he found the hidden path that he was on now was by listening to the first nagging suspicion that it existed. He kept faith that it was real and worked like crazy to turn it into a reality.

There in the moonlight, he made a silent promise to himself. He vowed to never stop exploring his earliest interests he'd had as a child. As he walked back to his bed and lay down, the goose bumps continued. Visions of California swirled in his mind. He thought about kissing Ella while overlooking the Golden Gate Bridge.

There was so much opportunity in the world, Jay could barely fathom it all. At school, he'd been taught that everything was known. Now, as he lay on his bed, he knew how foolish that was. If he was able to accomplish so many things in a single year, he couldn't imagine where it could lead in ten. There were still secrets, adventures, and opportunities waiting for him discover.

Visions of travels, Ella, and a bright future danced through his mind. Jay closed his eyes and fell into the deepest sleep of his life.

36

OPTIONS AND OPPORTUNITY

"I started exercising, reading, and writing... and then I found a girlfriend. Go figure."
–Jay Pencha

Jay awoke in the early afternoon. He had kept up his strict morning routine for a couple months, and wasn't about to stop now. He jumped from his bed and did the Five Tibetans. Afterward, he took his notebook down to the kitchen and grabbed a cold glass of lemon water.

After an hour, he grabbed some food, then finished his last remaining design work for his new job. By the time his parents got home, he had finished all of his work in just half a day. That feeling was ten times better than finishing any homework assignment he'd ever had. The work he just finished would start helping users in just hours. Jay hopped up to greet his parents as they came inside.

He held the door open as they walked up. "Hey, Mom and

Dad! Thanks for letting me sleep in!"

Debbie and Alan both lit up when they saw him, and they gave him hugs.

A moment later, Debbie put down her bags and smiled. "So, we got the texts you sent us... But we want to hear all about your trip!"

Alan shut the door behind them. "Yeah, you got hired at Livu! That's fantastic! When do you start?"

"It went great! We explored the bay area and Silicon Valley, and got to see the Livu offices and hang out on the CEO's boat! The CEO offered me a six-month trial spot like Gary just went through. I've already started working! In fact, I just finished one project before you got home!"

"That's wonderful," said Debbie.

"Are you serious? That is amazing! You haven't even graduated yet!" said Alan.

Debbie rustled Jay's hair, and Alan hugged him in disbelief. Jay gave both his parents another hug and stepped back. "Thanks for that note! I was exhausted."

"We figured you would be! This calls for a celebration!" said Debbie.

Alan walked one of the bags they were carrying into the kitchen. "We brought home dinner. Let's eat, and you can tell us everything!"

After dinner, they relaxed at the table. Jay had never seen his parents listen so intently. They didn't say it outright, but he saw a mental weight lift from their minds when they realized they wouldn't have to pay for P&C.

Both Debbie and Alan were excited, especially Jay's dad, who couldn't believe that he got a job without a completed high school degree, and with such a high salary.

"So, you'll never need to go back to college?" asked Alan.

"Nope," said Jay proudly. "But I will need to keep my skills sharp and keep learning, though. I like the work, so it's fun for me. I'll be reading books, learning on the job, and picking up bits of training as I go. There might be a new platform or technology that comes along. When it does, I'll learn it."

"You learn the new things that quickly?" Alan asked.

"Yeah, everything I learn makes the next thing a bit easier. And then they all compound together. The CEO of Livu said if I could learn what I did in just six months, he couldn't even imagine what I'll learn over the next few years. The only reason I thought learning design or coding would be hard before was because I had never tried it. After I started, I realized, it's not bad. In fact, it is even pretty rewarding."

"So proud of you, son. Cheers!" Alan said. He raised his glass, and all three of them clinked their glasses together.

Alan took a sip of his drink, with a smile from ear to ear. "So Gary isn't in the six-month trial any longer? He's now a full-time employee?"

"Yup, and he's got stock options that vest after five years and everything."

"Amazing," said Alan.

Debbie nodded. "It is, and we just want to make sure you know how proud we are of you."

"Thanks, Mom and Dad."

"We have some news, too," said Alan.

"Oh yeah? What's that?" asked Jay.

"Remember when you got your mom setup on Drivr?"

"Yeah... why?"

"Well, she's making more money than at her old job."

"Her old job?" Jay said, expectantly.

Debbie held her head up proudly. "Thanks to you, no more temp job and commute for me!"

Alan raised a finger. "But, that's not all. After that, we looked into a few other things you recommended. We got knocked off course a bit with... with...Gavin and everything... but we finally got the basement room listed on Airbnb as well. When you were gone this past weekend, we had our first couple stay here!"

"Wow, are you guys serious? That's great!" said Jay.

Alan continued while Debbie beamed with pride. "Those two income sources alone are plenty more than her last job, especially when you factor in everything like the cost of her time and the expense of commuting."

"Mom, that's so awesome!" said Jay.

"Thank you," said Debbie. "Now, I'm looking into longer term stuff too. We're not sure what it will be yet, but your father and I are thinking of starting our own business eventually."

Alan excitedly chimed in. "After you started working, and you and Gary launched your app, your mom and I got super inspired. I decided you might know a thing or two about the new economy. So, I'm getting a bit more entrepreneurial too!" Alan got a smile on his face, holding his Smartphone up to Jay. An email was open on the screen, and the message was from Gary's dad:

Hi Alan,
Let's meet for lunch by the Oxen offices downtown. If there is a time on Tuesday or Thursday that would work for you, let me know and we'll plan something. I hope Jay told you, but

we're looking to hire a new enterprise rep, and I'd love to get a chance to talk!
Best,
John Weinstein
Co-Founder, Oxen Software

Jay looked at Alan's new Smartphone, and then back at him. "Wow Dad, YOU reached out to John?"

"Hah, hah, very funny... yes I did. And I've been researching what they would need so I can be ready before we even talk. I checked out Oxen and their product. I've got to say, it sounds a heck of a lot better than the services I used to sell. We're meeting this Thursday," said Alan.

Debbie and Jay both locked eyes in amazement. Alan had shed enough ego to ask somebody for help. This was a miracle.

Alan gleamed with excitement. "Thank you both! You know, when you first started talking about anything outside the old college path... It felt so unnerving because it's all your Mom and I have ever heard."

"That's okay, Dad."

"But now," said Alan, "it's the only thing that makes sense. Unless you need a credential, why on earth would you wait four years to get started?"

Debbie smiled and nodded in agreement.

Debbie loaded Jay's plate with more food. "So, are you going to be able to balance all this work and still graduate?"

"Yea, I'll be fine. I can stop doing my schoolwork, and I'd still pass all my classes."

Debbie and Alan looked at Jay like he'd just said something horrible.

Jay refined his statement. "Of course, I would never do that, though... I'll still work hard!"

Debbie and Alan nodded, and Jay decided to not push his luck with anything too radical at the dinner table.

"Don't worry, I'm not going to drop out of high school or anything crazy like that," laughed Jay. "although Gary might."

Debbie and Alan both looked at each other in terror. Alan put up both his hands defensively. "Okay, now that scares me. Take it easy on us. We can only adapt to change so fast!"

They all laughed. Jay finished the rest of his dinner and texted Ella. He talked with his parents a bit more, and then headed over to Ella's house to watch a movie. The whole night he thought the same thing over and over in his mind. Before he started taking action, he never could imagine that his parents would change as much as they had. He thought they'd never discover the problems Gavin faced. He thought they'd never let him do anything outside of college. But after Jay got the Drivr job, taught himself design, and landed the job at Livu, he couldn't imagine them *not* being supportive. In the span of a year, it felt like all three of them had become different people.

On top of it all, he was dating Ella, and getting ready to move to San Francisco with his best friend. It had all been just fragments of an idea floating around in his mind at the beginning of the year. Now as he approached graduation, he'd made it all a reality.

PART IV

37

Spreading Truth

"If students have been pre-sold something for twelve years, how is it possible for them to treat it as an investment?"
–Gary Weinstein

The next day, Jay picked up Gary for school like normal. Swamped with work, Gary was now living his motto, 2.0 to go. He had the grades he needed to pass and get his high school degree, so he invested all of his time towards his job as a mobile engineer at Livu.

Mr. Moore asked how their trip went, and if they might want to share details of it with the rest of the class. The rest of the class was doing well in their individual pursuits, but Jay, Gary, and Ella had truly pulled off something great.

Mr. Moore had been so impressed by their trip, initiative, and success, he wanted to rest of the class to hear about it. With the end of the year approaching, the class was assigned a final presentation. Mr. Moore simply asked Jay, Ella, and Gary to tell their story. While Jay drove, Gary read him a new text message from Ella. She had already created and e-mailed them a presentation outline.

"She's on it!" said Jay, as Gary started looking over the presentation.

"Tell me about it," Gary replied. He looked over at Jay and raised an eyebrow. "So you guys started dating right after the P&C trip? How'd you make that happen?"

"We continued to hang out once we got back from Cali, and I asked her if she wanted to make it official. It's not computer science, Mr. Engineer. The only wrong way to make it happen is by stalking girls on social media."

Gary's face flushed with embarrassment along with a side smile. "I was just peeping the hunnies."

"You got the 'peep' part right... creep."

Gary let out a deep laugh. "Oh please... but seriously, you've gotta help me out with that stuff eventually."

"Done. I owe you one anyways for helping me make it in the real world. So, do we need to read through this outline or are you all good?"

"I'll check it out again before class," said Gary. He leaned over and bumped fists with Jay. "I owe *you* one for landing a job at Livu too. I can't wait to move out there! We're gonna be roomies!"

Jay grinned. "It's all good, and roommates it is!"

They pulled up at school and walked inside. Jay noticed the anxiety he used to feel about speaking publicly was gone. Now that he had achieved something, he felt obligated to share his story.

The only thing he dreaded about the school day was his last mandatory appointment with the school guidance counselor... Pemberton. By now, Pemberton would have checked Jay's file and know that P&C rejected him, and that he never applied to his backup school, SSU. That was going to make Pemberton furious. He could be intimidating 1-on-1, and Jay was glad he had prepped for their meeting. If Pemberton thought he was going to talk down to him about any of his choices, he had another thing coming. He had all his research packed with him; everything from his opportunity cost calculations, his job offer from Livu, to projections about what he could be earning by the time his peers were graduating college.

In a way, Jay realized he was standing up to Pemberton like Gavin should have done all those years ago.

Jay wondered how Gavin was doing and made a note in his phone to call him again tonight. It was mostly Gavin's fault that he was where he was. But... there had been a huge amount of pressure from society, Pemberton, and his parents. So many people had nudged him towards becoming something he wasn't. Pemberton wanted the prestige that came from saying one of his advisees got accepted into P&C. He succeeded in forcing Gavin into a tracked career path. Unbeknownst to Pemberton, it was a path that led to stimulant-infused, 80-hour work weeks.

Before the final presentation in Mr. Moore's class, Jay was going to have to face Mr. Pemberton. Before he could graduate, Pemberton got to take one more swipe at him.

He and Gary walked into school, and were determined to crush their final presentation. But first, he had the Indulgence Salesman to face... Pemberton.

38

THE INDULGENCE SALESMAN

"If you lower your expectations, you won't ever be let down."
–Mr. Pemberton, Guidance Counselor

Jay knocked on Pemberton's office door.

"You can come in," echoed Pemberton's loud voice from inside.

Jay walked in and dropped into the chair. "Hey Mr. Pemberton, I know we have our last scheduled appointment for college stuff today."

"Yes, we do. Thirty minutes scheduled here, and we need to go over your file. It's a disappointment that you failed to prepare well enough to get into P&C, but that's what safety schools are for, aren't they?"

Jay nodded. Pemberton had no idea that Jay was no longer buying what he was selling. Pemberton took out Jay's file, leaned back in his chair, and murmured to himself,

"Mmm...Mhmm... well, let's see."

Pemberton was doing his best to make this sales process look like hard work, thought Jay. He tried to be polite and listen as he droned on.

"I warned you that without more sports, you wouldn't get into P&C. Did you know Gavin is the first one from our school to make it into P&C? I think you know Ella? She got accepted to P&C."

"That is great for them," said Jay, flatly.

Pemberton shook his head, still looking at Jay as if he'd done something wrong. "But that is why we have safety schools for, and thank goodness we applied and got you into SSU. Hmm... I don't think your file is updated. It says here that you haven't enrolled in SSU yet? Jay, please tell me this is wrong."

"It's not. I'm not going to SSU... or any college."

"Wh-What?"

"Mr. Pemberton, we're not on the same page, and we don't have the same goals. This meeting is supposed to be for me, not for you. I'm glad I didn't get accepted to P&C. I'm glad I'm not going to SSU either."

"You're glad?! What's with the attitude?"

"It's not an attitude. After everything I've learned this year, I feel like I know a lot about the in-demand skills employers want right now."

"Employers want college, Jay." Pemberton let out a chuckle. "You'll find that out soon enough..."

Jay fought the urge to get angry. He knew Pemberton's laugh was an attempt to upset him. Jay didn't give him the satisfaction of showing any emotion, and he calmly continued,

"It used to be the case that you needed college to do anything. But... the smartest employers caught on, and now they want people who are creative with skills. Now, anyone with skills can choose to work for a technology company where they get to tackle challenges that all of humanity is facing."

Pemberton's face was red. He sighed and shook his head. "Oh goodness. Well, I guess you know everything, Jay. I'd love to see how far you get with your newfound attitude."

Jay discovered that the calmer he stayed, the more infuriated Pemberton became.

Jay smiled confidently. "I'm trying make your job easier... I'm not the only student who realizes we get to ask questions. I mean, all I've heard for the last few years is that college was great and without it, I'd be in trouble. But, that's just not true at all."

"Are you calling me a liar? I can still give you a referral, if you would like." Pemberton's eyes squinted.

"I'm saying the world's changing. I don't need college, I've already landed a job– "

Pemberton cut him off. "What's after that, Jay? What are you going to do... have a bunch of minimum wage jobs?"

Jay laughed. "I don't think you understand the type of job I landed at Livu."

"This is hilarious, Jay." Pemberton said as he scribbled on the referral pad. "You're so upset about not getting into P&C that now you're delusional."

"I was blind... but now I can see," joked Jay.

"THIS!" yelled Mr. Pemberton, holding up his referral pad, "is going to be a referral your parents need to sign because–"

It was Jay's turn to cut him off. "Because what? I dared to

learn, think, or speak?"

Pemberton fumed and started filling out the referral. "Every one of you kids from Mr. Moore's class has an attitude problem. His nostrils flared as he shook his head. "I guess for your file, I'll have to put undecided and refuses to enroll into SSU."

"No, I'm very decided. I got a job at a Livu."

"Well, God forbid you fall on times where you have to apply to every other job that requires a college degree, Jay."

"I'm not above working hard at any job. And speaking of jobs, since I got hired at Livu, I get a new job offer every few days. It looks like I picked a valuable skill to learn!" said Jay cheerily.

Pemberton's mouth was open. He laughed and shook his head. "Good luck with this attitude in the real world!"

"I've seen the real world, Mr. Pemberton, and I love it. I can't wait to get out in it, and I think you've been isolated from it for way too long."

"Your parents will have to sign this referral. I won't have students disrespect–"

"Mail it, please." Jay glanced at his phone and shrugged, "Our time is up! I don't want to be late for Mr. Moore's class, so I'd better go. Thanks for the debate practice!"

Jay got up while Pemberton sat in a state of shock. "I'm trying to look out for you Mr. Pemberton. If you ever want a clean conscience... you should stop guilting minors into buying bad financial investments."

Mr. Pemberton was still trying to argue as Jay walked out and shut the door behind him. Jay put his hands behind his neck as he walked to Mr. Moore's class. Now, *that* felt good to get off his chest.

Back in his cramped office, Pemberton was fuming. Stressed, he found a donut leftover from breakfast and gobbled it up. He picked up his phone, tapped a button, and after a few rings, the principal answered.

"Principal Davis?"

"Yes... Well do you remember the problem I was warning you about? Yes... exactly... like I said it's Mr. Moore."

"No, no, at this rate it doesn't look like we're going to hit our numbers."

"I think so too... we have to do something about it... Okay... I'll be right down."

39

SETUP

"Learn to wield technology effectively, and you'll always be in demand."
–Mr. Moore

Jay, Ella, and Gary huddled up in Mr. Moore's class. They quickly rehearsed their presentation that Ella had crafted. The rest of the class would be presenting today, but they would be presenting first. When the last of the students filed in through the door, they jumped into presenting the story behind their trip.

Jay thought back to who he was at the beginning of the year. The old version of himself was always afraid to follow his interests, constantly looking to Gavin or his parents for approval. He would have thought "expanding your definition of possible" or "inspiration" were corny phrases and words. But now he realized that without feeling, "corny" or judged, you could never accomplish anything. It was only possible to build your imagination after pushing past the discomfort that caused everyone else to quit.

As he stood there thinking, he completely forgot he was standing in front of the class. He looked at Gary and Ella talking, and realized he should jump in, too. He launched into his portion of the presentation, outlining how he had strategized, started learning on his own, and eventually built rapport with the CEO of Livu. He was speaking in front of a group of peers completely effortlessly. It was just a class of students now, but why couldn't it be hundreds, maybe even thousands of people in the future? As long as they were interested and he was bringing value, he didn't see any reason why the number of people would affect his talk. Jay let Gary end the presentation by telling the class how, "sick" Ryan Parker's boat, team, and offices were. The class and Mr. Moore roared with applause. The three of them took their seats, and Jay felt free. Senior year would be over in days, and he couldn't wait.

Jay noticed the other groups had also broken into teams. Some were in groups of two, and some were three or four. Mr. Moore's class was the first class he saw that seemed to bring everyone together instead of keeping them divided. He realized you couldn't get very far by competing with everyone. The best thing to do was to learn on your own, and then collaborate when you had something unique to bring to the table. It was way more fun; and judging by the size of his first check from Livu, it was way more profitable.

He listened to the other presentations and heard a variety of similar stories. Many of the students had landed jobs, were almost there, or had discovered new interests and income streams. Some of them were going to college, but their level of planning regarding choices of majors were backed by future career projections. Many of the students even, "proved" the value of their hypothetical majors beforehand by reaching out to industry experts.

Jay thought back to the start of the year. They all got to this point because they weren't afraid to ask a simple question, "College...or not?" They were all starting to figure out who they were and their real interests. Now every single student in the class was making an investment in themselves.

During the presentations, Jay scribbled furiously, taking notes. Two groups from the class had fascinating presentations focused on the "skilled trades" and "vocational" pursuits. For some weird reason, people looked down on these because you didn't need college. As Jay listened, he was starting to see "technology" in a much broader light. Like Ryan said on the boat, technology was simply a way to do more with less.

The students who were entering the skilled trades showed how technology was replacing everything that could be standardized. They went over an academic paper showing which jobs were under the greatest threat of being outsourced, automated or replaced. The paper showed that the jobs they picked were far from being replaced.

The last group that presented summed up everything even better. Their research showed that robotics, technology, and software would replace white-collar jobs first, while many "blue collar" jobs would be, "augmented by this technology." Anyone who had skills, and could wield technology effectively, would be able to earn more and do more long before robotics could replace them. The average white-collar college graduate might not be so lucky.

Jay listened and made notes in his notebook to stay

connected with everyone in the class who were doing cool things.

The last students to present told the class how upset their parents had been when they told them they wanted to learn to be an engineer, an underwater welder, a plumber, or a petroleum pipe fitter.

As the presentations wrapped up, the class clapped and several cheers went up around the room.

Gary let out a, "woooo woo!" and as he did, Mr. Moore's door creaked open. Pemberton's face poked through the door opening, glaring at Gary. "Try to control yourself, Weinstein!" He turned and frowned at Mr. Moore. "Can we speak with you in the hall for a moment?"

Mr. Moore looked confused. "We? I'm in the middle of class."

Pemberton nodded with a smug satisfaction. "Yes, *we*. The principal and I would like a word with you."

Mr. Moore turned to the class. "You'll excuse me. I think I'm in trouble with the principal."

Pemberton gazed at Gary a moment longer, then sighed and stepped out into the hall. The class let out a nervous laugh, and Mr. Moore walked out the door.

Gary turned to Jay. "They're trying to harass Mr. Moore for this class!"

Jay turned to Gary. "You really think so?"

Gary nodded. "Oh yeah, I think they only get government funding if they meet a certain quota of students who enroll in college. Mr. Moore's screwing that up for them."

Gary got up from his seat and pulled out his phone.

"What are you doing?" asked Jay.

"I'm going to stop Mr. Moore from getting blackmailed."

"What do you mean?"

"They're going to try and screw him over or something... I just know it. Plus, there's no more reason for me to waste my time here. I need a good drop the mic moment. This might be it!"

40

THE DARK SIDE

*"I don't care where the money comes from, I just know we
need more of it!"*
–Principal Davis

The door closed behind Mr. Moore as he walked into the
hall. Gary and Jay snuck up to the door and peered out. Ella,
along with the rest of the class, sat there bewildered. Before
Jay could walk out the door, she hissed, "*what* are you
doing?"

Gary and Jay turned back to her and the rest of the class.
Gary pointed to his phone as if it was obvious. "I'm gonna
record what they're saying."

Several students in the class whispered it might be a good
idea. Ella leaned in. "Just try not to get caught."

Jay laughed. "We'll try not to."

Gary held the door open, and whispered to Jay, "I think
they're around the corner in the hallway. I can hear them." He
tapped his phone a few times, and then looked at Jay. "I'm
recording... let's go!"

Jay turned to the rest of the class. "I dunno what Pemberton and the Principal want, but we need to keep them honest, so they don't screw Mr. Moore. We'll be right back!"

The students in the class agreed, and Jay and Gary slipped slowly out the door.

The hall was empty. As they listened, they could hear Mr. Moore and the Principal arguing back and forth. It was coming from around the nearest intersection. Gary and Jay crept silently along the hall wall until they came to the corner. The voices were louder now.

Gary motioned for Jay to stand back, and he got down on his hands and knees. He scooted up to the corner and slowly poked the camera on his phone around the edge. He gave Jay a thumbs up and held the phone at exactly the right angle to record the conversation, and still see the group arguing on the screen.

Pemberton and the Principal both looked angry. Mr. Moore remained calm, but was not being intimidated. Pemberton waved and pointed to a sheet of paper. "You don't understand how this works. If we don't get the right amount of students enrolled in college, we'll lose federal money!"

Mr. Moore looked at the Principal, and then back to Pemberton. "You two are serious? What is the *right* number of students? Do you both just bow your heads to this Soviet-style crap?"

The Principal started to stammer out a rebuttal. "I don't know what you mean; It's my job to make sure this school gets more Federal money! In order to get it, we have to do what they say!"

"*That's* what you think your job is? So, you're willing to do anything to get more money? I thought students might need to know how to make good investments... whether it's college or whatever skills they decide to learn!"

Pemberton grumbled and looked at the Principal as if he'd caught a troublemaker. "Mr. Mo–"

Mr. Moore cut him off, and now he was the one yelling. "Let's compare the students in Pemberton's class with mine. My students have all learned how to make money in the new economy, they have multiple options, and some have already landed great jobs! How are your students doing?"

Pemberton's face turned red, and his voice was now hovering on a yell. "*My* students all got into their first or second choice schools, some of which are VERY big names."

Mr. Moore shook his head. "So... you care about money, brand names, and appearances over substance."

Principal Davis pointed at Mr. Moore. "Think carefully before you say something you regret, Moore. We can't have most of the students who are in your class being interested in only gaining skills. Higher education is our first priority! Then, they can go work in technology or a blue collar job. Otherwise, we lose funding."

"Let me get this right... I've helped these students identify industries with opportunity, and then assisted them with learning the right skills to break into them. And somehow, that threatens the amount of money the school will receive?"

Pemberton shook his head back and forth, and sneered, "You've filled their head with lies! None of them have a chance without higher education. It's how I got to where I'm at... it's what has worked for years!"

"No, the only way they have a chance is by learning how to learn. All the best opportunities require skills! Why would I encourage them to take on debt and postpone their learning for four years?"

Pemberton threw his hands in the air. "Principal Davis, you and I know the value of higher education can't be measured. I'm not going to be lectured by some new teacher... wait a minute... what is that?" said Pemberton, angrily.

Gary and Jay both held their breath as Pemberton's gaze shifted directly to the phone. Gary's eyes grew wide, and he pulled the phone back around the corner. He whispered to Jay, "I'll take the fall, just get back in class."

Jay nodded, and darted back to the classroom.

"Who's there?!" yelled Pemberton, as he came walking around the corner.

By the time he turned the corner, Gary was on his feet, relaxing against the wall, pretending to read on his phone. "Oh, Hey, Mr. P!"

Pemberton moved aggressively to an inch away from Gary's face and snarled, "Give me that phone!"

Gary sidestepped Pemberton and backed away to create distance. "Not a chance."

Mr. Moore and Principal Davis walked around the corner and stared at the scene.

At that moment, Jay came casually walking out of Mr. Moore's door and locked eyes with Pemberton. "Oh... I was wondering what's going on?"

"Were you here the whole time too, Jay? I see Gary's lack of respect for authority has rubbed off on you, too." Pemberton said, fuming.

Jay smiled and nodded. "Questioning authority rubbed off...that's for sure."

"How dare you!" said Pemberton, as he took a step towards

Jay. He paused, and instead lunged at Gary who now had his phone recording again. "Give me that phone, you can be expelled for that!" snarled Pemberton.

Gary jumped back. "This is insurance, so people like *you* don't blackmail people like Mr. Moore."

Mr. Moore's face broke into a smile. "I can't believe any of this is happening, but thank you for...uh... looking out for me, Gary." He broke into a full laugh as Gary dodged Pemberton's hand again.

The Principal looked horrified at Mr. Moore for laughing. He scrunched his face up, holding his palm out to take the phone. "You heard Mr. Pemberton, Gary, give us your phone."

Mr. Moore's entire class was now pressed up against the doorway, with Ella at the front of the class. She, like Mr. Moore, had a smile creeping over her face.

Pemberton lunged crazily for the phone and Gary leapt back again. Gary moved alongside the lockers and turned to the class. "*This* is what happens when you don't buy what your guidance counselor sells! They get crazzzzyyyy!"

A few brave souls in the class were laughing now. Gary sidestepped Pemberton's attempt to grab his phone again, this time training the phone on Pemberton's wild eyed, bright red face. He was still recording.

The skinny, glasses wearing engineer had made high school obsolete. Gary Weinstein dodged the Principal and Pemberton, and took off running, holding his phone up behind him. To everyone's astonishment, Pemberton went jogging after him.

Gary yelled behind him as he ran. "It's been real, and it's been fun, but it hasn't been real fun! Except for your class,

Mr. Moore! Peace!"

Mr. Moore and the rest of his class broke into laughter. Principal Davis tried to herd the students back into class, citing "insubordination", but nobody budged.

Gary made it to the outside door just in time, and the laughter coming from the students prompted Mr. Pemberton to stop short of the door. He must have realized how insane he looked.

"Godspeed, Gary Weinstein," Jay said, to nobody in particular. He started a slow clap, and the entire class followed suit. Jay looked at Principal Davis and shrugged. "Add one more drop out to your numbers!"

Gary Weinstein had officially dropped the mic, and proven that not only did he not need college, but he also didn't need high school.

41

GRADUATION PARTY

*"The only way for our world to get better, is for each of us
to make a little progress... every single day."*
–John Weinstein

Gary's move to drop out only a few days short of graduation didn't surprise his parents. Most parents would freak out if their son or daughter dropped out of college... but high school? Instead of giving Gary a hard time, John and Suze decided to throw him a party.

They didn't care if Gary got his high school diploma, but they did care that he was blazing a trail in the real world. He had a great job, he was writing articles that got hundreds of thousands of readers, and he was about to move across the country with his best friend. To Gary's parents, those accomplishments had to be celebrated in a big way. While impoverished twenty-somethings across the country moved back home or went to graduate school to pile on more debt, Gary's statement was a powerful one.

When Jay's parents heard the news, at first they were

horrified. But after Jay patiently explained it to them, they started to come around. There was no denying it that Gary had way more options and opportunity than any piece of paper could provide. Not only that, but Jay tried to paint a picture of where the path he was on could lead over the coming years.

Alan and Debbie both started to understand the idea that investing in yourself compounded like money. As they pulled up to Gary's "Rebel Alliance" theme party, Jay's parents had started to come around. The three of them walked in, and Debbie helped Suze get things ready while Alan went off to talk with John. In the meantime, Jay bounded up the steps to go visit the rebel of honor.

As soon as he walked in Gary's room, before he could say anything, Gary greeted Jay breathlessly. "Hi, I've gotta show you something. Wait here!"

Jay rolled his eyes as Gary darted out. Moments later, Gary emerged holding two red party cups, and his laptop tucked under one arm.

He handed one of the cups to Jay. "Here, take this." He took the laptop out from under his arm with the other hand and raised his party cup high.

"The finest, for my co-conspirator. Tonight we drink deeply and celebrate!" proclaimed Gary.

Jay raised his cup, chuckling at his physically small, but mentally bold friend. "Thank you, sir! You seem extra excited about all of this."

Gary took a sip from his cup. "I'm extra excited!" he said, as he opened up his laptop and pointed to the screen. "About this!"

Jay looked at the screen and saw pictures of a house. It looked like the bay area of San Francisco.

"And this is?" asked Jay.

Gary yelled, "It's our new home away from home!"

"How are we going to afford a place like that in San Francisco?"

"We aren't. Well, we are... kind of... It's a subsidized deal. Just listen."

"Okay I am, but calm down. There's no rush!"

"There *is* a rush because deals like this don't come around often. When they do, you have to jump! We just have to interview with the homeowners, and we've got it. "

"Slow down! Interview?" asked Jay. "This isn't a scam is it?"

"No way! The owners are friends of my parents. They're getting ready to travel the world for a year. They want to keep renting out their house and want somebody there to watch over things."

"An entire YEAR?" asked Jay incredulously. "Good Lord, are they rich?"

"They've done alright. They both worked in technology, and now he's a photographer, and she works for a company that my mom used to work for. They're taking a mini-retirement around the world... or maybe it's more of a workcation. Whatever you want to call it, WE CAN RENT THE HOUSE AND GET A SWEET DEAL!"

"So, they're just going to let us stay in the house?"

"No, if it was that sweet of a deal, I'd be worried. They still want $1800 a month for rent, which is amazing. But we would have to rent out a few rooms in their house on Airbnb for them. They want to keep their AirBnB profile active, and all we have to do is help, and we get subsidized rent!"

"Holy crap. That's awesome," said Jay. "Let's go for it."

"Cool, I'll send them your email right now." Gary tapped furiously on his phone, and then looked up. "Done."

"Nice," said Jay. "Damn, it's nice to have parents that are entrepreneurs."

"Hashtag blessed, son," Gary raised his glass and gave a toast, "To all the hard work that's now leading us into the real world! Onward to victory!" Gary and Jay tapped their cups together and took a drink.

Jay leaned back in Gary's desk chair. "You know, it's weird that in the first three years of high school, I always dreaded getting ready for college. I was worried it'd be just like high school."

"Tell me about it," said Gary. "Most of college is just high school except you live on your own, and everybody drinks to forget it's like high school."

"Yea, I think the idea of college was only exciting to me because of the freedom. Now that we're moving out on our own and working, this feels like the type of freedom that I didn't even know existed." Jay said.

"True that. And when we want to do the college party scene, we can do it with money in our pocket, no debt, and with a way better story."

Jay and Gary toasted one more time, downed their drinks, and headed downstairs to the party.

Guests filled the house, and everyone was talking, laughing, or filling their plates with food. Jay's grandparents were visiting from out of town, Mr. Moore was there with his wife, and several of Gary's parent's friends circulated through the house and the outdoor patio.

Along the side of the room, Alan and John had been talking for a while. Alan was interested in working for Oxen, but he still seemed uncertain if he was cut out for it.

"I'm not used to contracts that large... Besides, I don't know if I could learn all the new technology?" said Jay's Dad to John.

John Weinstein nodded for a moment, and then looked at Alan. "Can I be blunt with you?"

"I'd rather you were."

"You're how old? Late 40's?"

"Uh, just turned 50."

Gary's Dad winced. "That's still so young! What if we each live for another 50 years?"

Alan looked delighted and sipped his beer.

"You're healthy... your life expectancy might be another 40-50 years. I think it'd be a shame if someone as talented as you decides to retire, take it easy, or stop looking for that next adventure."

"Well I'm not sure I can learn as quickly as these young kids."

John put his hands up. "One of my early mentors used to tell me, if you defend your limitations, you'll always get to keep them. I'm just saying, you still have decades ahead of you! Imagine how much you could do!"

Alan started to feel offended but remembered what Jay had been saying lately: feeling ignorant could either be a precursor for defensiveness or learning. He perked up and chose the latter. "Decades? Care to explain?"

"Sure!" nodded John. "You're so hesitant to jump into re-training now, but there is massive demand for people with your level of skills in sales. There's no doubt in my mind that in less that two years you could be the top producer in our company. Heck, we'd even let you work remotely after a while."

"You think so?"

"If you want to learn, then yeah. But if you're content to sit out of the game for another 50 years, by all means... It'd be a shame to give up a new career in a growing industry because you didn't want to invest a few months of training."

"Okay, I'm starting to see what you're saying. So you're saying these younger guys have a lot of the technical knowledge, but none of the sales experience?"

"Exactly! I'm saying you already have the stuff that they can't buy. Do you really think any of these kids coming out of Ivy League Colleges have that? You've seen some of the younger salespeople you used to work with. Hardly any of them are detail-oriented, and none of them keep trying after they hear "no" a few times. If you're willing to learn the technology basics we use, like our CRM software, you'd be deadly, and I'd love to hire you."

"I could definitely learn that!"

John smiled. "Why don't you come down to the office on Monday. Watch some of the sales team in action. If you can pick it up, we'll start a trial work agreement, and renegotiate when you get up to speed?"

"Deal!" said Alan. "I'll see you at the offices on Monday!"

"Perfect. Now let's get back to this party."

42

An Unexpected Gift

"You stepped up, so we did, too."
–Debbie Pencha

Jay and his parents got home late from the graduation party. When he woke up the next morning, he thought to himself how there was nothing better than waking up on the weekend with zero anxiety.

He scribbled down a few notes, and decided what his three most important tasks were for the day, and then got started on them. He did the Five Tibetans, and by the time he got downstairs, he found his parents were awake. Throughout the year, he had listened to his parent's conversations in the mornings, which were mostly arguments. But now, he could swear he heard them laughing and joking.

As Jay rounded the corner into the kitchen, he found a surprise waiting for him on the table. Several presents and two cards, wrapped and positioned perfectly, were sitting in front of his placemat. A smile crept across Jay's face. "What's all this?" He hadn't expected gifts for graduation.

"Morning, dear," said Debbie.

"It's a bit of a surprise. Think of them as graduation and early birthday gifts!" said Alan.

"My birthday's not for another two months," said Jay, smiling.

"We know," said Alan. "But by then you'll be out in California with Gary."

"Well, can I open them now? Where should I start?"

"Start with this," said Debbie, as she handed him a card. "It's a letter from Gavin. He's doing well. After that, we'll have some breakfast, and you can open your presents."

Alan smiled and nodded. "Read it, and then I have another surprise for you!"

Jay opened the card, still in shock by his parent's generosity.

Inside the card was a letter from Gavin, who had now been in rehab for a little over two months.

Dear Jay,

I can't say sorry enough. I thought I was doing something good by going to P&C, and at the time, that was the best path I was able to find. The more I hung around that crowd, and the longer I stayed at my job, the more brainwashed I got. There's a whole world out there, and I can't believe I tried to force you to do the same thing as me. You were right to be skeptical along the way.

I've been sober the whole time here, and looking forward to keeping it up indefinitely. I respect you for having the courage to stand up to me when I wasn't myself.

Rehab has given me a lot of time to read and to think. I did the most prestigious thing everybody told me to do, and then figured out what my ethics were after I got golden handcuffs (my salary) in a toxic culture. I never stopped to think about whom I was working for, or where my salary came from.

My salary came from the same people Mom and Dad trusted with their retirement savings. They lost most of Mom and Dad's money, and then ran to the government to pay their bonuses. Basically, my old employer made risky bets with their money, lost it, then used the legal system to get Mom and Dad to pay for those losses. The most insane part about it all is that I didn't have the courage to say, "That's not right, I'm leaving." I guess that's why everybody at my old work does the drinking/drugs thing. Deep down, we all knew there was no point to anything we did. We weren't creating value for anybody, just moving and hoarding 1's and 0's.

You seem hell bent on building and reinforcing your ethics now, and then fitting a job to them that matches. That's not easy to do, but I have no doubt that you're doing things right. I'm proud of you, bro!

Mom and Dad tell me you're working for an entrepreneur who started his own company. That's amazing. People twice your age don't have the balls to do that.

Mom and Dad are the only ones who talk to me a lot here, and, to be honest, I don't blame you for not talking much. There were many years where I was a jerk, and I have a long way to go before I make it up to you.

I hope we can catch up soon. Maybe you can help me get some skills. :) I'll need them to re-invent myself when I'm ready to leave.

Your (sober) brother,
Gavin

Jay's eyes were watery, and he wiped them with his hands. "I'm glad Gavin is doing better."

"We're glad too, and it doesn't hurt that he has a brother who's leading the way," said Debbie.

Alan sipped his coffee, and a grin stretched across his face. "Now cheer up, because I've got a surprise besides the presents!"

Jay looked at him quizzically. "What's the surprise?"

"Your dad got a job," said Debbie proudly.

Alan held his finger up. "Not just any job, but a job working for a technology company... Oxen!"

"Wow, are you serious?" said Jay. "That's great!"

Alan held his coffee mug, smiling proudly. "Thanks. I've been talking to Gary's dad a bit, and at the party he told me to come in on Monday. I'll be working on a trial basis for a few months, just like you are at Livu."

Jay shook his head in disbelief. His Dad used to be dogmatically skeptical of anyone who had money. He never thought that one day he'd be working for Gary's Dad... Let alone be looking forward to it.

"What made you say yes?" inquired Jay.

"Well, we were talking at the party, and he said something that really made me mad at first. He asked me what I would do if I lived another 50 years! I never thought about that. I mean, I might have another 50 years ahead of me! I've still got a few decades left, and it'd be a shame if I didn't make sure it was great!"

"Dad that's awesome. That's really big news!"

"Thanks. There are still quite a few technology basics that I'll have to learn. But let me tell you, from what John told me about their new sales hires, I've got some experiences that these kids are decades away from learning. Might as well teach myself the new tools, and jump in to show these kids who's the boss!"

"Yea, I might be able to show you how to use some of the tech stuff, too!" said Jay, with a smile.

"That sounds good. First, I need a computer for work, and I've got my eye on that old laptop you bought yourself."

"Oh... do you want one like it?" asked Jay.

"I was hoping you might trade me," Alan turned and handed Jay one of the wrapped presents on the table. Debbie was beaming in the background. "Alan, I think you might have ruined the surprise. Just open it up, Jay!"

A smile crept across Jay's face as he tore open the wrapping paper. It was a brand new, ultra thin and sleek laptop. "Wow, are you guys serious? This is top of the line!"

"Of course we're serious. I believe designers need a computer with a bit more horsepower!" said Alan.

Debbie handed him a card. "This idea came from Gary's mom and Mr. Moore."

Jay opened the card. It was a brief note from his parents, followed by several coupons. One was for an Audible Subscription, another for Kindle Unlimited, and even a few coupons for a few non-fiction books he wanted to read.

"Wow! This is really nice, Mom and Dad."

Alan smiled proudly, watching Jay unwrap everything in awe. "We said we'd pay for school, but after paying for rehab, things are a bit tight. But we ran some numbers, and these going away presents cost about the same as your college textbooks would have. And, I have a feeling this stuff will get way more use!"

Jay couldn't believe all the gifts. His parents had literally thought of everything:

The laptop, and Kindle subscription was just the beginning. There was a gluten-free cookbook, plus a few books that Jay remembered seeing on Gary's parent's bookshelves. And, there were a few sets of notebooks and pens for Jay to draw and sketch out designs, mockups, and ideas.

Alan patted Jay on the shoulder. "You stepped up big time this year, and we wanted to say thanks. Paying for Gavin's rehab until he can pay us back was not easy, and we appreciated all your help by figuring out how to save us from another five years of paying for P&C."

Jay gave his Dad and Mom a hug. "Thank you so much. You don't know how much I appreciate all this."

Debbie beamed with excitement. "We're proud of you, Jay."

"Thanks, Dad and Mom," said Jay.

Jay took the unexpected gifts upstairs and packed them with everything else he was taking to California. All his belongings and clothes fit on his bed. Now *this*, thought Jay, felt like freedom. There was nothing that tied him down, and he was ready to get out and see the country.

He looked at the array of technology sprawled out on his bed. He'd seen it all throughout his life, but after this year, he viewed each piece in a new light. All these tools that he now owned were better than the most powerful supercomputers of twenty years ago. They learned in Mr. Moore's class that the average smartphone had more computing power than the computers that the Apollo astronauts had. If NASA had used a weaker computer to get to the moon, there was no reason Jay couldn't use these more powerful supercomputers to create something meaningful. He was already using them to add value to a company that was 2,900 miles away! He no longer viewed the technology he owned to be used for entertainment and consumption. He viewed them as tools to create. It was a powerful feeling.

All the work and experiences that Jay had gone through this year landed him a job at Livu and changed him for the better. The reading, writing, speaking in front of the class, exercising, meditating, learning design, fighting with Gavin, dating Ella, and traveling had all led him to this one point. Now, as he prepared to leave home, he felt ready for the next challenge... Saying his goodbyes.

43

THE REAL WORLD CALLS

"I never imagined I could accomplish so much in a single year."
–Jay Pencha

Before Jay knew it, his senior year was over and he was packing to move for California. His job at Livu had been challenging, yet rewarding, and he couldn't wait to start working from their offices. Working remotely was a great perk, but he was eager to learn and work alongside an amazing team. Besides getting ready for his trip, Jay was able to finish and turn in a project for work. He double checked the final design files, and then sent them to his boss, George.

Jay took a break, and stood up to stretch.

He surveyed his room; it had been the only home he knew for eighteen years. Now, that was about to change completely. He had taken down his posters and bulletin board. The place looked empty. It was hard to leave, but he was glad that his parents would be able to rent out his room and bathroom on AirBnb. Gavin's rehab had been a huge expense, and his Dad had just started at Oxen. For now, Jay wanted to do all he could to help. Stepping out on his own would be a major step.

Everything he needed for his move lay packed and waiting on his bed. He had gotten rid of everything but the essentials. Simplifying was hard, but he felt a boost in his mental energy now that he had fewer physical possessions to keep tabs on.

There was only one day left at home, and he wanted to say his goodbyes to Mr. Moore and Ella. Saying "I'll see you soon" to Ella would be hard. They planned a lunch date, and to walk around downtown. Maybe the long distance relationship they were going to try would work out. He hoped.

Neither of them knew the first thing about long distance relationships. But, after Jay spent an entire year stepping out on his own, he had confidence that he could learn anything just by jumping in and doing them.

He grabbed some of his bags and took them down to the car. Jay thought back to when he believed a job meant that you were confined to one place, and shook his head in disbelief. The thought of being forced to stay in one place or town his whole life scared him.

He texted Ella. He had the car for one more day, and then he'd be making the final chauffeur trip with Gary out West. Ella's response came a moment later, and they texted back and forth a bit to finalize the details of the lunch date.

It would be the last time they'd see each other for a month, but he and Ella were already starting to plan a visit sometime during the summer. They were even throwing around the idea for their coastal road trip. Ella was so excited about that, and assured Jay that this time she'd get real approval from her parents.

Jay opened up a new message and sent it to Mr. Moore. He wanted to make sure he got to say goodbye and thank you. After a few minutes, he responded, and they scheduled a meet-up at his house. At least this time, Jay would be showing up at a normal hour, sans all the bleeding.

While Jay finished packing, Gary was busy planning the details of their cross-country trip. He didn't have any preference for where they went, but Gary had mapped out an extravaganza. Just about every major city in the country now had a small or thriving startup culture, and Gary made plans to ensure that they would visit every one of them. Their living situation was squared away, thanks to Gary. They signed a year's lease for the house in San Francisco, and they were thrilled. Outside of a place like Gary found, rents were crazy. If they had to, they talked about working remotely and moving to a place like Seattle, Austin, or maybe even closer to home.

But first, they were hungry to soak in Silicon Valley.

Jay's parents weren't going to take him leaving well, but he'd be back to visit soon enough. On a brighter note, Gavin would be getting out of rehab soon. Supposedly he was doing better, which made Jay relieved, but he also knew it'd be a challenge for him when he got out.

He checked the time. It was still early morning, and he had a few hours before his date with Ella. If he was going to make it on time, he needed to squeeze in a visit to Mr. Moore's first. He made his last trip of stuff to the car, and drove over to Mr. Moore's.

44

VALE!

"Eventually, more people will realize that the best way to become smarter is through reading."
–Mr. Moore

Jay pulled the car up to Mr. Moore's house. He couldn't help but think about the last time he was here, after his fight with Gavin. The place looked different during the day, and Jay was a long way away from the bleeding and scared mess that he had been that night. Mr. Moore waved from the porch. He was sitting in the same place he had been the first time, reading a book.

Jay got out of the car, waved, and walked up to meet him.

"Is reading all you ever do outside of school?" asked Jay.

Mr. Moore smiled. "It's the second best way I've found to get smarter."

"What's the first?" asked Jay.

"Thinking!" said Mr. Moore, with a laugh. "So you ready to head out West?"

"Yea, I think so. What ever happened with Pemberton and the principal? Are they really trying to get you fired?"

"Probably," confirmed Mr. Moore. "But I'm not worried about that."

"What? You're not staying in teaching? But you're such a good teacher!"

"Thanks! Pemberton and the principal will force me out soon enough. But, if I am such a good teacher, it only makes sense for me to teach the greatest number of students, in the most effective way possible."

"Yeah... I guess that's not possible at our high school, huh?"

"Not at all. Plus... all the standardized tests are designed to turn teachers into a commodity. Teaching, when done right, is an art. What can be standardized, by definition, isn't art. All of this is a great reminder for me that it's time to leave."

"Is that why you kept saying, 'what can be standardized can be replaced'? I assumed that's why you pushed us all to learn skills that weren't commodities?"

"Exactly right, standardization leads to marginalization, replication, and finally... replacement by technology. The entire education system is becoming fragile. But, I don't want to bore you with that education stuff!"

"Well, then, what's next for you?"

Mr. Moore clapped his hands and shrugged. "What's next for me? I'm going to help education transform into learning."

"And that means...?"

"My wife and I are going to join an education startup."

"Ohhhh! Nice!" A light bulb went on in Jay's head. "Wait, so you're coming out to Silicon Valley too?"

"Nope, I'll we'll be working from right here. Silicon Valley is great, but you can start or join a growing company from anywhere."

"Yea, that's what Gary has been saying. Do you still think it's a good idea for both of us to go out there?"

"Without a doubt!" said Mr. Moore. "You need to get in proximity with other ambitious people doing big things. It will shift your view of what's possible. If you stay close to home your whole life, you might never find out who you are, or what you're capable of. *That* would be a real shame."

"Yea, I'm starting to see that."

"It's the ideal place for you and Gary. You'll be able to work shoulder to shoulder with the best operators in the world. You can build up your net worth, network, and get the skills to start your own company."

"Mr. Moore, thanks for all the help this past year. I'm glad I took the leap and transferred to your class. I never thought I could learn so much from a teacher. I owe you a lot."

"Thank you, but it was my pleasure! Are you leaving today?"

Jay laughed. "Early tomorrow. All that's left is one last goodbye with Ella."

"Ahhh..." Mr. Moore's said, raising his brow. "So, you two are dating now? That's a bold move starting a cross-country relationship!"

"Yeah, we are, even though it's kind of terrifying."

"The challenges that scare you are those that force you to grow. That's a good sign. That reminds me! Wait here." Mr. Moore spun, and ran into the house. He reemerged a few minutes later carrying several books. "Here, read these."

"Wow, thanks!" Jay took the books under his arm.

Jay held up one of the books from the stack. "What is this one about?"

"When I deployed overseas in the military, my wife and I

were worried about our long distance relationship, too. But, it turns out, with a little bit of faith, reading, and staying busy, it's not that tough."

"I will definitely read these!"

"For us, that challenge and strain on our relationship was one of the best things that ever happened to us."

"What? Really?"

"Without a doubt. Plenty of people never shed their ego in relationships. Eventually, neither partner can stand to take risks anymore. They never learn that going through adversity together is the only way to build your relationships."

"Thanks. I'll read them and pass them along to Ella."

"Perfect. Now go spend some time with her! But make sure you get out to Silicon Valley to save the world! Okay?"

Jay laughed. "Right... no pressure, or anything!"

"Of course not... Oh! One more thing..."

"Yeah?"

"Remember the entrepreneur we talked about in class, Seneca?"

"Yeah, why?"

"When Seneca used to part ways with friends, instead of saying goodbye, he said, 'Vale.' That's Latin for, 'be worthy.' It was a reminder to each friend to retain the best parts of their character. But, it was also a challenge and call to action to keep improving."

Jay was quiet for a second, thinking through what Mr. Moore had just said. Then, he looked up and nodded his head. He walked over and shook hands with Mr. Moore.

"Thanks for everything, and Vale."

Mr. Moore patted Jay on the shoulder and smiled.

"Vale."

45

A LEAP WITH ELLA

"Why would I let anyone stop me?"
–Ella Johnson

From Mr. Moore's house, Jay drove to the downtown area where he and Ella were meeting for lunch. It was, as always, amazing to see her, and lunch was over too quickly. After they had eaten, they spent the last bit of time they had together to walk around downtown.

They walked hand in hand, passing the same bars and restaurants where Jay used to drive for Drivr. He laughed to himself about some of his customers. Ella noticed and squeezed his hand.

"What's so funny?" she asked.

"Sorry, I was just thinking about working for Drivr, and some of the people I would pick up."

"I can't believe we've done so much this year," Jay said.

"Me neither. What else are you thinking about?"

"Everything I guess. Missing you already...and..." Jay trailed off.

"Same here... and... what else?"

"I don't know if I'm going to miss this town. Part of me feels guilty for that."

Ella smiled and squeezed his hand again. "I think that's okay. I was thinking the same thing."

"Really?"

"Yeah, I don't think being restless is a bad thing. My grandfather used to say that's a good sign. Being ambitious and wanting to explore means that you're alive. But, leaving me here... Now you should feel guilty for that!" She crunched her nose laughing and poked Jay's ribs. He sidestepped away from her and a smile graced his face.

"You're the one who encouraged me to do it!"

"I was joking!!! Well, not really... But you know what I mean. This is hard, that's all. Are you going to miss me?"

"Of course I'm going to miss you," said Jay. He kissed her on the cheek. "You'll be out to California soon for our road trip."

"Yes, assuming my parents will let me..."

Jay swung his head to the side. "I thought you said they would!"

Ella looked at Jay and cringed. "I *almost* have them sold! You work out the details, and give me a few more weeks."

"I'm going to get your ticket in two weeks, so the clock is ticking, little lady."

"Like I said... I've got the ticket, and we can split the road trip," Ella said insistently.

"Fine! It's crazy that it's almost here."

"Yeah, but you know what... I don't think any of this stuff is crazy..."

"What do you mean?"

"You and Gary getting jobs out there... us starting a long distance relationship. It's adventurous!"

"Agreed," Jay said, as he brushed her hair out of her eyes. "Besides, plenty of people make it all work. I just came back from Mr. Moore's, and he and his wife went through an entire deployment. He said that it actually helped them."

"Really... so you were talking about me?" Ella's face blushed as her eyes lit up.

"Only everywhere I go! Plus, I need all the tips I can get."

"You and me both. You're the first boyfriend I've had who's not crazy."

"That's what they all say," said Jay, laughing and dodging a soft punch from Ella.

"Your bromance with Gary doesn't count."

"Ha-ha..."

Ella looked worried for a minute, and then spoke, almost choking up. "I'll come visit for the road trip, but you have to promise you'll come visit me at P&C, okay?"

"Done," said Jay sincerely. "I promise I will. I'll be back a bunch anyways. I'll be back to see Gavin when he gets home. Plus, I'll be home for Christmas!"

Ella smiled and pushed him away playfully. "I guess when you break it down like that it's not so bad. Besides, if we like each other enough to try something crazy like a long distance relationship, you know...there might..."

"Might...?"

"There might... be something here?"

Jay laughed and looked at her. "Well, I sure hope so! Hey, I didn't know P&C students could be this emotional. I thought you all were cold and calculated?"

"Hah hah. Very funny. It wasn't too long ago that YOU

were thinking about going there!" said Ella.

"You're right. Don't remind me. I hope you know I still think it's impressive that you got accepted."

Ella smiled. "Thanks for noticing that it wasn't easy."

Their walk had come full circle back to their cars. They had parked next to each other, and they stood for a moment in between the two cars. Jay hugged her, and Ella leaned into him, pressing him against the car door. She whispered to him, "I'm glad we started dating."

He kissed her and smiled back. "Me, too."

"However, we have to make it happen, I'm going to see you in July. And, don't you dare buy my ticket, I've already looked at them, and I am buying my own! You plan the trip, and I'll be out there in July."

Jay smiled at her. "Deal, and this time I'll have my own room, so I don't think we'll have to listen to the Weinstein snore."

"Now you're talking," responded Ella, with a grin.

They said their goodbyes, kissed one more time, and then drove their separate ways.

Jay felt worried, but brushed it aside. He thought back to everything he learned this year. He took a deep breath and repeated, "The uncertain path is the only one that's certain."

46

PARENTAL GOODBYE

"We're naturally protective. But we know if you don't get out on your own... you'll never be able to protect yourself."
–Alan Pencha

Back at his house, Jay had already said goodbyes to his parents. Now, with Gary waiting out in the car, they all stood around the kitchen table. Alan and Debbie had watery eyes, and if he didn't leave soon, Jay was going to start crying too.

He grabbed his water bottle and said sheepishly, "I love you guys, but Gary's waiting... we've got to head out soon."

"We know," groaned Debbie.

Alan looked from Debbie to Jay. His voice cracked as he spoke up. "Be sure to call when you get a chance."

"I will, Dad."

"Jay, you have a lot on your plate, but we just want you to remember that Gavin's struggle isn't yours. You worry about you when you're out there, okay?" said Debbie.

"Thanks, Mom, I know."

Alan put his arm around her. Both of their eyes kept

watering, and Debbie wiped away the tears. "We hate that you're leaving... but we're also proud that you're not hanging around here. So many of our friends have their grown children living at home. It doesn't sound like a bad idea to me, but I know that's not what's healthy for you. Getting out and seeing the world is the only way to grow up."

Jay gave his mom a hug.

Alan rubbed Debbie's shoulders and wiped his own eyes. "You know, I used to get cynical when anybody talked about making the world a better place, or finding work that matters. But the more I hear you talk about it, the more I think the only thing that's crazy is not looking for work like that."

Jay smiled with a tear rolling down his cheek. "Well, both of us are working for amazing companies now, so I think we've got the world problems covered."

Alan wiped his eyes again and chuckled. "You're making the world a better place and you're making a leap to do that right now. Don't ever quit, okay?"

"I won't, Dad."

"Well you need to get going," whispered Jay's mom. "Don't forget about your old mom and dad."

Jay laughed. "You know I won't!"

"Remember that between the two of us, we might still have a thing or two to teach you," said Alan.

"Only a thing or two?" Jay laughed. All three of them turned their heads to the front door as the thump of rap music started outside.

"Good Lord, is rap music all Gary's listens to?" asked Alan.

Jay grinned. "Just about... Well, I guess I'm heading out... I love you guys. We'll be safe, and I'll call you when we stop for the night!"

Debbie nodded. "Okay, please be safe driving!"

"We will be mom. Don't worry."

The three of them walked to the door, and then stood on the porch. Jay hugged them one last time, and then waved and got in the car with Gary. They pulled out of the driveway, and they were off.

Jay kept waving, and as he and Gary drove down the street. He watched the figures of his parents in the mirror as they got smaller and smaller.

47

THE BEGINNING

"I am a learning machine, homie."
–Gary Weinstein

In the car, Jay and Gary were both silent for a few minutes. Eventually, as they got on the interstate, Gary turned the music down.

"You know, I'll miss this town."

"Yeah, me too" said Jay. "It's been one heck of a year."

"Agreed. We crushed it," said Gary.

Jay looked over at his best friend. "I'm glad you came back from Silicon Valley after your Bootcamp. There wasn't even a reason for you to come back to graduate. But you returned from the promised land bearing good news."

"No problem-o," said Gary, as he pushed up his glasses. "As long as you help me meet some girls out in California–"

Jay cut him off laughing. "I knew it! I knew you'd demand payment!"

"Well duh, I saved you from like a million years of learning all the wrong things! Hundreds of thousands saved, thanks to this guy," said Gary, pointing to his chest with a big grin.

"I know. I owe you big time."

"Don't mention it, homie."

"You know at a certain point, I'm going to have paid you back."

"I know!"

"That means no more chauffeuring you around!"

"Hah! Not until you get your own car, son!" shouted Gary.

"Hilarious, but I don't know if I'll even need one out there."

"Yeah, I was thinking the same thing," nodded Gary. "So, what's gonna happen with you and Ella? You guys are doing the long distance relationship thing?"

"Yes we are," Jay said. "If there is anything you taught me this year, it's that you can only learn about things by taking the leap and doing them. Reading about them from those who do them is good, but ultimately, it's no substitute for taking the risk myself. And taking that risk with Ella... that's one worth taking."

"Now *that* is some big thinking. You know what else is?"

"What's that?"

"Declaring what we are becoming," said Gary, as he rolled down the window and yelled to the world, "I am a full-stack engineer and entrepreneur!"

"You're getting that good already?" asked Jay.

Gary looked incredulous. "How do you think any of this works?"

"What? What do you mean?"

"Do you think anybody gets what they want without believing it's possible first?"

"Well–"

Gary cut him off. "I have ideas. I form them into visions. And I hustle my glasses off every day to create them. That's where I'm headed son," said Gary proudly. "Words have power, and I am a one MEAN full-stack engineer... and entrepreneur!" he yelled.

Jay couldn't help but smile. "So, saying it out loud is supposed to help?"

Gary looked at him. "Of course. If you never sell yourself on your ideas, nobody else will. If you don't have a vision then where are you gonna go? Have I let you down yet? We've got to keep leveling up!"

"True, true." Jay suspended the nagging voice of inner disbelief and mumbled. "I am a senior UX/UI designer."

"Ohhh... That's wimpy! I don't buy it and I know you don't."

"I'm a senior UX/UI designer!" yelled Jay.

Gary raised his eyebrows. "Now, that's what I'm talking about!"

Jay went on, "And I am going to be the first designer at Livu to get as many stock options as the engineers!"

Gary put up his hands. "Woah, woah, slow down there."

They both laughed, and Jay got serious for a second. "Can you believe we're actually doing this?"

"Yes I can!" said Gary, looking down at his phone. "Do you need directions? What's the next road we need to get on?"

Jay shook his head. "No directions needed. It's a straight shot... 80 West."

"And what's after that?" asked Gary.

"Twenty-nine hundred miles between us and Silicon Valley."

###

About the Author

Chad Grills is the editor of Life Learning, and the author of several fiction and non-fiction books. He speaks at various colleges, graduate schools, and technology events.

In the past, he's worked everywhere from a Hedge Fund to the Army Infantry. While in the military, he deployed to Iraq and Egypt. He provided security for the 56th Presidential Inauguration, and was in the military's 2011-2015 Defining Moments radio and TV advertising campaign.

When he's not traveling, he and his wife are based near Washington, D.C. He's currently working on his next book, and a near-term science fiction trilogy.

For essays, interviews, reading recommendations, short stories and more, checkout
www.ChadGrills.com

Books by Chad Grills

Non-Fiction:
Veterans: Rebuild America
Future Proof
Business Ideas

Fiction:
College or Not?

Short Stories:
Take These Pills
While You Were Bleeding
Call It Murder
Quick Fix
First Patrol

These books are available for free as part of Amazon Kindle Unlimited.

Paperbacks and Audio versions of most books can be found at:
www.amazon.com/author/chadgrills

For the latest updates, essays, ideas, book giveaways, and more, visit: www.ChadGrills.com

Connect with Chad

Chad loves hearing from readers, and you can connect with him on:

Twitter: @ChadGrills
Facebook: Chad Grills
Amazon: www.amazon.com/author/chadgrills
www.ChadGrills.com